Magic in Her Blood

Book One of The Enaid Chronicles

ATL Doyle

Somewhat Grumpy Press

Published by arrangement with Somewhat Grumpy Press Inc. Halifax, Nova Scotia, Canada.
SomewhatGrumpyPress.com
The Somewhat Grumpy Press name and Pallas' cat logo are registered trademarks.

ISBN 978-1-998555-06-2 (paperback)

ISBN 978-1-998555-07-9 (eBook)

February 2025 v2

Author's Note

Many of the places mentioned in this book are real, and I did my best to describe them as accurately as possible. I have also included aspects of various mythologies and folklore as an homage to cultures that I love that have fuelled my love of history and storytelling.

I hope reading this stimulates and encourages you, Dear Reader, to delve deeper. Visit these places if you can. I do not claim to be an expert in any of it, so please do not assume that the elements of the myths and folklore that you read herein are canon.

I have tried to include some elements that are as close to accurate as possible, both with lore and places, but this story is my own, with artistic licence taken. My depictions of various creatures are of my own imagining. In my acknowledgements, I recognize some of those who've helped guide me, provided authentic source materials, and inspired me. I encourage you to seek out those sources at your leisure.

I am an ardent lover of history and hope to honour the cultures from which these myths and lore originate.

Thank you for taking this journey with me.

For those who feel like they don't belong and long for a place
they've never been to.

For the Wanderers and the Rebels.

And the Unseen.

Death must be so beautiful. To lie in the soft brown earth, with the grasses waving above one's head, and listen to silence. To have no yesterday, and no to-morrow. To forget time, to forget life, to be at peace.

—Oscar Wilde, *The Canterville Ghost*

Chapter One

Freydis envied the dead. She'd danced with Death countless times throughout her long life. Flirted and teased, and yet Death refused to take her home. Instead, Death often came for those she loved or simply used her as its instrument.

She'd lost track of how many funerals and how many cemeteries she and Vetus had attended, although this was the first at which she'd worn the face and body of an old woman. Her wrinkled, age-spotted hands trembled as she wiped the tears from her wind-burnt cheeks.

Vetus, however, looked as he always did, ageless and stoic. Huddling against him, Freydis was grateful for the subtle warmth his magic wrapped around them. Icelandic autumn air tore through the cemetery, and overhead, black clouds threatened rain.

Good. Astrid loved the rain.

Freydis closed her eyes, listening to the words the cleric spoke. His steady, rhythmic voice carried away on the wind. Her mind wandered several decades into the past to when she'd served as a nurse aboard a hospital ship in the European theatre of the Second World War. For Freydis, it was her penance: atonement for the darker parts of her past she longed to forget. It was on that ship full of death and destruction that she met Astrid.

Astrid had been a light in that terrible darkness, and she was the only human, other than Freydis's father, who knew what Freydis truly was and loved her anyway. Immortality had given Freydis many things, but Astrid gave her the sense of belonging she'd always sought.

And now Astrid was gone.

A wave of nausea jolted her back to the graveside. Despite the cold, a film of perspiration formed on her brow. An accompanying chill snaked down her spine. The magic she'd used to craft the glamour she wore was failing. She'd never tried to hold a glamour for so long before, and it drained what little strength she had left amongst the grief. Resting her head against Vetus, she inhaled deeply. He smelled cool and crisp, like a winter-kissed evergreen and freshly fallen snow.

"I'm so tired, Vetus," Freydis sighed. "I don't know how to live or where I belong anymore without her."

She searched his familiar face, a silent plea for an ounce of his ancient wisdom. The distant look in his eyes told her everything—more than words ever could. While he might have been standing beside her in that tiny cemetery, his mind was far away.

Turning his eyes to meet hers, he murmured, "It is never easy to say goodbye, Freydis, especially when it's forever. But time passes, and you learn how to bear it. You learn how to continue without them."

Vetus wiped a lingering teardrop from Freydis's cheek, his hands warm and gentle. They watched as the casket was lowered into the cold, damp earth—her last connection to that place safely resting within. Freydis fought the urge to climb down after her.

Vetus placed his arm around her shoulder, gently squeezing for encouragement, as they turned and walked to the car that was waiting for them. Freydis was grateful for his presence and the comfort it always brought her.

Slowly, she began to release the glamour she had worn to blend in for all those years. Vetus eased Freydis into the car, and once inside, signalled to his driver to leave. The smell of leather and newness from the rental car assaulted her heightened senses as her magic unravelled. The crunch of the gravel beneath the tires and the incessant sound of the windshield wipers grated on her as she gazed distantly out the window. Freydis wondered how she could feel so numb and so raw all at once.

"Dea," Vetus murmured, breaking their silence, "Have you given any thought to what comes next?"

His use of her nickname, the one her mother gave her, always felt bittersweet. Exhausted, she offered a shrug in reply. She hadn't let herself think that far ahead. She didn't even know who she was anymore without Astrid.

They completed the remainder of the trip in silence until they arrived at her modest wood-framed chalet. Vetus, ever the gentleman, walked around to open the door for her. Her glamour was completely gone. Her previously snow-white locks now hung in chestnut waves around her face. The wrinkles had smoothed from her fair skin, and the strength of youth chased away the weakness of old age from her body.

Vetus met her tired gaze with a warm smile, no doubt in response to her looking like herself again. Freydis could see the care and concern he felt in his emerald-green eyes.

"There is nothing left for you here, Freydis." His tone made the hairs on her neck stand on end, and she could feel the heat rising in her cheeks. "Perhaps it's time you—"

"I know," she snapped. "I just need some time."

A tight smile remained on his face, though it did not quite reach his eyes. An icy, unrelenting stare betrayed his true emotions. Freydis forced herself to return the smile as Vetus leaned over to kiss her forehead, leaving without another word.

Her grief made arguing cruel and pointless. Vetus stalked back to the car without a backward glance. He'd always struggled to understand Freydis's incessant need to live as though she were human. Especially with her complicated past. Humans feared and hated what they did not understand. History was proof enough of that. She couldn't possibly believe she'd be welcomed as one of them if they ever discovered what she truly was.

Astrid was unlike any human he'd ever known, and he'd known many. Humans like Astrid were a dying breed, but the years spent with Astrid held Freydis back. He knew he had to help her find her way forward from this.

Comfortably seated in the vehicle, he pulled a cellular device from his suit jacket pocket. He hated being tied to it, but operating in the human realm made it necessary. His long fingers knew the number by heart. Ophelia would know what to do. She knew Freydis almost as well as he did, albeit from a distance.

"How is she?" Ophelia's familiar voice greeted him.

"Exhausted. Using so much magic for such a long time has drained her dry—she worries me."

"She will be alright, Vetus. I will keep eyes on her. We will see her through this, just as we always have."

Vetus leaned his head against the car window. "Do we still have that residential property in Boston?"

"Yes. Why do you ask?" He could hear her smile in her voice.

"Freydis needs a fresh start, a new life. I have contacts there who can help. Can you arrange it?"

"Anything for you." Ophelia paused. "Meeting others like herself would help her too, Vetus."

Vetus sighed, "Thank you, Ophelia."

He disconnected from the call and returned the cellular device to his inner jacket pocket. Still leaning his head against the cool window, he closed his eyes, twisting the amethyst ring on his finger as his thoughts drifted.

Freydis crossed the threshold to the place she'd called home for decades, and the silence she found waiting for her was suffocating. Aimlessly, she paced the rooms, the evidence of a happy life all around her, but she only felt numb. A picture of a much younger Astrid sat on a shelf in the hall. Delicately, she picked up the picture and held it close to her heart.

Freydis squeezed her eyes closed and whispered, "Please tell me it's all a dream."

They had never defined their relationship—it was complicated. Freydis wouldn't have called it romantic, although there were moments. A penetrating gaze, a lingering touch, or comfort in a lonely moment was not uncommon. They gave each other the simple pleasure of another's touch.

Astrid had been a widow when Freydis had met her, her young husband killed in action, driving her into service as a nurse. She'd told Freydis she'd promised her God that she would never remarry. She'd said their friendship was all she needed to be fulfilled until she joined her husband in eternity. It suited Freydis.

She'd been with men and women over the centuries. Nothing serious, but they satisfied her physical desires. She never let any of them become more. But it was different with Astrid—a steady and comfortable companionship without judgement or expectations.

And now it was gone.

Unable to bear the empty house, she grabbed her coat and retreated outside, startling a snowy owl from a nearby tree. She was a child when last she saw one of those majestic beasts. Iceland was full of beauty and often reminded her of Norway, her homeland.

In the shadow of two great mountains, her tiny Icelandic town sat alongside a harbour that opened to the Northern Atlantic Ocean. The wind had picked up since earlier, carrying the frigid salty air off the harbour. Wrapping her coat tightly around herself, Freydis walked along the water for the better part of an hour. It gave her time to think, and she realized that, while she was pretending to be human for so long, she had forgotten why she had come to Iceland in the first place. Her mother's ancient edict, "Find my people to find yourself," echoed in her mind.

Listening to the water splash against the pier, Freydis remembered the calmness of her mother's voice whenever she spoke. Even as they hauled her away, her voice remained steady and calm. Thinking of her mother always brought a tightness to her chest and a tidal wave of painful memories.

Closing her eyes, Freydis could see the soldiers once more, binding her mother's hands as they placed a black bag over her head, leading her away to Vardøhus Fortress. Witchcraft was the charge they laid against her; Freydis's first example of many to come of how humans destroy what they fear or do not understand. She'd been so young.

Lost in her memories, Freydis was unaware of the eyes that watched and followed her from the water, eyes that watched her the whole of her life. Eyes that understood the source of her pain.

The street lamps burned brightly in the twilight when Freydis returned home to find the snowy owl perched in the tree once more. Its large green eyes fixed on her. Before she went inside, she turned to face the creature.

"My mother used to say that your kind knew the way to the underworld," Freydis scowled at the owl. "Is that why you're here? Did you take her from me?"

As if trying to understand, the creature cocked its head and ruffled its feathers. Freydis watched its display and nearly jumped out of her skin when it abruptly screeched as it flew from the tree and dove toward her before sweeping up and over the treetops. Freydis shook her head and unlocked the door.

Once inside, Freydis made herself tea in her favourite mug. A gift from Astrid, it was white with black letters that said, **Go Away, I'm Reading**. She grabbed Astrid's pink knitted cardigan from the kitchen chair where it always hung and wrapped it around herself. It smelled faintly of her flowery perfume. She picked a book from the bookshelf and, with her tea, sat in Astrid's recliner chair, trying to distract herself from the aching loneliness she felt. The weariness of the day seized her within moments, and she fell mercifully into dreamless sleep.

The days melted into weeks while Freydis navigated through her grief. She hadn't eaten anything substantial, and all she wanted to do was sleep. The reality of waking each time to an empty house always brought fresh tears and anger that she'd woken at all.

On one occasion, she nearly tore the house apart, hoping against the odds that she would find even a single dose of that sweet relief she used to know. Something to help her forget. Something to make her numb. She wouldn't find it.

She tried seeking solace in what little magic she knew but could barely manage a glamour to change the colour of her hair.

Concerned neighbours brought food and gestures of comfort, but she wouldn't answer the door. Even if she did, they wouldn't recognize the young woman she had become without her glamour.

When she finally managed to get out of bed, she filled her emptiness with paranormal documentaries and takeout until she finally started to accept her new reality. It would be Vetus, as always, who would finally break through the wall of her despair.

A shrill cry from the telephone startled Freydis awake, and her knees shook as she tried to stand. By the third ring, she answered. Her voice sounded raspy as her vocal cords awoke from their lack of use.

"I know you need time, but I think a change of scenery would also help," the familiar voice said.

Rolling her eyes, Freydis felt the faintest grin pull at her lips. Recognizing the musical tone of her cautiously optimistic friend, she relented, "Okay, Vetus. I'm listening."

"I have an acquaintance at Harvard University in Boston. He owes me a favour," Vetus said.

Freydis sighed, "Okay, so?"

"Well, I know how much you love history. I thought, since he is the dean of the History Department, *and* he happens to have a vacant assistant professor position, you'd be a perfect fit."

Freydis had never been to America. She certainly wasn't prepared to teach. It had been over two hundred fifty years since she last found herself at university.

"I'm not interested in being a professor's assistant right now, Vetus."

"I figured you'd say that," he chuckled, "which is why you will be an assistant professor in name only."

"Yeah, right," Freydis grumbled.

"I'm serious," he protested. "As a faculty member, you would have access to the libraries. I thought it might be the perfect opportunity to continue researching your mother's people."

Vetus knew her well and played her love of history and old things against her. She didn't mind, though; it was one of his more endearing qualities.

The prospect of a new opportunity, though intimidating, was also exciting. For most of her life, before Astrid, Freydis had been hoping to find others like herself. The place where she truly belonged. Perhaps America might have some of the answers she was looking for.

Standing in the disarray of her scattered memories, Freydis realized that, throughout her many lives, she'd never accumulated many personal possessions of any significance. She had a small collection of items she held very dear: her favourite mug, several books, a small Scottish dirk, and a few other mementos from each life she'd lived and the people she had loved. Her most prized possession, though, was a hastily written note from her mother, which she kept tucked inside a well-worn copy of Marcus Aurelius's *Meditations* for safekeeping. It didn't take her long to pack.

Freydis's favourite mug still sat on the counter next to the sink, half full of last night's tea. After dumping the contents down the drain and giving it a quick rinse, she dropped a fresh teabag into the mug and waited for the water to boil. She chuckled to herself at how Astrid would have scolded her for not washing the mug properly if she'd been there. She glanced around the tiny robin's egg blue kitchen. The room looked the same as it had every day for several decades but felt emptier now.

A knock at the door interrupted her rumination, and without waiting for her to answer, Vetus strolled in. Still in her pajamas, tea in hand, Freydis sat down at the table and watched as Vetus instructed his driver to collect her luggage.

He placed himself at the opposite end of the table and began absentmindedly flipping through the morning newspaper. Freydis continued to watch him as she sipped her tea. Most would have found the silence awkward, but there had been many similar moments between them. It felt natural to be with Vetus. Something deep within her felt connected to him in a way she couldn't seem to put into words. It was as if the magic within them, or perhaps the immortal part of each, recognized one another.

Regardless, his presence always made her feel safe and at ease. After her mother died, Vetus had been the only consistent person in her life. He was the only other non-human and immortal being she knew. In all their years of friendship, he never talked much about himself. Freydis realized she knew truly little about him, personally, except his Irish heritage.

"Thank you, Vetus—for everything."

Without looking up, he cleared his throat and waved his hand dismissively. He closed the newspaper and glanced at his watch. Freydis was notoriously late for things, but she passed it off as a symptom of feeling like she had an infinite amount of time. Hastily, she rinsed her mug and stuck it inside her carry-on before she finished getting ready to leave.

Stopping at the threshold, she turned to take everything in one last time, knowing in her heart she would never return.

"Goodbye, Astrid," she whispered to the empty house and, with a heavy sigh, locked the door behind her and handed the key to Vetus.

He reached for her hand, and they walked to the waiting car. Once again, he opened the door for her. It was in those difficult moments, endings and such, that she appreciated their comfortable silence most.

Chapter Two

Boston in midwinter was unexpectedly like Iceland, only wetter. Freydis was glad for one less adjustment, though there had been many others. She was still getting used to seeing her "normal" face in the mirror. Over the years, Freydis had modified her appearance to age alongside Astrid and spent the last decade with an old woman looking back at her. This wasn't the first time she'd started over, though. It would take time for this new life to take root.

Freydis spent several weeks settling in and becoming familiar with the people and the city. Boston boasted a rich history, which increased her hope of finding some evidence of her mother's people. If she only knew where to start.

The biggest downside was city living. As a rule, Freydis avoided cities. They were crowded and noisy. How people could live without nature in their concrete jungles would always baffle her.

Boston's saving grace was the abundance of bookstores, at least ten within walking distance. There was a certain magnetism about bookstores that always drew her in. She liked to call book shopping "treasure hunting," and it was one of her favourite hobbies. Books would always be her refuge and escape.

Walsh's Book Nook was the closest shop, located only a few blocks from her apartment. The façade of the shop was adorned with beautiful stained-glass windows that radiated a kaleidoscope of colours to the world from the brightly lit interior. The inside was small but inviting. Ceiling-to-floor shelving, the kind you needed a ladder for, lined the walls, overflowing with many volumes. Despite the small space, a few comfy chairs were scattered about for use by the patrons. The register was located at the back of the shop, which Freydis found odd, but then again, she supposed that the people you typically find in a bookstore are rarely prone to theft.

As always, it was the smell of the place that made the experience so rich—new paper and ink mixed with the sweet, musky smell of well-loved words from aged tomes.

Freydis had a ritual whenever she found herself among so many books. She walked along the shelves, slowly running her fingers over the bindings, caressing and reading the titles, waiting for the one that would call out to her, a whisper only she could hear. The leather-bound ones, with embossed lettering and a gilded edge, were her favourite.

Barely into the ritual, Freydis was interrupted by a vibrant, clearly extroverted redhead calling to her from behind the counter. She approached Freydis, waving so vigorously that Freydis had a mental image of her hand flying off. The woman's smile was the kind that lit up entire rooms, and it burst through the gloomy demeanour that Freydis often found herself in lately. With pep in her step, she moved toward Freydis with her hand outstretched in a friendly greeting.

"Hi! I'm Cass! Welcome to my family's bookstore," she beamed. "You must be new around here? I never forget a face."

After barely taking a breath, Cass continued her verbal assault, telling Freydis all about the history of the shop, her family, and where to find each genre. Freydis couldn't help but watch her, feigning attention to her words. Long red ringlets framed her face perfectly, but it was her emerald-green eyes that made Freydis pause. Vetus had emerald-green eyes that were very similar. The colour reminded her of the new spring grass that comes after winter.

After a moment, Freydis realized that Cass had stopped speaking and was staring at her with a strange but curious look.

"I'm Freydis," she offered back, "and yes, I'm new here. I arrived a couple months ago."

Cass oozed happiness, yet unlike other happy-go-lucky humans, Freydis didn't find her insufferable.

"Well, feel free to have a look around. We have lots of *treasures* waiting to be uncovered."

Cass smiled and left Freydis standing, somewhat perplexed. Had she read her mind?

Freydis continued her ritual and fortunately found a few books longing for a new home. For some reason, she couldn't let go of the feeling that Cass reminded her of someone. Underneath all that exuberance was calm confidence, and it was palpable. Astrid had been the same. Thinking of her now was bittersweet. Freydis wondered if there would ever be a time when her memories didn't fill her with endless grief.

With the ritual successfully completed, Freydis walked to the back of the store, ready to make her purchase and leave.

"This is going to sound weird," Cass held up her hands. "I promise I'm not weird...but are you busy later?"

Freydis schooled her features and shook her head, immediately wishing she was busy.

"Well, my boyfriend's brother is launching a book he wrote tonight, and Ethan and I promised to go for support. Wanna come?"

Freydis desperately wanted to think of an excuse or reason why she wouldn't be able to go, but nothing came to her. Forcing a smile onto her face, she replied, "Sure. Sounds like fun."

Cass burst out laughing. "I wouldn't say fun. Ethan's brother is a computer science engineer. It will probably be incredibly dull, but I am thrilled you will come!"

Damn bookshops and their siren calls. Freydis finished her purchase and agreed to travel with Cass to The Coop, Harvard University's and MIT's shared campus bookstore. It was there that Dr. Marcus Wolfe, a computer science engineer, would be launching his book. Freydis hadn't known many scientists personally, but what she did know didn't inspire any ideas of fun.

"We can meet here at the store," Cass offered.

Freydis nodded, "Sure. Sounds perfect."

Freydis entered her apartment, and the lock clicking into place behind her made her instantly relax. Had socializing always been so exhausting? Or perhaps she'd spent too long living like a little old woman.

Freydis lay down with one of her new books, hoping to have a quick nap before meeting up with Cass later that evening. She tried to let go of the regret she felt for agreeing to go. Maybe it was exactly what she needed to finally bring herself out of the grief and despair she had been drowning in.

The evening air was mild for early April and hinted at the promise of a warm spring. Cass was waiting outside the bookstore, as agreed, and the man standing with her was textbook tall, dark, and handsome. At first glance, Freydis knew he must be an athlete by how he stood: relaxed but poised for action at any moment. He had a friendly face and smiled as Freydis approached.

"Freydis, this is Ethan," Cass said, beaming. They were an adorable couple, clearly in love and extremely comfortable with each other. Ethan let Cass shine brightly, content to simply bask in the warmth of her. They laughed and joked the whole way to The Coop.

Stepping inside, Freydis felt like a child in a candy shop. The bookstore was multi-leveled and boasted bookshelves everywhere she looked. It was breathtaking. Tapestries bearing the campus colours hung from various locations around the store, and a curving staircase led the way to the open balconies lined with bookshelves above. It had been ages since Freydis had been to such a place. It was love at first sight. She would never tell Vetus how right he'd been to suggest this place. He'd never let her hear the end of it.

Awestruck, she followed Cass and Ethan to the area cordoned off for the book launch. A small and chatty crowd waited patiently for the event to begin. Off to the side stood Marcus in a sunflower yellow t-shirt, blue jeans, and sneakers. He was tall, and his dark, unkempt hair gave him the look of a "mad scientist."

Cass had filled her in on Marcus's particulars. As an MIT graduate born to wealthy parents, Freydis expected him to be unapproachable, but when he noticed their presence, he smiled warmly and waved them over. Ethan and Marcus greeted each other with some sort of a brotherly "secret handshake," followed by Marcus politely kissing Cass on the cheek. Freydis stood quietly by, watching them, her heart rate increasing as her palms began to sweat. She frantically wiped them dry on her pants.

"Marcus, this is Freydis," Cass introduced. "She is new to the area, so we brought her along. Try not to bore her."

Marcus laughed off the friendly jab and grasped Freydis's hand, locking his dark eyes with hers as he introduced himself. She felt as though time had slowed, and instantly, butterflies filled her stomach.

Holding up his right hand, he said, "I promise not to bore you."

Marcus pretended to keep a serious face, but his eyes held a mischievous gleam. She smiled sheepishly, hoping she wouldn't embarrass herself in front of him.

When it was time to begin, Cass, Ethan, and Freydis made their way to stand with the others in attendance for the launch. Freydis couldn't stop staring at Marcus. He looked nothing how she had imagined. The crowd welcomed him with a round of applause, and he jumped right into his presentation.

He started by giving a brief personal history, followed by his academic career and the "why" behind his chosen field of expertise. He described the ins and outs of electrical engineering and, more specifically, computer science, where he specialized in machine learning and artificial intelligence.

With a seamless segue, he finally arrived at the part of the presentation describing his newly published book. Up until that point, Freydis, though desperately trying to concentrate on his words, found herself imagining several inappropriate things about this man she just met. It had been several decades, after all.

The book outlined the possibilities and potential that artificial intelligence could offer society in the future. His ideas were innovative and exciting. He argued that his AI-enhanced software, combined with a hardware technology akin to tissue nanotransfection, could be introduced to the human brain, drastically improving brain performance, the prognosis of certain diseases, and even repairing damage. A similar technology was already seeing minor successes in the medical world, and with improvements, his could even tackle aging and mortality.

It also held the potential to help resolve societal inequities on a level where certain differences would no longer influence people's successes and failures. It could be done at a surprisingly low cost when compared to the future it could promise.

It was brilliant and revolutionary, and picturing it wrenched Freydis out of her daydreams, filling her with trepidation. At no point in his entire talk did he cover any possible complications or consequences of the procedure or the potential ramifications this technology could have for humanity.

When the time came for questions, Freydis could barely contain herself. Her thoughts were moving at the speed of light. At the first opportunity, she hammered him with questions.

"Isn't this procedure incredibly dangerous?"

"It is minimally invasive, which mitigates most of the risk, but like any procedure, the risk is not zero," Marcus answered.

"Who will install the implants?" she continued. "Will it be reversible?"

"Every procedure will be conducted by rigorously trained, highly skilled technicians, overseen by my team and our medical staff. Reversing it will be possible but is inherently more dangerous."

The questions poured from her mouth as fast as they popped into her head, but Marcus fielded them expertly, to the delight of the audience watching their intellectual tennis match.

"Who will be responsible for maintenance and the overall operating system?"

"I will," Marcus smiled. "My team has developed a state-of-the-art program that has passed multiple ethics reviews and evaluations."

Marcus responded to each question with confidence, although his answers did little to calm the unease and apprehension she felt. After a few questions from others in the crowd, Marcus offered the opportunity for people to get their copies of his book signed.

Freydis purchased a copy and waited in line. When her turn came up, Marcus greeted her with the same warm smile she saw earlier. Overcome with a sense of self-consciousness due to her outburst and interrogation, she handed him her book without making eye contact.

"Hey—Freydis, was it?" Marcus drawled.

She nodded, meeting his gaze. He opened the book, scribbled a quick dedication on the inside cover, and handed it back to her.

"I can tell I didn't give you all the answers you were looking for, but I would love to take you for a bite to eat after this, and we can discuss it further."

His invitation caught her completely off guard, and she looked at Cass, who was within earshot, standing with Ethan. Cass gave her a wink and thumbs-up as though it had been her plan all along. Freydis rolled her eyes and shook her head at the childish grins on Cass's and Ethan's faces and reluctantly agreed to his offer. Cass and Ethan wasted no time saying their goodbyes, and Marcus assured them he would see Freydis made it home safely.

❦

Marcus hurriedly finished signing books and the obligatory small talk that came with it. He couldn't stop thinking about Freydis. He found himself continually looking where she waited patiently for him to finish up. He'd surprised himself by inviting her out after his book launch, but he had to spend more time with her.

She was beautiful in a way that he couldn't put into words. Her wavy shoulder-length hair fell gently around her face, its chestnut hue accentuating her stormy grey eyes. It was her fiery intellect that attracted him most. The way she challenged him and showed genuine interest in his work was refreshing, and although he never cared about what other people thought before, he was hell-bent on proving his vision worthy in her eyes. He made a mental note to thank Cass for bringing her into his life, no matter what that evening might bring.

Marcus took Freydis to The Longfellow bar, only a few minutes walk from The Coop. The atmosphere was relaxed and fun, which eased the tension between them. Their chemistry was unmistakable. Marcus spent very little time discussing his book and the ground-breaking possibilities such a technology might herald. He was too preoccupied with finding out everything he could about Freydis.

"So why come to Boston?" Marcus asked. "It must be very different than Iceland."

"I needed a change of scenery, and a friend pulled some strings to set me up with a job."

"What about your family?"

"My parents died a long time ago," she smiled ruefully. "And I'm an only child."

"I'm sorry, Freydis, I—"

"It's okay," she reassured him. "I have a few close friends that might as well be family."

Their conversation lasted until the bar closed, and as promised, Marcus ensured Freydis made it home safely. On his way back across town to his condo overlooking the waterfront, he couldn't stop thinking about when he would be able to see her again. When he finally settled into bed and closed his eyes to sleep, his memory traced the lines of her face on his eyelids.

Once home, Freydis made herself a cup of tea before bed and replayed the night's events over and over in her head. She grabbed her phone and dialled Vetus's number. She never knew where in the world Vetus might be, but he always answered.

"Hello, Freydis," Vetus said. "Is everything all right? It's well after midnight where you are."

"Everything is fine...wonderful actually," her words poured excitedly from her lips. "Did I wake you?"

"No."

"Okay, good. I met some people today. It was bizarre actually, but this girl, Cass, she works at one of the bookstores near me, and she invited me to a book signing tonight."

"I'm glad to hear you're settling in. This is the happiest I've heard you in a long time. Did you buy the book?"

"I did. The author is Cass's boyfriend Ethan's brother. He's a scientist—an engineer, actually. He's very handsome, Vetus; you'd like him."

"Probably not my type, Dea," Vetus drawled.

"That's not what I meant." Freydis rolled her eyes. "Cass introduced us. You were right about needing a fresh start. After the book signing, he took me out for drinks, and—"

"You misunderstood me, Dea, if you thought I meant for you to jump into a relationship with another human," Vetus's voice was taut. "And so soon. You've only just laid Astrid to rest. Take some time to learn to be by yourself again."

"First of all, it was only drinks. And second, that is so easy for you to say," Freydis shot back. "You have other people, Vetus, others just like you. You won't introduce me, so I only have you, wherever you are. I don't want to learn to be by myself. You are supposed to be happy for me."

"I am happy you're making new connections in Boston," Vetus's voice was monotone.

"And you are happy that I found new friends...including Marcus. Right?" Freydis urged.

"Good night, Freydis."

The line went silent.

Vetus might not get older in looks, but he could be a grumpy old man sometimes. It never mattered who Freydis had a relationship with. If they were human, Vetus never approved, but what other choice did she have?

Thoughts of Marcus quickly replaced her lingering annoyance with Vetus's attitude. Freydis was smitten with him. She could barely recall all the things Marcus had said. She would have listened to him recite the alphabet and been content to be in his presence. It had been ages since she'd felt the excitement of meeting someone and having an instant connection.

Despite her infatuation, a nagging anxiety cautioned Freydis about how quickly she was falling for Marcus. Was Vetus right? *Was it too soon?* She'd barely moved on from her grief of losing Astrid. But Marcus was charming, attractive, and smart. *And he'd said all the right things.*

Chapter Three

Freydis had never been camping in the traditional sense, and by mid-August, Cass had convinced her that getting out of the city would be an excellent way to end the summer. It sounded like a lot of work, but the chance to submerse herself in nature would be worth it.

Cass had shown her just about all there was to see around Boston. She needed some time away from the city.

Marcus and Ethan chose Long Pond Campground, the place where they had spent many carefree childhood days in the wilderness with their family. As they unpacked and set up the site, the brothers' excitement was palpable. Freydis could easily imagine them as children.

The campsite was a small clearing in a wooded area with an established firepit. A lake for swimming was visible through the trees, and Freydis was almost certain it was at the perfect angle to watch the sunset.

Cass and Ethan went to find firewood, so Freydis made her way to the shore, slipping off her sandals to dip her toes in the cool water while Marcus finished setting up the last tent.

Freydis and Marcus had spent the last few months getting to know each other, but despite their obvious mutual attraction, neither had made any real moves toward taking the next step. Freydis knew Marcus was busy with his new position at Anderson Technology and Robotics. The time needed for his research limited their opportunities for quality time. He had spent his entire academic career for this very chance to make a difference and contribute something meaningful to society.

This camping trip would be the first opportunity they'd had to spend consecutive days together since they met. Freydis was cautiously excited, but the thought of losing herself in another "human" relationship was daunting. There was a lot she would never be able to share with him. She would never be able to be her true self with him. The obstacles they faced seemed insurmountable.

A flash of something large and iridescent in the water drew Freydis's eye. She waded a little further in to try and get a better look, but it was gone as quickly as it had appeared. She bent over and plucked a flat stone from the lakebed.

Coming up to the water's edge behind her, Marcus said, "I can't believe you've never been camping. Not once? Really?"

"I have, but not like this," she said, skipping the stone across the water. "My father was a fisherman. I spent most of my time near the water."

"So, you can catch our supper then?" Marcus asked wryly.

She swallowed and gave him a tight smile, "It was a long time ago."

Freydis started out of the water and felt something grab her ankle. Before she could register what was happening, the grip gave a hard tug, causing Freydis to fall forward onto the sharp, wet rocks. The grip released, allowing Freydis to scramble on. Marcus rushed toward her and helped her up. She winced at the sight of blood blossoming from the cut now on her hand.

If it hurt, Freydis barely noticed it; her mind was racing. Had something grabbed her, or had she been caught up in something and slipped? Before she could stop him, Marcus hurried to get the first aid kit. Gently, he cleaned the wound and applied a small bandage. Freydis laughed at how serious he was being.

"I'm alright, Marcus; stop fussing over me."

"Infections are serious business, Freydis. Who knows what kind of bacteria is in that water?"

"I heal fast," she said, rolling her eyes.

Freydis laughed, earning a goofy grin from Marcus, though his brow was still furrowed with obvious concern. She leaned over and kissed him on the cheek. He looked at her, his eyes full of longing. Freydis thought for sure he was about to kiss her, but the moment was gone almost as quickly as it came, interrupted by Cass and Ethan's return.

They spent the evening around the campfire, laughing and enjoying each other's company. Ethan brought his guitar, which surprised Freydis. He didn't seem like the musical type. Cass sang. She had a beautiful voice. Freydis closed her eyes and listened to the duet. Her mother had always been singing when Freydis was a child. She'd forgotten how much she enjoyed listening to someone sing.

Ethan played and Cass sang until well after midnight. Their fire had burned down to the last few glowing embers, twinkling as though they were communicating with the stars in the night sky. Freydis watched as Ethan knelt to put his guitar back in the case. Despite the dim lighting, Freydis noticed that he had retrieved a small velvet box, poorly concealed in his hand. His face was tight with determination.

Ethan knelt on one knee in front of Cass, taking her hand into his own. His eyes were full of certainty and hope. Freydis elbowed Marcus, who had begun to nod off, drawing his attention to the couple.

"Cassandra Walsh," Ethan began, "I have loved you more each day since the day we met. You are the answer to my prayers and all my dreams come true."

He paused, swallowing deeply as he fought the tremor in his voice. With tears in her eyes, Cass reached out and cupped his cheek with her free hand.

Ethan continued, "I want to spend the rest of my life with you. Will you marry me?"

Cass leapt toward him, knocking him onto the ground, the two of them barely missing the dying fire. Through their giggles and kisses, Freydis heard Cass answer yes, earning a cheer from Marcus.

Freydis couldn't recall a time when she'd had so much fun, and she wondered if she would ever find a love like theirs for herself.

With summer over, Freydis decided to use her credentials as assistant professor to access the multitude of libraries on campus. She was thrilled to have the freedom to do so without the obligation of actual professorship. It had been almost a century since she had access to a proper place to research, and the thought of having something to focus her energy on was refreshing. It might lead to information about the others like her mother.

Standing amid the dusty stacks, Freydis tried to remember something, anything her mother might have said that she could use as a clue. She'd once said that she wasn't born on this planet but came from somewhere else. Somewhere beyond the stars.

As a child, Freydis found her stories exciting and magical, but as she stood in front of a section on extraterrestrials, Freydis began to think her mother might have been a little crazy. So, if she wasn't an alien, maybe she should start with the obvious.

The section on the occult was considerably large for a university campus. Freydis ran her fingertips along the vast collection of old books, hoping her intuition or the magic in her blood would guide her. She found herself drawn to the books on witchcraft.

Out of the corner of her eye, she swore she saw someone duck behind one of the stacks toward the front of the alcove she was in. She quickly pulled the few tomes she'd been eyeing from the shelves and steeled herself against the fear that started to creep into her mind.

As she exited the alcove, she looked around briefly for whomever had been lurking around, but the area was empty. Still, she couldn't shake the feeling that someone or something had been watching her.

Freydis left the library with a few promising books she hoped might hold some evidence of her mother's people. At least reading them would make her feel like she was working toward something and quiet the guilt she felt for ignoring her mother's words.

For centuries, a sense of existential dread made digging too deep terrifying. What if she never found them, or they didn't exist at all? What if everything she thought she knew about her mother and her past was a lie or some fairytale her mother told her? Perhaps time had twisted the story she'd told herself, and she was only chasing shadows. How would she face eternity if the persona she'd built for herself was a lie and her life really had no purpose?

She hadn't seen much of Marcus after their camping trip. He explained that there had been a big breakthrough with the technology his team had been working on, but he texted often. She was secretly very glad to hear that she was on his mind.

When she wasn't preoccupied with academia, she was with Cass. In less than a year, Cass and Freydis became very close. They were like opposite sides of the same coin. Where Cass was bright and bubbly, Freydis was serious and reserved. Together, though, they brought out the best in each other. Freydis hadn't realized how much she missed companionship.

Every Friday morning, Freydis would meet Cass early for tea, and they'd spend the day together. It almost always included browsing bookstores, followed by a walk near the waterfront.

The first signs of autumn were beginning to show. A crisp but gentle breeze accompanied them as they strolled along the pier, delivering an air so salty they could taste its residue on their lips. The rising sun painted the changing leaves lining the boardwalk in hues of gold and scarlet. It was a picturesque New England morning.

Freydis inhaled deeply, "Autumn starts so late here. I'm used to it coming earlier in Iceland. It's my favourite time of year."

Cass smiled, "I like the fall too. Mom and I used to travel to Salem every Autumn Equinox. I still go, but it's not the same without her, you know?"

Freydis smiled tightly and nodded, "How long has it been?"

"Three years in December," Cass murmured, "but it hurts as bad as if it were yesterday."

"It's good that you still make the effort to go. I bet she'd be thrilled." Freydis tried to sound encouraging, but she knew all about the pain Cass felt.

"I bet she'd haunt me if I didn't." Cass's chuckle was genuine, and Freydis felt the tension in her chest slip a little. She was grateful to have Cass in her life now.

Freydis and Cass were deep in conversation when they were uncharacteristically interrupted by the ringtone of Cass's cell. Cass pulled the device from her sweater pocket, and the blood drained from her cheeks as she glimpsed the call display.

"I'm so sorry, Freydis. I have to take this."

Freydis smiled and went back to watching the naval traffic that polluted the harbour.

"Hello? Yes, this is…," Cass's voice faltered. "Yes, of course, you were clear."

Cass remained quiet, listening to the caller briefly before lowering the phone away from her face. Her hands trembled as she fumbled the phone back into her pocket. Sensing something wasn't right, Freydis approached Cass, who'd forced a smile onto her face.

Freydis returned the smile, "Everything okay, Cass? You seem a bit shaken."

"I'm fine," Cass said brusquely. "Wrong number."

Freydis didn't believe her lie but decided not to push her any further. "Okay," Freydis smiled brightly, "wanna grab lunch?"

Later that evening, Freydis tried reading one of the books she'd purchased earlier that day. No matter how she tried to focus on the page in front of her, her mind drifted repeatedly to Cass and the phone call on the waterfront. She had never seen Cass like that before. She remained off for the rest of the day. Even the odd time Freydis had seen her have a squabble with Ethan, Cass had always been unshakable.

Freydis's cell chimed with a text message notification. It was Cass, as if thinking had conjured her out of thin air. The message was an invitation for Freydis to go with her to Salem for the Autumn Equinox the following weekend. Freydis wanted to support her friend more than anything, but the thought of travelling to one of the most infamous historical sites of witch trials and executions made her skin crawl.

Without answering, she placed her phone on her nightstand and downed the last mouthful of tea from her favourite mug. She shuffled down in her bed and fixed her pillows from reading position to sleeping position. Turning off the lamp, she lay in the dark, looking at the light from the city outside as it poured in through the window, making shadows dance on the walls and ceiling. As she lay there, the sound of rain on the windowpane lulled her into a fitful sleep.

Freydis stood silently watching as soldiers led her mother, almost willingly, and tied her to the stake. Even in a dull grey rough-spun dress, Freydis thought, she was the most elegant and graceful being she had ever seen. Her mother's stormy grey eyes, a mirror of Freydis's own, scanned the crowd, finding Freydis despite her attempts to hide herself. If her mother was afraid, she was unable to tell.

Freydis's mind was racing, and her heart ached, desperate for a plan, wanting to scream at her mother to save herself. But she kept her lips firmly sealed.

Frantically, Freydis scoured the crowd that had gathered. Where was her father? Why wasn't he there? *Coward.*

In her hand, she clenched a scrap of parchment, her mother's last words to her, as tears streamed down her face. Her mother smiled sadly at her, but her eyes remained resolute. The executioner carried the torch to the pyre as the rain began to fall. The flames, in bright defiance, licked ever higher. Inhuman howls flooded the courtyard as flames swallowed the others.

Freydis crumbled to her knees.

A single tear rolled down her mother's cheek, and just before she let go, she looked up, stoic as always, and gave her final breath to the night sky.

Freydis woke in a cold sweat, her pajamas soaked and clinging to her. It was not the first time she had dreamed of her mother's death. It always felt as real in her dreams as it did the day it happened.

The pastel pink of the sky out her bedroom window indicated it was just before sunrise. She peeled off the sweat-drenched clothes and stood in a steamy shower, letting the hot water relax her and wash away the remnants of her dreadful sleep.

After her shower, she retrieved her cell from her nightstand before making her morning cup of tea. Reluctantly, she scrolled to and read the message from Cass once more. She would accept the invitation, she knew, regardless of how she felt. Maybe it would give her some closure of her own. Maybe somehow, it might honour her mother's sacrifice. Either way, it meant a lot to Cass and that was enough for Freydis.

Cass slid gently out of bed and tiptoed out of the room, hoping to let Ethan sleep a bit longer. She loved rising with the sun when the world was quiet and peaceful. Those moments in between: night and day, light and dark, were full of magic. It was why she always made a big deal about the Equinox.

Her mother had taught her all the magic she knew, though her mother was only human. Cass's magic, she knew, came from her father, some faerie prince who had claimed to love her mother but left her before Cass was born.

Her mother never married, and though she never admitted it, Cass knew she always believed he would return someday. When her mother died, Cass used every bit of magic she knew to try and bring her back, but it wasn't enough.

Cass glanced at the gold and silver filigree ring she wore on her right ring finger. It was inlaid with an amethyst of the deepest purple she had ever seen. After her mother's death, an envoy from the faerie Winter Court had brought condolences on behalf of the prince and the ring. It was a gift from her father, they'd said, and with it came a message that should she accept his gift, she would be recognized as a vassal of the court with all proper entitlements.

The implications of that offer were far beyond what she could have imagined. The ring on her finger was a daily reminder of the court's expectations. Glancing from the ring to the man still asleep in her bed, she wondered if the sacrifice she made by accepting her father's "gift" would ever take him from her. Ethan was her solace.

It was shortly after her mother's death that Ethan came into her life and embraced every part of her, even the magic. He didn't understand it, and she wasn't sure he completely believed everything she told him, but he never held her back from exploring that part of herself.

That was why, when he came home last night saying he was coming with her and Freydis to Salem, she wasn't entirely shocked. His announcement that Marcus wanted to come made her raise an eyebrow. It was entirely out of character for *Mr. Oh-So-Rational*.

The trip to Salem had a two-fold purpose this year. Cass wouldn't have missed it for the world, but inviting Freydis would give her the opportunity to come clean. Cass knew she was supposed to keep Freydis focused on the search for her mother's people, to be someone who could fill in the missing pieces of who she was and why she existed at all. Hopefully, she could still accomplish what she set out to do.

Chapter Four

Freydis filled the kettle with water and plugged it in. When she received a message from Cass saying Ethan and Marcus were coming with them, it wasn't until she read his name that she realized how much she had been missing Marcus. At least having him there would give her a pleasant distraction.

Freydis pinched the bridge of her nose in a futile attempt to squeeze away the tension headache she had woken up with. Regretting her decision to go with Cass to Salem wouldn't make the trip any easier. She forced herself to focus on the positives.

Living with Astrid had made her feel like she had somewhere to belong. She thought losing Astrid meant losing her identity all over again, but perhaps Cass and Marcus could help her belong here.

A knock on the door jolted Freydis from her daydream. She looked at the clock on the wall to confirm that she wasn't late, but it was still too early for Cass to have arrived to pick her up.

Another knock on the door hurried Freydis, and she opened it without looking to see who it was. Vetus stood outside her door, shadowed by a man so otherworldly that, for a moment, she wasn't sure if he was real. Meeting his gaze took her breath away. He was slightly taller than Vetus, who also towered over her, and even though he wore casual clothes, he looked like he should be wearing chain mail and brandishing a sword like the great knights of old. Her reaction to his presence was visceral, and it unnerved and intrigued her.

"Are you not happy to see me, Dea?" Vetus asked, brushing past her. He never waited to be invited in. She gestured sarcastically to his handsome companion, who, surprisingly, *did* wait for an invitation. She could sense that Vetus's question was loaded. Freydis closed the door and took a deep breath.

"I'm always happy to see you, Vetus," she said, embracing him. "Just a little surprised that you're here. I am leaving shortly to go to Salem with Cass, remember?"

His apparent desire to start being more present in her life, just as she was preparing to go on another trip with Marcus, seemed too on the nose to be a coincidence and irritated her. She'd only just found out Marcus was coming this morning, though. *Vetus couldn't possibly have known, could he? Is that why he brought Mr. Tall-Dark-and-Handsome?*

"Marcus and Ethan are coming too," she said, although she wasn't sure what compelled her to say it.

"You are making a mistake with that boy," Vetus spit out the words like poison arrows meant straight for her heart. "They aren't all like Astrid, Dea."

Despite the attempt to soften the blow, his words found their mark without mercy. Vetus had never spoken harshly to her before. She wasn't even sure she heard him correctly and paused for a moment, allowing the weight of his words to build up pressure inside of her. She glanced from Vetus to the mystery man who accompanied him.

He was alluring and magnetic. She could tell he wasn't human just by looking at him. She'd always felt the same quality about Vetus, although he was better at pretending to be mortal. The man's dark-brown hair was a stark contrast to his silvery eyes, which sparkled mischievously as he stared at her.

"Where are my manners?" Vetus feigned embarrassment. "Freydis, this is Rowan MacArtur. He works for my family, but he is more like a son to me."

Freydis could feel the heat rising in her face, and she desperately tried to calm herself. She didn't care who the stranger was, but to call him a son was a slap to her face. She had known Vetus for nearly three and half centuries, and he'd never mentioned him. The whole situation felt more and more like it was a set-up.

"What the hell is that supposed to mean, Vetus?" A dam had broken, and she couldn't stop the flow of words now. "You show up here after I don't hear from you for what—more than a month? And with some random stranger, to lecture me—like you have any right to an opinion."

Vetus sat silently at the kitchen table, not breaking eye contact.

Freydis continued, "We have been friends nearly my whole life, but I know almost nothing about you. I've never asked anything of you, never pushed you to talk about yourself because I always thought we respected each other if for no other reason than that we both carried the same burden of immortality—"

"Stop," Vetus interrupted. "It is not a burden to live forever; it is a gift. One that you make seem abhorrent and are content to waste, over and over, dallying with humans like you are one of them."

At that, Rowan smirked, though he quickly changed his expression when Freydis shot him a look.

"Who even talks like that?" Freydis's voice grew louder. "You forget, Vetus, I *am* partly human. I am as much a part of their world as I am yours, if not more. You talk about them as if they are something less and then seem surprised that I would be insulted."

The kettle had been whistling, though Freydis didn't know for how long. At some point, Rowan walked over and opened the cupboard. Coincidently, he retrieved her favourite mug and placed a teabag inside, followed by the boiling water. Though she was intrigued by the gesture, it was presumptuous of him to go through her cupboards. Strangely, she didn't mind the intrusion, although she was rather distracted by Vetus and his unwanted opinions.

Rowan stood before her, his sweet, earthy smell like the air after a summer thunderstorm wafted around her. He held the steaming mug in his outstretched hand, and his lips again quirked into a smile at the corner, but his eyes were gleaming. Gods, his presence there at that moment was unnerving and slightly irritating, but she forced herself to smile and take the mug.

"I know this is about Marcus," Freydis hissed. "I've known you didn't like the idea of me and him since I first told you about my feelings. You can't stop me from having a relationship with him, Vetus."

Vetus remained silent, his expression unchanged. Rowan moved as if to join him at the table, but instead, with the same grin as before, he pulled out a chair and offered it to Freydis. She only glared at him, fighting her own smile, hoping he would take a hint. *Who does this guy think he is? He hasn't said a word the whole time, and he just carries on as though this weren't the most awkward situation he could be in.* Rowan returned her glare with a shrug and sat down in the chair himself, completely casual, as though he was unaware of the tension in the room.

"What do you want to know?" Vetus asked. Freydis looked at him incredulously.

"Have you not been listening to me at all?" *Had he always been this insufferable?* Vetus sat across from her, waiting expectantly.

"I don't have time for this today, Vetus," Freydis shook her head and sighed. "Cass will be here to pick me up shortly. Maybe you and your 'son' here should spend some time getting to know the area. I will call you when I get back."

Freydis walked to the door and opened it. The obvious gesture that it was time for them to leave hung in the air like a thick fog. Rowan was the first to get up, and as he passed her, she was sure he gave her a wink before he carried on down the hall. Vetus stopped in the doorway, and without turning, he said, "I am only trying to protect you, Dea."

"I've never asked you to," Freydis replied coldly, shutting the door before he could say anything else.

Rowan watched as Vetus emerged from the building with a grin lighting up his face. He couldn't imagine what Vetus had to be happy about. Only moments before, Freydis had given him quite the tongue-lashing. She was not at all how he had imagined. She was bratty and stubborn and beautiful. Even "beauty" wasn't a true enough word to capture her.

Still, he was drawn to her like the tides are pulled by the moon. He couldn't get the image of her out of his head. He knew she was haunted. He could see she wore her pain like armour, but her stormy eyes gave her truth away. He didn't know why but seeing her made him want to risk that storm and all her ghosts to save her, not that she needed it. He could tell she was fierce, not fragile, battered but never broken. He knew he would give up immortality itself for just one moment in her arms. He also wondered if he'd bumped his head.

"What are you grinning about?" he asked Vetus after he'd crossed the street. Rowan stood with his arms crossed. "I would never dream of speaking to you like that. Why put up with it?"

"She is exactly like her mother. More so, every time I see her."

"So, you knew her mother?" Rowan asked.

"At least as well as you did," Vetus replied, touching the lower left side of Rowan's torso. Rowan's hand moved to the area, the site of a grievous wound he had suffered in his youth. He'd been stabbed by a legendary blade that left an unhealable wound. Vetus had found him dying and taken him to an arcane healer. A woman. He looked at Vetus with wide eyes and nodded slowly as understanding overcame him.

Rowan watched as Vetus approached the car waiting for them and dismissed the driver for the day. They would indeed do some sightseeing, as Freydis suggested. It had been an age since Vetus used the old ways to the Otherworld, and he was feeling nostalgic.

Shaken from the surprise visit from Vetus, Freydis was quiet for almost the entire drive to Salem, staring blankly out her window at the dark clouds gathering in the sky. She listened half-heartedly as Marcus told them all about the latest developments in his research. They were seeing real progress in the lab with the initial clinical trials, and if things continued at a similar rate, human clinical trials would soon follow. Freydis found his passion and excitement refreshing.

Humans were innovative and creative. They didn't let their mortality limit them and keep them from pursuing more, which she couldn't say about the few immortals that she knew. Her mother barely spoke about her immortality, and Vetus was the most predictable person she knew. They behaved like nothing should ever change, and the old way was the only way.

"How's the hand?" Marcus asked. "You really should have seen a doctor, you know."

"Hmm?" Freydis said. "Oh, my hand? Good as new." She offered him the palm of her hand, which showed a faded, almost invisible scar.

"That's incredible," Marcus said. "It's like nothing ever happened." He sounded surprised, sending a surge of awareness to her. She pulled her hand away.

There was no way Freydis was going to let Vetus influence the way she felt about Marcus, even though in truth, she really didn't know what she felt for him.

There were several ways they could have chosen to celebrate the Autumn Equinox in Salem, but Cass told Freydis the first thing she always did was visit the Salem Witch Trials Memorial. The memorial was not at all what Freydis had imagined. If Cass hadn't described it on the drive, Freydis would have overlooked it entirely.

It was a modest little park located next to an old cemetery. The area was surrounded on three sides by a low stone wall with the occasional stone slab jutting out. In the middle was a small grassy patch with a few trees scattered about. It wasn't strong, but Freydis could feel a low thrum of unsettling energy all around her. Cass explained that it was believed the same species of trees was used for the hangings.

The four began to walk the first section of the stone wall. Closer inspection revealed that the stones jutting out were marked with victims' names and other details. As they passed each epitaph, Cass laid a single white lily upon the stone—to symbolize the victim's innocence.

Freydis tried to listen intently and reverently to Cass as she read each name aloud but found herself distracted by that energy and an increasingly agitated Marcus. Ethan must have noticed also because he slowed his pace to match his brother's and spoke to him in a low, calming voice, too low for Freydis to hear what he was saying. As Cass was finishing her ritual at the final stone, Ethan suggested they grab something to eat before checking into their hotel for the night.

Freydis was relieved to leave the memorial behind as it conjured up many painful memories. Still, she found that all she could focus on at that moment was Marcus. She had never seen anything ruffle his feathers that way in the time she had known him. She tried subtly to get his attention as they walked to supper, but he proceeded as though she weren't there at all. It wasn't until after they had all sat down and placed their orders that Marcus finally spoke up.

"It amazes me how many people, mostly innocent people, have been wrongly killed or imprisoned because of some ridiculous superstitions and weak-minded beliefs." He sat a little taller. "That is why I deal with science and facts, not feelings. If they had done the same, that memorial wouldn't even be necessary."

"Excuse me?" Cass asked incredulously. Freydis could sense a sudden shift in Cass's usually happy demeanour. Her tone and the redness that flushed her cheeks betrayed the illusion of calm that Cass was struggling to maintain.

"All I'm saying is there isn't anything that science can't explain, at least eventually," Marcus's tone was matter-of-fact, almost arrogant. "Salem is the perfect example. Religion, magic—neither is real. There was nothing supernatural about what happened here. Just ignorance."

Magic isn't real. The words were barely out of his mouth before Freydis felt as though all the air had been sucked out of the room. She knew intimately that what he was saying was wrong. She knew magic existed, but she would never be able to say it.

The shock she initially felt from his words was soon replaced by an urge to defend Cass. *Why had he come on this trip at all if that was how he felt?* Doubt and memories of Vetus's visit earlier that day began to creep into her mind but were interrupted when Cass spoke.

"Well, that is a very narrow-minded way of looking at it."

Freydis watched as Ethan covered Cass's hand with his, as though by instinct, a clear display of concern and an attempt to comfort.

"I think what Marcus meant," Ethan said, "is that they were limited by the times they lived in. Things weren't understood as they are now, and if they'd only known then what we know now, many lives would have been spared."

He looked at his brother, "Right, Marcus?"

Freydis twinged with discomfort at Ethan's attempt to make peace between the two people he loved, though she admired him for it. Her thoughts returned to her argument with Vetus earlier. She immediately felt pity for the man who had been there with Vetus. *What was his name again?* She had been too preoccupied with Vetus to remember.

He was stunningly handsome, though—the same type of ethereal beauty that she would have ascribed to Vetus.

Otherworldly and captivating.

Marcus stood abruptly, jarring Freydis out of her thoughts, and tossed a few bills on the table.

"Sure, that's it," he said, leaving the table without another word. Freydis forced herself not to follow him. She was there with Cass, after all.

Their meals arrived, and though they no longer felt like it, they ate in mostly uncomfortable silence, punctuated with a bit of small talk.

Walking back to where they had parked the car, Ethan received a text from Marcus saying he had gone to the hotel and checked in. It was then that Ethan explained Marcus's outburst.

"Our parents were very religious when we were children and raised us to be the same. Everything changed when our sister died."

His words slammed into Freydis like a freight train, and Cass whipped her head around, her expression full of hurt. Ethan continued to speak, though the words stuck in his throat.

"Charlotte was ten. Marcus was fourteen, and I had just turned thirteen. At age nine, she was diagnosed with an aggressive, rare form of brain cancer. As he had been taught his whole life, Marcus prayed, constantly, and when she died, his faith died with her." Ethan paused for a moment to collect himself.

"Mom and Dad threw themselves into their work, and I had always been into sports, so I found an outlet for my grief. I don't think Marcus ever did. At her funeral, I heard him promise her he would find a way to make sure what happened to her wouldn't happen to anyone else."

When he finally stopped speaking, Cass wrapped him in her arms, tears filling her eyes as the weight of his words brought understanding about why Marcus had been so upset. Freydis, familiar with the all-consuming grief of losing someone you love, wanted desperately to get to the hotel. To Marcus.

Chapter Five

Time behaved differently in the Otherworld, and when it was only autumn in the mortal realm, the snow already dusted the ground in the lands of the Winter Court. Nearing the yearly height of his power, the Winter King, Vetus's father, would be in high spirits, or at least that is what they hoped for.

The disused entrance to the Otherworld Vetus and Rowan came to was located in Mount Auburn Cemetery. Vetus had led them to the edge of a lake that was almost a perfect circle.

"There used to be an entrance near here...somewhere." Vetus rubbed his chin as he looked around. "It looked a lot different when I was here last."

Without warning, Vetus began to walk toward the water. Rowan grabbed his arm.

"I don't think drowning yourself will help you remember."

Vetus winked at him and placed his foot in the water. A frozen path appeared on the surface of the lake, and in the middle arose a stone doorway at the end of the path.

Rowan shook his head in disbelief.

"Even after all the human interference in this place, the old magic still remembers." Vetus gave Rowan a mischievous grin. "You'd better keep up or you might get wet."

Rowan followed Vetus along the frozen path and through the doorway. It landed them a lengthy walk to Midhir's palace, a minor inconvenience, but it would allow the crown prince to sort out what exactly he intended to say to the king.

"How long has it been since you last saw him?"

"Not long enough," Vetus muttered.

"Do you think the king will actually help you?" Rowan asked.

The Winter King unnerved Rowan. He found it difficult to reconcile the fact that the crown prince he loved as a father and the soulless wretch that sat upon the twisted blackthorn throne shared blood.

When Rowan was only a child, Vetus had saved him after his mother and father had been butchered before his eyes. Rowan tried desperately to protect his mother when his father fell, but he was struck down, pierced by a legendary blade, the wounds from which no living being could survive. But thanks to Vetus, Rowan *did* survive, and Midhir made him his ward.

It wasn't kindness but curiosity that moved Midhir. How did a half-fae, half-Fir Bolg survive such a wound? And why, as the years passed, did that same boy who should have been mortal like every other half-fae being suddenly become immortal?

Vetus's voice was grim, "I doubt it. He has never helped before where she was concerned."

The snow crunched beneath their boots as they walked, echoing through the forest, startling some ghostly blue will-o'-the-wisps. The gnarled trees resembled grotesque beings frozen in time, but it was what they concealed that made treading off the known path so treacherous. The creatures of Winter knew better than to challenge their prince, but their loyalty belonged to the Winter King alone.

Vetus's and Rowan's modern clothes had been replaced by Winter Court regalia as though the land recognized them and their destination. It probably did. The Otherworld was known to have a mind of her own.

Vetus's Burberry suit was replaced by a midnight-blue doublet with silver embellishments and his father's sigil emblazoned on his chest. Black breeches and leggings covered his legs down to his black leather riding boots. A rich black velvet hooded cloak, fastened with a palladium brooch in the shape of a crown of thorns hung over his shoulders. The finishing touch was a simple palladium circlet adorning his brow.

Rowan, on the other hand, exchanged jeans and a simple shirt for a black gambeson underneath a palladium cuirass, also engraved with Midhir's sigil, and black riding breeches. Identical black leather riding boots now replaced his running shoes. Unlike Vetus's, Rowan's cloak was midnight-blue with silver embroidery. A livery collar bearing a crown of thorns, denoting his rank, hung around his neck.

Now, they were fit to stand before the king.

For most strangers, winter magic was unpredictable and unkind to those who had the bad fortune of finding themselves in the lands of winter. For Vetus, however, the magic was in his blood, though neither blood nor magic would sway the Winter King.

Marcus stood in the shower, hot water rushing over him like flames, burning away the tension in his body. He'd meant everything he said at supper, but the look of shock and hurt on Freydis's face pained him. *Why was she so bothered by his comments?* It didn't matter. He'd hurt her somehow. He would make it right. She was the only thing that had ever made him want to forget the world, his work, and his worries. The pull she had on him was terrifying and wonderful, and why he chose to come to Salem. His work would wait.

Marcus didn't anticipate the memorial to be so triggering for him. He would apologize and try to explain himself, even though he wasn't sure he could. He truly believed science could and would eventually explain all the mysteries in the world, and with time, Freydis would understand that.

Out of the shower, he pulled on a clean plain white t-shirt and his dark blue jeans. Ethan texted, saying they were back from supper and invited him to the hotel bar to grab a drink. He hoped Freydis was still in her room as it would be the perfect and possibly only chance to catch her alone and make his apology.

Reaching her room, he stood frozen, desperately trying to find the words, when Freydis opened the door.

"Marcus?" Her look of initial surprise melted into a smile that went all the way to her eyes.

"I came to apologize for earlier, I...," he started his apology, but his voice faltered when she slipped her fingers into the waistband of his jeans. Pulling him inside, she closed the door behind them. All the words and thoughts he'd had before were gone.

She removed her hand from his waist and slid it up his chest to his neck, her eyes following her motion like a predator sizing up its prey. He could feel the heat of her body next to his own. She entangled her fingers in his hair, sending waves of desire from his head to his toes.

With her face barely inches away from his, she looked at him, her grey eyes luminous and longing. She smelled like lavender. He hadn't noticed before. He'd never been so present with her, like nothing else existed. His heart hammered in his chest.

He couldn't count the number of times he had pictured being with her. He had always thought he would be nervous, but as her soft, warm lips pressed against his, everything became instinctual. He placed his hand on the small of her back and pulled her against him, deepening the kiss. She moaned and he felt her relax into him. Her body responding to his touch was better than he had imagined.

Freydis hadn't expected Marcus to be outside her door when she opened it. She was about to leave to go meet Cass, but there he was. He smelled like soap and fresh linen.

All the emotions that were building inside her all day, from that morning with Vetus to the walk back to the car with Ethan, screamed for release. Seeing Marcus outside her door, she decided to give in to the need to let go. Thank the Gods he didn't pull away. She wasn't sure she could handle rejection. She leaned back slightly, ending their kiss, and looked into his wide brown eyes.

"You don't need to apologize," she said in a husky voice. "I forgive you."

He traced his fingers along her jaw, back to her lips, and leaned in to kiss her once more.

Freydis moved slowly backwards, drawing Marcus in, careful not to break their kiss. They were nearing the edge of the bed...

"Freydis, I was just—Oh! Oh God, I'm so sorry," Cass's words cut off abruptly as she burst into the room. She turned quickly, covering her eyes like she had walked in on something far worse. Freydis could see several different emotions pass across Cass's face and had to stifle a giggle when she looked at Marcus with his scarlet cheeks.

"I just—you said you were coming—and then you didn't, so I...," Cass was speaking with her hands, clearly at a loss for words.

Freydis watched as Marcus let himself fall back against the bed, staring up at the ceiling and running his fingers through his hair. She could still feel his lips, still taste him. He turned his head to look at her, and she gave him a reassuring yet apologetic smile.

"I'm so sorry, Marcus. I was just heading out to meet Cass, and when I opened the door, there you were," Freydis blushed. "Can we chat later?"

"Yeah, sure," Marcus said, sitting up, "I was going to meet Ethan at the bar for a drink anyway." He rose from the bed, adjusted his clothing, and walked out of the room. When they were sure he was out of earshot, Freydis grinned and Cass squealed.

"Oh my God, Freydis, I am so sorry I interrupted—what was that?"

Freydis smiled, "He came to apologize for earlier. I forgave him."

"Yeah, obviously," Cass said, laughing as they left Freydis's room.

A darkening sky greeted Cass and Freydis as they made their way from the hotel back to the Witch Trials Memorial. Dusk, the bridge between day and night, had arrived with the setting sun barely visible on the horizon. The place looked and felt very different with the absence of the tourists. It wasn't the memorial they were there to see, however.

Located next to it was The Burying Point, the oldest cemetery in Salem and among the oldest in the entire country. Cass slipped quietly inside, careful not to be seen by curious onlookers. Freydis followed but immediately froze upon entering. The air was electric, and her feet felt heavy and reluctant. Magic—old magic—lay thick in the air. Cass must not have noticed that Freydis had stopped following her until she turned to speak.

Silently, she beckoned for Freydis to join her.

Exerting her will, Freydis lifted her leaden feet and moved to join Cass near a modest memorial stone. The inscription was well worn from centuries of exposure to the elements, though it was clear that care had been taken to preserve what remained.

"This is the grave of one of the magistrates who presided over the Salem Witch Trials," Cass said.

As the words left Cass's lips, the air around them dropped several degrees, their breath now visible on the night air. The grass beneath their feet began to shrivel and die. Freydis stood, staring. Pure hatred filled her as memories of her mother's death taunted her.

"I haven't been honest with you, Freydis," Cass whispered. "I know that you are not human. I know about your mom and your magic."

Thunder rumbled and lightning tore across the sky. Hearing Cass's confession, Freydis turned, locking eyes with her friend. She watched as Cass swallowed deeply, regret written all over her face.

"Why did you bring me here?" Freydis asked quietly, clenching her fists at her sides, holding desperately onto the last sliver of control she had left. "How could you bring me here, to this place, knowing about my mother?"

"Please, I can explain. I never meant to cause you any more pain."

Cass was standing before Freydis, arms splayed open by her sides, and her voice was soft and reassuring as though she was comforting a frightened animal, "I have magic, too, nothing even close to yours, but my father wasn't human."

Freydis couldn't speak for fear of what she might say to Cass, and the betrayal she felt at that moment was excruciating. She clenched her teeth and exhaled through her nose as her eyes fell to the ground where the grass had died.

"I wanted to have this conversation with you since the day we met," Cass said. "Are you familiar with the fair folk?"

"Faeries?" Freydis replied, not quite sure where the conversation was headed.

Cass nodded. "They go by many names. My mother always said my father was a fae prince, and honestly, I never really took her seriously until a delegation arrived after her death and gave me this."

She raised her hand, wiggling her fingers to draw Freydis's attention to the amethyst ring.

"My father sent me this. It came with a message. Accept the gift, and I would be entitled to the provisions of my heritage. I had no idea that meant I was bound by oath to do their bidding."

Freydis was only barely familiar with the fae courts and their bizarre rules and traditions. It did explain why she felt so comfortable with and drawn to Cass. Something within her must have recognized the magic.

"I still don't understand. Why bring me here to tell me?" Freydis moved closer to the gravestone, leaning against it for support. She was lightheaded after using her magic. She watched Cass bend down and place her hand on the patch of dead grass where Freydis stood only moments before.

Cass's face became a mask of concentration as she uttered a few words in a language Freydis thought sounded familiar. After a moment, she raised her hand, and in the spot where the dead grass had been only moments before was newly grown green grass.

"My magic has always been one of healing," Cass explained. "I hoped to show you that. I want to help you find your mom's people and help you heal. You aren't alone."

Freydis could feel her anger slipping as tears filled Cass's eyes. Cass continued, "At the Equinox and in this old cemetery, I knew my magic would be strong enough to show you. I can barely feel it at home."

"But how did you know about me?" Freydis asked coldly; a thousand questions flooded into her mind.

"Do you remember the telephone call, that day at the waterfront? I had been contacted before you arrived here by the Crown Prince of the Winter Court. He told me that I was to find you and make you feel comfortable and welcome. I was given a brief historical account of your life. When I saw you in my family's bookstore, I nearly died of shock. I knew immediately you were who he had spoken of. Please, Freydis, forgive me. I never meant to mislead you."

The pain in Cass's voice was tangible, and in her heart, Freydis knew that Cass didn't have a malicious bone in her body. She didn't know who the Crown Prince of Winter was, but by the Gods, she would find out how he knew so much about her and why he was interested. Then something occurred to her.

"What about Ethan and...," she hesitated, not sure she was prepared to hear the answer if she finished the question.

"No," Cass replied, "Ethan and Marcus are completely human."

Freydis sighed with relief, although she wasn't sure why. It would have been easier if Marcus had been more than human. It would give her something to throw in Vetus's haughty face. Freydis reached out and took Cass's hand in hers.

"Let's head back," she said, and the two friends walked to the hotel under the star-filled sky in silence.

Chapter Six

The closer they drew to the Winter Palace, the more restless Rowan seemed to grow. Vetus decided to send him in search of food and fulfillment of his other appetites while he went to speak with the Winter King.

"Meet you back at the stables?" Rowan asked as Vetus approached the large double doors leading into the great hall.

"Yes, of course," Vetus called over his shoulder as he motioned to the sentries to open the doors.

Carved from obsidian, the doors were engraved with mirror images of a great dragon, each inlaid with rubies where the eyes should be. Precious stones encrusted the bodies of the winged beasts like scales. When the doors were closed, a crown made of thorns, Midhir's sigil, was visible between the two dragons.

The great hall of the Winter Palace was built around a giant clump of twisted blackthorn trees as old as time itself. Their gnarled and twisted trunks had been fashioned into the ornate throne of the Winter King. The large upper branches of the canopy appeared to support the cathedral ceiling above from which large chandeliers of bone hung. Ghostly blue flames burned brightly from the chandeliers like stars in the night sky. Similar blue light gleamed from the sconces that lined the hall. Closer inspection, however, would reveal the sconces as small cages holding blue will-o'-the-wisps like those Vetus saw in the forest on his way to the palace.

Perched on his ancient throne, Midhir, King and Lord of the Winter Court, glowered at Vetus with his onyx eyes, a hint of a cruel smile on his face. Beside the king, a smaller yet no-less-ancient hawthorn tree had been fashioned into another throne, but it remained empty. The tree bloomed with clusters of small white flowers that, from a distance, made it appear covered with snow.

Vetus's mother had left the Winter Court ages ago. None but Midhir believed she would ever return. Her empty throne was a painful reminder of her absence. Vetus bowed deeply and reverently before his father, waiting for his invitation to speak.

"My son," Midhir's voice echoed through the empty hall, startling a raven that had been perched on a macabre chandelier above, "to whom do I owe the credit for your long-awaited presence?"

"*Ard Ri*, I come before you a humble servant of Winter to request the aid of Your Gracious Majesty."

Vetus's words tasted of bile on his tongue, but his father was susceptible to vanity, and he would need all the help he could get to convince him to provide the aid he sought.

"How fortuitous," Midhir purred. "I, too, had hoped to request a great boon from you."

Of course. Vetus knew it had been too easy securing a private audience with his father. He cursed himself silently for not foreseeing his father's ruse. The king never gave a favour without the expectation of reciprocation, a common characteristic among faeries.

"Tell me, Father, what must I do in exchange for your help?" Vetus waited as his father's empty eyes crept over him, slowly searching for any sign of weakness.

"As you know," the king began, "for many years, I have held possession of the Dagda's cauldron, one of the four treasures of the Tuatha Dé Danann, our blood of old. Your brother, Lir, has recently discovered that Fragarach, Nuada's sword, has been kept from us by the Summer Queen."

The king paused, steepling his long, bony fingers before him. Vetus was well-loved by the queen, his aunt, and his father's disdain for their relationship was blatant.

"As the queen has refused to return it to me, your brother is determined to declare war against the Summer Court in my name."

The king's announcement unsettled but didn't really surprise Vetus. His fiery younger brother looked for any excuse to start a war.

"In exchange for the help you seek," Midhir continued, "I had hoped that you, my son, would return to me the Spear of Lugh that I had gifted to you so long ago. I wish to guarantee your brother's success. With

Summer conquered, all Otherworld can once again be united, as the Dagda intended."

Vetus took several steadying breaths, weighing the situation in his mind. He knew he must choose his next words wisely. His father obviously had no idea that Lugh's spear was no longer in his possession. He needed to buy some time.

"I shall consider what you ask, Father, but first, you should hear my request."

The king inclined his head in acknowledgement, though his eyes burned with impatience.

"I would like to ask your help to locate an ancient race, not of this earth. They were exiled here several millennia ago, and I have some urgent business with them, though they seem to be impossible to find."

The king raised his hand, a command for silence. He stood and moved to be at eye level with his son.

"No. You will not continue in this folly with that—that abomination," the king hurled the insult at Vetus, aimed straight at his heart. "I thought you had moved on from such madness."

"Father, please," Vetus sighed, "I will—"

"Here is what you *will* do," Midhir hissed. "You will give me that spear and aid your brother in his war, or I will have the girl killed, though not before I pull her apart, piece by piece. I will fracture her mind and use her body to my delight. There will be nothing left of her for you to recognize."

Vetus's hand clenched the hilt of his sword, forcing him to stay calm. The Winter King was trying to provoke him, but that didn't make his words any less true. He swallowed hard and averted his gaze in false deference to his father, vowing in the deepest recesses of his being that, someday, he would kill Midhir, King of Winter. Vetus bowed and turned to leave.

As the sentries began to open the great doors, his father's final words echoed behind him, "You have until the new moon, Vetus Mac Midhir. I will have your fealty. One way or another."

The Lusty Leprechaun was a seedy little pub barely a stone's throw from the Winter Palace. The proprietor, Dizzy O'Gratin, ensured that he catered to all manner of patrons and their appetites. Many soldiers of Winter filled their bellies and their beds thanks to Old Dizzy.

"Commander," Dizzy called to Rowan. "What'll ye have, lad?"

"My usual, boiled bacon and cabbage. Better bring me a pint too."

Dizzy was aptly named because everything he did was done in a frenzy. He'd had a nasty falling-out with the Summer Queen, and afterward, she tortured him senseless. He fled to Winter and opened the pub and remained off-kilter ever since.

Rowan greeted a few familiar faces with nods, smiles, and idle banter while he waited.

"Commander!" a soldier called. "Slummin' with us lesser fae today, are ya? We thought you'd have some fancy lunch at the palace."

"Dizzy makes the best bacon and boiled cabbage in all of the Otherworld, Devlon," Rowan smiled. He knew each soldier by name. "But I mostly come for the ale."

"Well, enjoy yourself, sir." The soldier clapped him on the shoulder and joined a noisy group on the other side of the pub. Rowan was one of the only officers to mingle with the lesser fae, and they loved him for it.

When the food arrived, Rowan plunged into the salty dish with enthusiasm, only stopping long enough to gulp down a mouthful of Dizzy's frothy homebrew. He hadn't realized how hungry he was. Finishing off the ale a little too quickly, he turned toward the bar to ask for another, but a beautiful fae woman blocked his view.

"Curious," she purred as she approached him. "I haven't encountered one of the Fir Bolg in over a thousand years. I don't believe we've met."

Her movements were lithe, and the pale blue gossamer gown she wore left nothing to the imagination. It was not uncommon in the Otherworld for clothing to be more optional than ordinary, but Rowan had been spending a lot of time in the human realm, and he'd forgotten that fact.

She placed her soft, cool finger underneath his chin and closed his gaping mouth.

He cleared his throat, "No...No, my lady, we definitely have not."

"My name is Leannán, but you may call me Lea."

Her smile was intoxicating. She extended her hand in greeting. Rowan held it, placing a kiss on the back of it.

"I am Commander MacArtur, but my friends call me Rowan."

"Mmm, Rowan."

The sultry way she spoke his name sent a wave of desire through him to all the right places. She moved around behind him and was so close he could feel her breath on his nape. The tiny hairs on his neck stood, and all his focus was drawn to the warmth of her body so close to him. She inhaled deeply.

"How did a half-breed become a commander in the Winter King's service?" She continued to stalk around him as she spoke. "You must be very special."

Rowan swallowed and tried desperately to remember what it was he was supposed to be doing.

"Why don't you come with me, Commander, and we will get to know each other a little better."

He'd lost track of time, but surely, he had a little more to spend a few minutes with the beautiful stranger. He placed his payment on the table and followed her out of the pub.

Vetus was waiting for him, two white horses already saddled. Seeing Vetus was all Rowan needed to snap back to reality.

"Leannán, My Lady, welcome home," Vetus said. "Finished the king's business already?"

"I have. Did you have need of my...services, Your Highness?" she asked. Rowan watched her ogle the prince and could feel the heat rise in his cheeks.

"No," Vetus replied, clearing his throat, "you are kind to offer, but no."

Leannán inhaled deeply. Rowan recognized the gesture from earlier when she had sniffed him in the pub.

"How long has it been, Sweet Prince? Surely, my senses deceive me," Leannán said.

"Enough!" Rowan bellowed, drawing his sword. He didn't know why or what he would do with it, but he wasn't going to let anyone speak to his prince that way. Vetus held up his hand to Rowan, a silent command to stand down. She giggled.

"Leannán, it has been a *delight* seeing you, but we must take our leave," Vetus said.

She smirked at Rowan and bowed deeply.

"And Leannán," Vetus added, "leave the boy alone."

"As you wish, My Prince," she said, winking at Rowan. They watched her turn and stalk back into the pub. Rowan swallowed deeply as the realization struck: she was a predator, and he was almost her prey.

"I...I don't know what came over me," Rowan stammered, "but I would have given her my very soul had she asked for it."

"That was Leannán Sídhe," Vetus sighed. "She is a dangerous seductress. She feeds off the life force and desires of her lovers and can even assume another's face to trick her unsuspecting prey. Pure evil, that one. Stay away from her, Rowan. Your father's bloodline makes you vulnerable to her magic."

From the moment they met, Vetus had been both a teacher and protector for Rowan, a debt Rowan wasn't sure he could ever repay. He had found the healer who saved Rowan's life when he was only a boy. Vetus was unlike any Winter fae he had ever known, and Rowan loved him like a father.

Rowan noticed Vetus's face was pale and entirely unreadable. He knew that look. Something was wrong.

"Tell me," Rowan said as he mounted the second horse.

"He will not help, though he did make his own request of me."

"Of course he did," Rowan muttered.

"He wants Lugh's spear and for me to assist Lir in his war against the Summer Queen. Apparently, she has an artifact in her possession that my father greatly desires."

"Okay, so why does your face look like that? The war?" Rowan asked.

"No, not the war," Vetus's tone was grave and tinged with fear. "I no longer have Lugh's spear in my keeping, and I haven't the slightest idea where to find it. If I don't arrive back here by the new moon, with the spear and ready for battle, Midhir will kill Freydis."

Rage and fear surged through Rowan. The horses shifted underneath them, sensing their shared anxiety.

"We aren't going to let that happen. There must be something...," Rowan wracked his mind for a solution.

"Not something," Vetus replied, "someone. We are going to see the Summer Queen."

Freydis had been so tired that she had fallen asleep in her clothes, still wearing her shoes. Glancing at her phone to check the time, she saw she had two missed calls and three text messages, all from Cass.

It was 9:00 a.m., and Cass had invited her to join her and the boys for brunch at 10:00 a.m. Grateful for the extra few minutes, she lay back on the bed and thought of Marcus and her hands in his hair, aching to feel him against her.

Freydis was in the middle of changing out of her dirty clothes when someone knocked on her door. Hurriedly, she threw on the complimentary hotel robe, tying it tightly around her waist, and opened the door.

"I brought breakfast," Marcus's sheepish grin lit up his whole face, "I didn't know what you'd like, so I grabbed a bit of everything?"

Freydis burst out laughing and welcomed him in.

"Coffee?" he asked, pouring two cups and handing one to Freydis. She held the cup up to her lips and inhaled the rich aroma. Without taking a drink, she placed the cup on the dresser beside her.

"I tried to apologize last night," Marcus began, "but that didn't go the way I'd planned."

Freydis chuckled but quickly realized that this was one of those important moments when someone was about to bare their soul. She sat on the edge of the bed and smiled, encouraging him to continue.

"My sister died when we were children," Marcus blew out a breath. "Cancer. But, when she first got sick, I prayed and prayed for a miracle. All my life, I had believed that God listened to my prayers. I thought, if I was good and prayed hard enough, He would save her."

He had been pacing as he spoke, and as he paused to consider his next words, he sat beside Freydis on the bed and began studying his hands.

"She died anyway, and that's when I knew for certain that God and magic and all those things that required faith were all lies."

Freydis swallowed hard and reached over, taking one of Marcus's hands in her own.

"Science is like magic," she offered. "At least, that's how I feel."

Marcus caressed her hand with his thumb and looked up at her; unshed tears lingered in his eyes.

"There are many things about science that I don't understand, and that makes it seem pretty magical," she said.

Marcus didn't wait for her to speak any more words. He reached out with his free hand and cupped her cheek gently as he leaned in to kiss her. She twisted her hand into his shirt, pulling him closer. This was what she had wanted last night. Just him. Before she forgot, she weaved a small glamour to hide the scars that covered her body. She didn't want to have that conversation.

The kiss began soft and slow, and Marcus groaned as it deepened and became more urgent. He slid his hand from her face, down her neck to her shoulder, gently slipping off the robe. His hands were warm as they caressed her bare skin. She'd forgotten what it felt like to be touched this way.

Freydis clumsily pulled his shirt off over his head. He smiled and continued kissing her, his lips moving from her mouth, along her jaw, and down to her collarbone. She inhaled deeply, breathing in the scent of him. With each kiss, Freydis craved his touch even more. She tangled her fingers into his hair as he kissed her.

Gently, he nudged her to lean back on the bed as he continued kissing her, each kiss moving further down her body, sending waves of pleasure through her. Gods, she wanted him.

His hands explored every inch of her. And without any coherent thoughts and without interruption, they finished what they had started the night before.

Brunch was served buffet-style in the small dining area of their hotel. The smell of toast and coffee wafted through the air. Freydis arrived hand in hand with Marcus, greeted by goofy grins from Ethan and Cass.

Freydis grabbed a muffin and made herself a tea before returning to join the others. Sitting there with Marcus and the others felt so comfortable. They could be her people. Perhaps this is where she could belong.

It was a lovely thought.

It didn't last long as Vetus's words, "wasting time," echoed in her mind and chased it away. Yes, Cass knew her truth, but Marcus wouldn't. They would all grow old and die without her, like every other person she'd loved. She gritted her teeth, forcing the doubt from her mind, and sipped her tea as Cass outlined their plans for the day.

They were interrupted when Marcus's phone rang. He picked it up nonchalantly, but his face paled at the name on the call display.

"Excuse me," he said to no one in particular, "I have to take this."

Marcus left the table to take the call, giving Cass and Ethan the opportunity to gush about Freydis and Marcus finally making the long-anticipated move to get together. When Marcus returned, all life and light had left his face. Freydis, sensing something gravely wrong, stood and took his hand.

"That was the CFO of Anderson Technology and Robotics. They are pulling my funding. I need to get back."

Chapter Seven

The lands of Summer were always lush and awash with colour. The fresh, fragrant scent of flowers filled the air, and the countryside buzzed with the presence of life all around.

Rowan and Vetus had ridden hard and fast. Were it not for their fae blood, the horses would likely have dropped dead from exhaustion. They hadn't made it far across the border when a small contingent of the queen's personal guard met them on the road.

"Hail Vetus, Prince of Winter!" The soldiers reined in their horses and saluted. "Her Majesty, the Queen of Summer, bids you a warm welcome. We expected a greater host to be travelling with you."

Vetus inclined his head slightly to acknowledge the lieutenant of the Queen's Guard. Rowan snickered. The queen was renowned for having spies in every corner of the Otherworld. Though Vetus was her nephew, the queen would not appreciate the informality and abruptness of their visit.

"We aimed to travel light and fast. I have no time to wait for any retinue. I must see the queen at once. It is a matter of great urgency," Vetus said.

The lieutenant nodded in understanding and motioned for them to follow him. The roads in the Otherworld often had a way of changing and moving, and the trip to the Summer Palace was faster than Rowan remembered. He hadn't visited the Summer Palace since he was a child, but it was exactly how he remembered it.

A great emerald spire pierced the bright blue sky. Beneath it lay a sprawling stonework castle perched atop the edge of a cliff that dropped off into a shimmering sea below. Surrounded by trees and gardens, the castle could almost be mistaken for an ancient ruin. It was hauntingly beautiful.

Once inside the busy palace courtyard, the travellers were met by a stableboy who collected their horses and promised to see them well cared for. Rowan mussed the boy's hair before following Vetus up the stone steps toward the large rowan-wood doors leading into the Summer Palace.

Rowan was named after the sacred rowan tree. When he was a boy, his mother had explained that his name meant "courage," "wisdom," and "protection." He had failed to live up to his name when he couldn't protect her.

Despite his shame, the summer magic sang through him, and he could feel his blood humming along. He hadn't spent much time in the Summer Court since he had become the ward of the Winter King, but it recognized him all the same.

Vetus came to an abrupt halt in front of him, causing Rowan to bump into his backside, earning him a grunt from Vetus, who was now staring down two heavily armed sentries.

"I am here to see the Summer Queen. I must speak with her immediately," Vetus said. His words were met with a deafening silence.

"As the Crown Prince of Winter, I command you to open these doors. I must speak with the queen." Vetus was visibly angry now and reached for the sword that hung at his side. Rowan grabbed his arm before Vetus could draw the blade, giving him a reassuring smile.

"Will one of you gentlemen please advise His Royal Highness when the Summer Queen will be receiving us?" Rowan asked.

A tall, bronze-skinned fae woman emerged from a garden nearby and approached them. Her vermilion eyes were feline, and her golden hair was entwined in an intricate arrangement of braids and flowers.

"Your Royal Highness, my name is Eden. I am a handmaiden to Queen Tarynn. She has instructed me to show you your rooms and see that you are fed. You must be weary from your travels."

"We appreciate the queen's hospitality, but I must insist, our audience with her cannot wait." Vetus's voice was raised, and Rowan could see a redness appearing on Vetus's face as his temper began to flare. They didn't have time for one of the queen's infamous games.

"The queen is not here," Eden said nonchalantly as she motioned for Vetus and Rowan to follow her. Rowan could feel a tightness in his chest, and he began to sweat. He hadn't felt so powerless in a very long time.

"When will she be returning?" he asked. He knew that Vetus could not wait. Vetus needed to convince the Summer Queen to avoid the imminent war with Winter by giving him Nuada's sword or at least agreeing to lend it to him long enough to pacify his father.

Perhaps if Vetus could remove the reason his brother had created for declaring war, they would have time to find Lugh's spear, and Freydis would be safe, for now. He would not let Vetus lose her.

"Her Majesty has gone to Alfheim, to the elves, as an honoured guest of their Mabon celebration." Eden's words shattered all hope they had of securing the Summer Queen's help. Rowan watched the blood drain from Vetus's face, and the pit in his stomach grew.

"Great Morrigan's tits," Rowan muttered, "she won't return in time."

His comment earned him a glare and raised eyebrow from Vetus. "Seanmháthair would skin you alive if she heard you take her name in vain like that." Rowan's face heated.

Looking around, he realized that they'd made their way to the western wing of the Summer Palace, where the guest lodgings were located. Eden led them to a pair of doors: a noble's suite and adjoining servant's quarters.

Normally, Vetus would waste no time teasing Rowan about being given a room for a servant, but he hadn't been himself since they'd left the realm of Winter. When Eden left them, Rowan paced the hallway as Vetus closed his eyes and leaned his forehead against the rough wooden door.

"What can I do?" Rowan asked. "Let me help you."

He would do anything he asked of him.

He remained silent, giving his offer time to penetrate the despair Vetus was drowning in. After several moments, Vetus raised his head and turned his deep, emerald eyes to Rowan.

"Go to Loch Cé and speak to Ophelia. Then, I need you to go to Boston. Protect Freydis. You are the only one I trust as much as myself," Vetus nodded to himself. "She must be safe. Ophelia will make the arrangements. I will handle the Winter King."

Rowan stood in shock. He was a warrior. He would gladly give his life for Vetus, but he did not expect Vetus to ask him to be a glorified nanny.

"As you command, My Prince. I will give my life to keep her safe." Rowan bowed deeply, and when he stood, Vetus placed a hand on his shoulder and smiled.

"Freydis will be furious about this, but she cannot know she is in danger. Try to keep a low profile, and should she recognize you, try not to take her reaction personally," Vetus laughed and embraced Rowan. "Good luck, Son."

Marcus kissed Freydis goodbye as the gang dropped her off and promised to call her later after he knew more about his funding. Cass decided to go with Ethan to drop Marcus off at his office.

"Did you want to say it out loud?" Ethan asked him. "I know you're running your speech over and over in your head."

Marcus gave him an odd look, "Into reading minds now?"

Ethan chuckled, "You're moving your lips as you think."

Marcus sighed, "I need to make them understand. We are so close."

Anderson Technology and Robotics owned a modest six-story building located on Alexandria Tech Square in Cambridge. From the outside, it looked like all the other buildings on the street, but walking through the main entrance was like travelling to the future.

An open concept, the main level was a fusion of glass and metal. Displays of past-project miniatures and future prototypes were meticulously laid out throughout the room. A small café was located next to the inconspicuous security desk. A single set of elevator doors was set into the wall slightly behind the desk, and from its position, the entire room, including the large conference area off to the right, was completely visible.

Each additional floor was dedicated to a different aspect of the company. Marcus's office and the research laboratory were located on the third and fourth floors, respectively, while the executive offices and Marcus's destination were on the fifth.

Approaching the elevator, Marcus retrieved his employee pass from his wallet and nodded in response to the security guard's greeting. He was sure the guard was new, but they all looked the same in their uniforms. Marcus swiped his pass, and the elevator door silently opened. Stepping inside, Marcus adjusted his position to accommodate the retinal scan required to operate the lift.

Unlike most elevators, this one ran a rudimentary version of an artificial intelligence program called Automated Lift Interface, which remembered each user's floor preference and provided each user with a personalized greeting. It was affectionately known by all as ALI. The voice they'd used belonged to Marcus's assistant, Tina.

"Good afternoon, Doctor Wolfe," ALI began. "To confirm your destination as the third floor, Research and Development, please say, 'ACCEPT,' or manually select the floor of your choice using the keypad on your left." Marcus jabbed his finger at the button for the fifth floor, and his thoughts about what he planned to say continued to run rampant through his head.

Marcus stormed into the CFO's outer office to find Tina and other members of his team already sitting and waiting at the conference table there. Another door at the rear of the room stood slightly ajar, and Marcus could hear the muffled side of a telephone conversation just wrapping up. Almost immediately after Marcus sat, the CFO of Anderson Technology and Robotics emerged.

"Kind of you to join us, Marcus. I know this must come as quite a shock." The CFO continued to explain that, despite the progress they were seeing, the board and investors had grown impatient.

"After consulting with your team, I was left to understand that we are weeks, if not months, away from human trials. The board and investors have voted to redirect the funding elsewhere. I am sorry, Marcus."

The room was silent, all eyes on Marcus. He desperately wanted to tell them he would figure it out—that he had a plan; he just needed time. *Think, damn it, think.*

"Sir, can I have a few minutes with my team so we can process this?" Marcus asked.

The CFO nodded and left the room. As soon as the door closed behind him, all hell broke loose. Everyone began speaking at once, fear and frustration filling the room as the tension mounted around them. Speaking turned into shouting when Marcus finally slammed his hand against the table. Silence followed.

"I know you are all upset. So am I," Marcus ran his fingers through his hair and inhaled deeply. "I'm sorry I've been distracted lately and didn't see this coming."

"There has got to be someone willing to fund this project," Tina said.

Murmurs began around the table from the others in agreement.

"What about the military?" another researcher asked. "We have worked on other projects for them before. Nothing of this scale, but they have the budget. I can reach out to our past contact."

Marcus stroked his five-o'clock shadow, listening to the different ideas being bounced around. He had always hoped his technology would be used in the healthcare field, but maybe the military avenue was worth exploring and was the necessary evil stepping stone to get to where he really wanted to be.

"Tina, can you get started on a proposal and have a look at the Federal Business Opportunities website? We need a timeline for when the next broad agency announcements will be released. Let's reach out to our past contact at DARPA while we finalize our pitch. At this point, I am willing to try anything," Marcus said.

And he meant it.

A sprawling garden grew beneath the window at which Vetus stood, watching the dryads and pixies who'd arrived with twilight. Despite his Winter blood, he always felt connected to this place, and it was easy for him to understand why his mother hated the Winter Court.

The youngest sister of Queen Tarynn, Maeve had been betrothed to Midhir to broker peace between the courts, and for a time, their union brought the intended stability. Midhir loved Maeve, and though he had always been ruthless and cold-hearted, it was her departure that made him wicked. A departure he blamed entirely on Vetus, though he never said so outright.

A knock on the door made Vetus's heart leap into his throat. It was too soon to be the queen, and Rowan was well on his way to Arbor Castle on Loch Cé. Opening the door, Vetus came face to face with the last person he had expected.

"Vetus, my love, how good to see you."

Petra, the Fomorian princess, stood before him, looking the same as she had half a millennium or more ago when Vetus ended their betrothal and left the Winter Court for the love of another. Her raven-black hair and violet eyes were striking compared to her nearly translucent skin. The smile on her face did not reach her eyes.

Seeing Petra reminded Vetus of the time a kelpie kicked him in the guts and left him just as nauseated, but in the heart of Summer, it was even more shocking. The Fomorians were not loved by the Summer Court. The queen could not have known of her presence, or she would never have gone to Alfheim. No greater threat to the Otherworld had existed since the dawn of time.

"My Lady, I had not thought to find *you* here," Vetus half-bowed to her and politely kissed the back of the hand she extended to him.

"Aye, but you are exactly who I intended to find," she said.

A chill crept up his spine as Petra moved to close the space between them. She pulled him into her embrace, and he could feel her warm, acrid breath on his face.

"You left without saying goodbye."

Her words lingered in the air, and Vetus swallowed gently as he felt the tip of her jewel-encrusted iron dagger against his throat.

Rowan stood in his new, fully furnished apartment and marvelled at how thorough Ophelia had been. He was surprised to learn that the building that held his and Freydis's apartments was owned by Vetus, or more accurately, by one of the shell corporations he used when navigating the human world.

The decor was minimalistic, and a mix of earthy colours adorned the walls, matching the furniture perfectly. The refrigerator and cupboards were stocked; the dressers were full of clothing, and in the closet hung expertly tailored suits and outerwear. A small, well-hidden drawer at the bottom rear of the closet held a carefully stowed cache of weapons and other items that might prove useful while tasked with keeping Freydis safe. Ophelia missed nothing.

After he had explored what he hoped was his *temporary* new residence, Rowan lay on his very comfortable bed. Letting his mind wander as his eyes became heavy, he couldn't stop thinking about the past few days. He thought about Vetus and the fear and desperation he had shown at the Summer Palace. He couldn't recall a time when he had seen his mentor so out of sorts, so close to losing control.

There *was* something about Freydis, something that made you want to protect and be near her. He felt the same way, though he couldn't quite explain it. One thing was certain, though: he was there, willing to lay down his life if required.

Rowan slept, though he wasn't sure for how long. Lights from the city seeped in through his bedroom window, casting shadows around the room. Reaching for his bedside lamp, his hand bumped into something solid, knocking it to the floor. Flicking on the light, he noticed a wooden box, not much bigger than a book, lying overturned on the floor.

When he picked up the box, he noted Vetus's sigil, the Serch Bythol with an Algiz rune at its centre, adorned the lid. The box hadn't been there when he fell asleep. Opening the lid revealed a single key and an unsealed envelope. Inside was a letter from Ophelia:

> Rowan,
> I hope your accommodations are acceptable.
> Here is a key to Freydis's apartment. If you require anything,
> place a message in this box. I will receive it.
> ~Ophelia~

Rowan removed the key and returned the box to his bedside table. He felt very strange having unlimited access to Freydis. He knew it was the only way to keep her truly safe, but it felt like a violation all the same. He decided that a quick reconnaissance of the building and immediate surroundings would be helpful and resolved to not use the key unless he believed her life was in immediate danger. It didn't ease his guilt, but it helped.

Chapter Eight

A warm trickle of blood snaked from where Petra's iron blade pierced and burned Vetus's skin. Her presence was a clear indication that, even after several centuries, the emotional wounds he gave to her had not healed but festered. He wasn't sure he would be able to talk his way out of this one. There was no excuse that he could provide that would satisfy her. He had walked away from their betrothal without a word of explanation.

Petra had been promised to Vetus through a bargain between Midhir and the Fomorian king, meant to end the centuries-long war between the two races. The match was political, and while he had initially agreed to the arrangement, he had never loved her.

"My Lady," he murmured, "there are no words I can offer that will mend the grievance between us, but I swear, I never intended to offend you."

Her eyes blazed with fury as she pressed the blade deeper, drawing more blood and a grimace from the prince.

"Offend me?! You ruined my life!" she hissed. "I was scorned by my father and my subjects. Used and discarded. And the peace that was promised from our union never came. There was nothing left for me after you."

Slowly, Vetus lowered himself to one knee before her. She watched him, keeping the pressure on the blade. He hoped the act of submission would buy him time. *How had she known he was there?*

"Where is she now?" Petra said. "I want to watch your heart tear in two while I take from her, piece by piece, what she stole from me."

Petra was out for blood, and for the first time in his very long life, Vetus was relieved that the woman he loved was no longer living.

"She's gone, Petra. For centuries, I have wandered alone, missing half of my heart."

"Was it worth it?" she snarled. "We could have been happy for eternity, and you lowered yourself for a slave."

"She was worth every moment, from the very first, and I will love her long after this world has faded from all memory. I chose her then. I would choose her now, even with this blade at my throat. I'm sorry you have suffered, but there is no threat that frightens me more than knowing I will live forever and she will not be with me."

Petra howled with rage at his defiance. He knew that it was a gamble, but if he could get her to lose focus, even for a split second, he might yet find a way to overcome her.

"Go ahead," Vetus said, "reunite us for eternity."

He felt the pressure ease slightly off the blade. With a surge of adrenaline and centuries of honed skills as a warrior, he seized the blade, burning his hand, and wrenched it from her grasp. Using his momentum to grab her throat with his uninjured hand, he lifted and pinned her against the wall.

"My Lady, it is your good fortune that we are both guests of the Summer Queen. You have spilled the blood of the Crown Prince of Winter, the penalty for which is death."

Vetus drew a steadying breath, "I have wronged you. Grievously, and for that, I offer you mercy. Please, take it and leave. If you are found here, neither I nor the entire host of Fomor will save you from the queen."

He paused, not relaxing his grip, and held her gaze until he was certain she would go. Petra eventually nodded in agreement as tears filled her eyes. Vetus lowered her to the floor and released her. Without another word, she left as quickly as she appeared, and Vetus was left waiting once more for the Summer Queen.

Freydis lay on her bed, relieved to be home. Salem had been an emotional rollercoaster ride, and the power that came to her that night in the cemetery was unlike anything she had ever felt before. Truth be told, it frightened and thrilled her. It felt intoxicating when the power was surging through her, and she wanted more, but the grass had withered under her feet. Now more than ever, she needed answers.

What was she? What had her mother been? Solveig never showed that kind of power. Her mother was a skilled healer and had taught her how to use glamours, but that was it. *Vetus may be able to help.* She tried to call him, but he didn't answer. *Odd*, he always answered.

She willed her weary legs to the kitchen to make a cup of tea to help her think. Her mind was a mess with thoughts of magic, Marcus, and her mother. Tea would help. Tea always helped.

But the tea was gone.

Damn it. How had she not noticed she was getting low? The last thing she wanted was to venture back out. She craved solitude. She needed it. But at that moment, she wanted tea more. She understood deeply why wars had been fought over it.

Freydis grabbed her jacket and walked out the door. Slipping her arms into the sleeves, she stuck her hands into her pockets to reassure herself that she had brought what she needed. It was then she realized she had left her wallet. She walked back inside to grab it and froze. An overwhelming swampy scent filled her nostrils, making her stomach lurch and skin crawl. Her wallet sat on the bedside table. The room was too quiet. Something was wrong. Her skin prickled with the feeling of being watched. She reached to grab the Scottish dirk from the top drawer when she was hit hard from behind.

The blade fell from her hand onto the floor. She managed to twist herself around to face her attacker before she was pinned on her back to the floor. Their face wasn't visible under the hood they wore, but they were impossibly strong as she struggled to free herself from the iron grip. Foul-smelling breath made her want to gag while she fought to keep the attacker's knife from finding its mark. The strange blade appeared to glow a sulphur yellow.

Freydis tried to call on the magic as she had in the cemetery, but it would not answer. What little strength she had began to fail. Her arms trembled, allowing the blade nearer, when she heard someone yell her name. Her attacker turned their head toward the voice, which was all the opportunity Freydis needed.

She thrust her hips up, twisting her body as she did. The movement knocked the assailant off balance, allowing Freydis to wrench herself free enough to reach the dirk she had dropped. As quickly as her fingers wrapped around the hilt, she drove the blade upward through the chin of the hooded assassin. A guttural sound escaped the attacker's lips, and foul-smelling ichor dripped from its mouth and down the blade still held firmly in her hand.

Her heart was racing. Exhausted and lacking the strength to shove off the dead weight, she lay still, trying desperately to suck air into her compressed lungs. Though it felt like an eternity, it was only seconds before Rowan heaved the body from her like a discarded trash bag and scooped her up into his arms. His silver eyes searched her for injuries. After a moment, a grin pulled at the corner of his mouth. "As fierce as she is lovely."

His smile faded as he sat her on the bed. Rowan furrowed his brow and carefully brushed a rogue lock of hair from her face and tucked it behind her ear. The intimacy of the gesture made Freydis's toes curl and her cheeks flush. His hands were warm but rough. Warrior's hands.

"Are you hurt, My Lady?"

"Please," Freydis groaned, wiping the black ichor from her hands onto her pants, "call me Freydis. What was that thing?"

"An assassin. Likely sent by the Winter King."

Rowan gave the body a push, flipping it over to reveal an eyeless face beneath the hood. Black ichor dripped from its mouth and the wound under its chin, staining the carpet where it had lain.

"A Fomorian would be my guess." Rowan grimaced.

"Assassin? I don't—I'm sorry, Rowan, right?" she asked.

He nodded as he bent to retrieve the assassin's blade, which still glowed ominously as it lay beside the body. She watched as he inspected it carefully, turning it over in his hands before tucking it into his belt.

"What are *you* doing here? Where is Vetus?" Her voice cracked a little, and her body began to tremble. She pulled her knees up to her chest to try and hold herself together. It had been more than a century since she engaged in hand-to-hand combat, and her body had clearly forgotten the cost. "He's with you, right? I tried to reach him, but he didn't answer."

"He's not here...it's complicated. He sent me to keep you safe."

"What? Safe from what? Did he know someone was trying to kill me?" she whispered the final question to herself.

"No, he wasn't certain," Rowan answered. "It was a precaution."

"I—I don't understand. Why would he send you?"

"I am a better fighter than he is," Rowan said matter-of-factly.

Freydis rolled her eyes, though a grin tugged at her lips, "Thank you...for being here. For saving me."

Her eyes moved slowly over him. Gods, he was stunning. A subtle hint of dark stubble, matching his dark-brown hair, shadowed his chiselled jaw. His sculpted body of corded muscle was visible underneath his plain black t-shirt, and for a split second, she wished it was her hands, not her eyes, moving over him. Rowan inclined his head and met her gaze.

"You saved yourself, My Lady."

They stayed looking at each other in silence. It should have been awkward and uncomfortable, but they were the only two people in the world that existed at that moment. Heat rose in Freydis's cheeks as she smiled and lay back on her bed, breaking their connection. Rowan cleared his throat.

"I, uh...I will check to make sure there are no more surprises and get rid of that," Rowan said, gesturing to the crumpled body on the floor. "And while you do look rather sexy all dirtied up, you might want to clean yourself off and try to rest."

Freydis scoffed at his comment, but she was shaken to her core. She didn't know why, but every fibre of her being wanted him to stay.

"Rowan?" Freydis asked. "Where will you go? I mean, do you have somewhere to stay?"

He turned to face her. "Is that an invitation? Tsk tsk, what would your human think? What's his name..." He tapped his chin with his finger, pretending to think.

"His name is Marcus, and it wasn't an invitation," she cringed at the lie as it left her lips.

"I am three doors down from you. Just moved in. You won't be alone," he said.

Rowan finished checking the rest of the apartment, and after reassuring Freydis that everything was secure and safe, he left, using a glamour to disguise the body draped over his shoulder.

Freydis peeled off her stained clothes and discarded them into the trash.

In the shower, the hot water eased her weariness. Freydis had no idea how she was going to sleep that night, so she grabbed a book off her nightstand and read until exhaustion claimed her.

The mood in the boardroom at Anderson Technology and Robotics was as tense as a fully drawn bowstring. Tina, Marcus's assistant, was tapping her pen on the table. The other members of the team sat rigid, waiting for the government representatives to arrive.

Sweat dripped down Marcus's back, and he was glad he decided to wear his suit jacket instead of only a dress shirt. Everything hinged on this presentation—all his dreams. The research, resources, and time would mean nothing if they could not secure the funding to continue the project.

The presentation would be in three parts. Tina, joined by the team's biomedical specialist, would introduce the team and their initial study of artificial intelligence as applied to healthcare, focusing on biomedical AI and its ability to monitor electronic signals from the body in real-time. Marcus made sure they knew to explain their findings using relatable concepts like implants detecting irregular heartbeats or high blood sugar.

Once they felt the representatives understood the medical basis for the technology, Marcus would outline the potential defence applications, drawing their attention to the fact that AI in defence is not a new concept. Unmanned Aerial Vehicles and other technology already existed and were used, so this would simply be another tool for their information-age toolbox. Artificial intelligence, particularly the implants Marcus designed, was an innovative technology with exponential potential.

Marcus quickly scribbled a note in the margin of his speech, reminding himself to avoid mentioning the potential risks that this technology could present. Operator bias or AI terrorism would not sell this idea. Homing in on the positives, like algorithm-based decision-making capabilities and mission success probability calculations based on the biological factors of the soldiers, as well as the potential for artificial biological improvements akin to updating software on a computer, would be his focus.

The most difficult part of the presentation would be the actual proposal. Marcus had no doubt they would send the absolute best people to receive this information and take it back to the other stakeholders. He would not be able to bullshit his way through it.

A chime from Tina's cellphone alerted the group of the government representatives' arrival, so she made her way to the elevator to go down and escort them up. Marcus looked around the table at the remainder of his team. Their nervous faces mirrored his own. He wondered if this was the time to give a pep talk.

"Any last words?" he said. A collective nervous chuckle went around the room just as the elevator doors opened to reveal Tina, followed by a man in full military dress and two women. Marcus shot to his feet and plastered on his best fake smile.

"Dr. Marcus Wolfe, team," Tina said, gesturing around the table, "this is the US Defence Department's Chief Financial Consultant, Vivian Ashford; Director General of Research and Development, Major General Jim Fox, and the Deputy Chief Scientist from the Defense Advanced Research Projects Agency, Dr. Claire Ellis."

Tina waited as the representatives shook hands with Marcus and the team before seating themselves.

"Let's begin."

Marcus did not hear a word of what was said, as he was too focused on the facial expressions and body language of their guests. He did not hear Tina the first time she said his name, inviting him up for his portion of the presentation. There was an awkward moment of silence before he realized everyone was staring at him.

As Marcus outlined the potential defence applications of the technology, he noted the excited whispers between the representatives and the occasional nod of approval at his ideas. The time had come for him to lay out their proposal.

"As you can see," he began, "This technology would be an asset to homeland security, not to mention internationally. According to industry sources, no one else in the world has advanced to this level with this kind of tech. Our proposal is simple: I would lead the project with my team, alongside any government participants, as I hold the patent for the tech. We would commit to human clinical trials with demonstrable data within two years in exchange for funding and access to required resources when necessary. We are open to negotiating the terms, with the exception being that my team and I stay involved with the project long-term. You have the detailed proposal in the folders in front of you. Thank you. I will now field questions."

A box of Irish Breakfast tea waited outside her apartment door when Freydis awoke from a dreamless sleep. It was her favourite. Accompanying the tea was a hastily scribbled note:

Ceann Fíochmhar,
I noticed you were out.
—R
Ceann Fíochmhar. Fierce one.

Smiling to herself, she retrieved Rowan's gift, caressing the words on the note as if the ink and paper could feel what was in her heart.

After making herself a fresh hot cup of tea, she texted Cass, asking if she was free. Cass was the only person Freydis could really ask about magic. If someone was trying to kill her, she had to get a grip on it. Not knowing almost cost her dearly. Thank the Gods for Rowan.

Cass arrived within the hour, as bright and bubbly as a brook in springtime, and Freydis filled her in on the attack.

"Oh my God, Freydis! Are you alright?"

"I am fine. It got startled, which gave me time to kill it, but I couldn't summon any magic. Not a drop. How could that happen?"

"Well, you haven't exactly used your magic much for a long time—"

"Try like, ever," Freydis interrupted. "The first time I can remember doing anything other than a glamour was with you in Salem."

"Magic is energy," Cass explained. "When you use it, you are manipulating that energy, and because it doesn't come from thin air, it has to come from somewhere, which is why you probably get tired after casting glamours, right?"

"Okay, but I couldn't even feel it when that thing attacked me. Did I lose it? The magic, I mean."

"No, of course not. You cannot lose it." Cass laughed. "Magic is a part of who you are. You just need to find its source or trigger."

Freydis dropped her head into her hands. She could feel a tightness in her chest. She had no idea what caused her magic. She had been angry in Salem when the grass died under her feet like she had drained the life right out of it, but she had used a glamour when she was with Marcus, and she was definitely not angry then. *Different magics for different emotions? Perhaps.*

"What about how I am feeling? I was upset in the cemetery when I…well, you saw what happened."

"Well, there is only one way to find out," Cass smiled. "Let's experiment."

Freydis watched as Cass retrieved a small wilting plant from the windowsill in Freydis's kitchen. Cass sat the pathetic thing between them on the table. Freydis twinged with embarrassment. She couldn't keep plants alive no matter how hard she tried.

"You know how to use a glamour on yourself, but have you ever created one around something else?" Cass asked.

"Not for centuries," Freydis paused, "Glamouring myself is the only magic I have mastered, but it can't be much different, right?"

"Well, not really," Cass replied. "The biggest difference is the intent. Glamours fall under the illusion category of magic, which is basically manipulating perceived reality. Nothing changes, only the perception of it does. Try glamouring this plant to look like something else."

Freydis took a deep breath and tried desperately to focus on the task at hand. After a few failed attempts and some encouragement from Cass, Freydis glamoured the little plant to look like a teapot. Arbitrary, but successful!

"Okay, great," Cass beamed. "Now, let's try enchanting something."
Failure.

"That's okay," Cass reassured her. "What about conjuring?"

The only thing Freydis could conjure was a string of obscenities that would have made the foulest sailor proud, and Cass blushed.

"This isn't working," Freydis groaned. "Maybe that night in the cemetery was a fluke. Maybe my mother was wrong about me having 'gifts,' and all I am capable of is little more than carnival tricks."

She rested her forehead against the table. She needed to speak with Vetus. Why hadn't he returned any of her calls?

"Let's try one more thing," Cass said.

"*Fine,*" Freydis sighed without looking up.

"Here," Cass pushed the dying plant toward her. "Bring it back to life."

She sat back and folded her hands in front of her. Freydis looked at her with disbelief.

"You've got to be joking," Freydis scoffed. "That is more difficult than all the other magic I have tried and failed at, in case you've forgotten."

Cass merely held her gaze until Freydis relented and pulled the plant toward herself. She searched the recesses of her mind for the memory of that night in the cemetery and focused on the way she felt when the grass withered beneath their feet.

At first, she felt nothing except frustration and disappointment. She forced herself to concentrate and felt a flicker in her gut. It was subtle, but it was there. She reached out to that feeling, willing it to grow. Freydis closed her eyes, and with the feeling held fast inside her, she put her hands on either side of the little terracotta pot.

An unmistakable surge of energy erupted from somewhere inside her chest, and her eyes flew open in time to witness the little plant that had been struggling to survive blacken and turn to dust.

Several silent moments passed with Freydis staring at her handiwork. When she found the courage to look up, all the colour had been drained from Cass's face, and her wide eyes were full of questions. Questions...and fear.

Chapter Nine

*H*ortus Vitae. "The Garden of Life" was the moniker for Queen Tarynn's throne room. Flora beyond imagination decorated the magnificent hall, crowned by *Crann Bethadh*, Tarynn's ancient oak throne and the living inspiration for her sigil. The room hummed as an army of pixies buzzed about like hummingbirds, tending to the life all around them.

Tarynn perched comfortably on her throne as Vetus genuflected before her. From a distance, one might've easily mistaken her for a child. Her diminutive stature and eternal youth were a clever ruse she used to appear less threatening, but Vetus knew, underneath her flame-coloured hair and jade gown, she was as dangerous as she was beautiful.

"Beloved Nephew," she purred, "how delightful to have you here to welcome us home from our journey. Has His Vileness, the Winter King, changed his mind about his war? Or is this visit meant to trick us into lowering our guard?"

"Mo Bhanrion," Vetus pleaded, "I have not come at the king's behest, though it is true he hungers for war. He seeks Fragarach, which he believes is in your possession. Release the sword to my keeping, and I swear no war shall befall the Summer Court."

Vetus waited, head still bowed, for the queen to acknowledge his words. Tarynn was an ardent enforcer of protocol and pretense, and she would seize any opportunity to exploit weakness.

"Pity," the queen sighed. "I had hoped the rumours of your purpose here were wrong. Even *if* I had Nuada's sword, I would not let Midhir anywhere near it."

"If?" Vetus raised his head as the question slipped unbidden from his lips. *Had he heard her correctly?* "Your Majesty...where is the sword?"

"In Alfheim, with the elves. I knew Midhir would seek the sword. I entrusted it to their keeping." She smiled innocently, "Alas, you've come uninvited and will leave empty-handed."

The wicked smile on her face infuriated him. Tarynn loved to play games, and though she was usually the lesser evil among the two courts, her games could drive a person mad or even turn deadly. Vetus stood patiently waiting for her to dismiss him, but Tarynn just looked at him, feigning innocence, whilst twirling a strand of her hair between her fingers.

"There have been whispers that you search for more than just some ancient relic." She narrowed her eyes. "Whatever could possess you to stray into the human realm so frequently and for so long? You are keeping secrets, Nephew.... Secrets can be deadly."

A chill moved along Vetus's spine. She couldn't know everything or she wouldn't have mentioned it, as doing so would mean overplaying her hand. He almost laughed at her false concern, though he remained cautiously silent. She was a master of keeping secrets.

"If you have nothing more to say," she waved a delicate hand dismissively as if she were shooing a fly, "you may leave."

Vetus bowed deeply, clenching his fists. Not only could he not prevent the inevitable war between Summer and Winter by securing that damned sword, but he no longer possessed Lugh's spear. Midhir would find perverse delight in this failure, Vetus was certain.

Tarynn moved closer, approaching him as he stood. She reached her long, pale fingers to his neck, tracing a finger over the wound from Petra's blade.

"Nephew, you are injured."

The queen gasped as Vetus instinctively seized her hand, moving it away from where Petra's blade had pierced him. Her eyes flashed with rage. It was forbidden to raise a hand to her. His fear did not diminish his insolence.

"One of several wounds from this trip, My *Queen*." He brought her hand to his lips, kissing the back of it before releasing her. "I will recover."

With his subtle insult hanging in the air, Vetus left the queen's presence and prepared for his return to the Winter Palace.

Cass had no words to describe what she had witnessed. Freydis had unbelievable power for someone who seemed so unfamiliar with magic. If her eyes could be believed, Freydis had the power of death at her very fingertips. Cass wanted to help her friend, but the thought of what a power like that could mean...it terrified her.

"I—I don't know what happened," Freydis whispered, breaking the heavy silence.

"Freydis, I have never seen or heard of anyone having that kind of power. It's like you absorbed the life right out of it." Cass gestured to where the plant had turned to dust.

Freydis looked down at her hands spread out before her, then back to Cass. "What am I?"

"Did you ever see your mom perform magic like—like that?" Cass asked.

"Never," Freydis shook her head. "She taught me glamours, and she was a very skilled healer. I watched and helped her heal countless people. She never harmed anyone."

"Well, I will see if I can get more information about this type of thing from some of my acquaintances, but Freydis, you shouldn't use this magic. It's dangerous, and without a high level of control, it could be deadly."

"I understand."

Cass stood up and moved to hug Freydis. "I have to go, but don't worry, we will figure this out."

When the door closed behind her, Cass stood in the hall and drew in a long, deep breath. She had been trembling and didn't even realize it until she was alone. She needed to speak to the Winter Prince. There were obviously details he failed to mention about Freydis.

Rowan checked in regularly, usually in the morning, for tea. There was no point in him pretending he wasn't there, and hopefully, his presence would deter any future attacks. Their conversations were easy and comfortable, and they spent many of them laughing. The more time he spent around her, the more Freydis enraptured him. She was like music he didn't know the words to, but the melody filled him, body and soul. And he knew that once he learned the lyrics, she would become his favourite song. It terrified him.

"How long have you known Vetus?" Freydis asked.

"I was only a boy when we met. He saved my life."

"He does have certain heroic qualities, doesn't he?" she laughed. "He saved my life too. I wonder why he didn't introduce us sooner."

He loved hearing her laugh.

"I am a very busy man." He puffed out his chest and, in a haughty voice, continued, "Responsibilities, you know."

She rolled her eyes in pretend annoyance, which made him want to tease her even more. Every time he saw her, she wore a mask of seriousness and caution that he so desperately wanted to penetrate, and little by little, she began letting him in. He hadn't really thought much about what the future might hold for him outside his role in service of the Winter King, but it was clear to him that he would give anything to be in her presence, now and always.

Chatting with Rowan was easy. Too easy sometimes. She wanted to tell him things she had never told anyone else, about her magic, about how intoxicating it was when she drained the life from the grass in the cemetery and turned the little plant to dust. But she wouldn't tell him. Or anyone else, for that matter.

Freydis poured herself another tea and gestured to Rowan's half-full cup, "Would you like a top-up?"

"Trying to keep me here longer, eh?" Rowan smirked. "What number is that for you? Must be the fourth cup since I've been here."

"Don't judge me," Freydis laughed. "Bostonians are known for their relationship to tea."

"If you mean trying to steep the whole harbour, you'd be correct. You'd have been traumatized if you'd been here," Rowan teased.

"You speak as though you were."

"Yes, Ma'am, I was." Rowan paused, and as if on cue, someone knocked on the door. Freydis moved to answer it. "Nearly forty-six tons, wasted."

"Gods, the horror." Freydis was mid-laugh as she opened the door and came face to face with Marcus.

Her breath hitched. Freydis did not expect Rowan to still be there when Marcus arrived. Marcus kissed her, and she moved aside to let him in. He turned immediately toward Rowan, who continued to sip his tea, acting oblivious to the intrusion or awkwardness his presence seemed to cause.

The tension in the room was palpable. To be fair, Marcus did not know Rowan existed.

"Who are you?" Marcus asked.

"Marcus," Freydis said, "this is Rowan. He lives down the hall. He helped me take care of a pest problem a couple weeks ago. He stopped by to check that I had no lingering issues."

Rowan stood, downed the rest of his tea, and reached out, gripping Marcus's outstretched hand in greeting. Both men glared at each other, their handshake lasting a little too long. Rowan finally released his grip, giving Freydis an easy smile.

"Until next time," Rowan said, departing without another word.

"Next time?" Marcus asked, looking at Freydis with more than a hint of suspicion. "What does he mean, 'next time'? How often does he 'stop by'?"

"It's not like that, Marcus. He is a friend."

"Well, whatever he is, I don't like how he looks at you."

Freydis prickled at his words, though she understood how Marcus felt. He had not expected to find Rowan there when he'd arrived, but she didn't belong to Marcus. He did not get to decide who she would spend her time with. Freydis took a deep breath and tried to change the subject.

"Any word on the funding?" she asked.

"The committee was pleased with our presentation and submitted a counter-proposal," he sighed. "They are willing to let me and my team lead the project, but they will only agree to the funding if we speed up the timeline for human trials."

"Well, that is doable, right? I mean, if anyone can make it happen, it's you." Freydis smiled at Marcus and kissed him, slowly, deliberately, and she could feel the tension melt from his body.

"When do they want you to start human trials?" she asked.

"Six months."

"Wow. That is not a lot of time. What are you going to do?"

She watched and waited as Marcus considered her question, picking at the dry skin around his fingernails. He looked at her and shrugged, "What choice do I have? They want me in Virginia at DARPA headquarters to finalize the contract before Christmas."

Freydis smiled sadly. She knew what this project meant to him. Marcus was good, and he wanted to help people. He wanted to change the world. But would the end justify the means?

Night had fallen when Vetus arrived at the edge of Winter. Whispers followed him from the Summer Court, so he was not surprised when he found his brother Lir waiting at the southern gate of the Winter Palace. Vetus reined in his mount, their warm breath visible in the night air. Vetus placed his hand on the cold metallic hilt of his sword, gripping it tightly with anticipation. Crown Prince or not, Lir had little respect for his elder brother.

"The stench of Summer still clings to you, Brother, though it is preferable to the smell of treachery underneath," Lir sneered.

Ignoring the insult and invitation to confrontation, Vetus sat taller in his saddle.

"Lir, I am surprised to find you here. Aren't you supposed to be planning a war against the Summer Court?" Vetus said. "I am honoured you found the time to welcome me home."

"Father knows about your little visit to Tarynn, though you seem to have returned empty-handed. A shame that that pretty girl of yours had to pay for your incompetence."

Lir's words slammed into Vetus like a battering ram. Digging the heels of his black leather boots into the belly of his horse, Vetus surged forward, with Lir's insidious laughter ringing in his ears. He would kill the king if he had harmed Freydis. His only hope was that Rowan had been there to intercede. Surely, word would have reached him...

Hooves pounded through the courtyard, and Vetus's black velvet cloak flew behind him like an ensign carried into battle. He reached the main entrance to the palace, and after dismounting quickly, his boots hammered hard against the cobblestone floor. The echo through the corridor made it sound like he was being chased to the great hall.

The grand double doors stood open, a vast gaping maw that would swallow him whole. The hall was full of fair folk from all over the lands of Winter. His father was hosting a great celebration, but for what, he did not yet know. The crowd parted at Vetus's arrival, but otherwise, his presence barely caused a ripple. As he approached the throne, his father stood and raised his hands to quiet the din.

Silence came immediately, and Vetus could feel hundreds of eyes on him as the court watched and waited. The pounding of his heart in his ears was so loud he would have sworn those gathered could hear it. The air was tense with anticipation, like a predator ready to pounce. He inhaled deeply, trying to calm his racing heart, and the air burned the lungs in his heaving chest. Slick with sweat, his hand instinctively grabbed the cool metal hilt of his sword. However, Vetus stopped short of drawing the blade because to do it here would be the highest act of treason.

"Fair folk of Winter, welcome," the king said. "Now that the crown prince has arrived, we can begin. My son, please join me and take your place at my side."

Those who filled the hall murmured and shifted uneasily. Vetus realized that the crowd was also unaware of their purpose there that evening. Cautiously, he made his way to his father's right hand and turned to face the anxious crowd.

"Tonight, we gather in this place to issue recompense for an ancient debt incurred by His Royal Highness, Vetus Mac Midhir."

Vetus's head whipped toward his father to see him wearing a cruel smile that showed his stained, jagged teeth. A creeping dread moved through Vetus as he swallowed hard and searched the crowd for a face he hoped never to see again.

The crowd was at a dull roar. He spotted his brother, Lir, now dressed in an immaculate midnight-blue tunic, his red hair standing out like a beacon. On his arm, in a tightly fit, sea foam-coloured gown, was Petra.

Once again, the host that filled Midhir's hall parted, allowing the pair to move unobstructed. Begrudgingly, Vetus had to admit they made an attractive couple, but what game was his father playing? It was obvious Petra's presence at the Summer Palace was not a coincidence.

"Princess Petra, daughter of Balor, King of the Fomorians, has accepted my offer to join in sacred union with my son, Lir Ruadh Mac Midhir. A prince had been promised, and a prince she shall have."

"*Ard Rí*," Vetus spoke through his clenched teeth, "I must speak to you privately."

Midhir raised his hand to silence him and continued addressing the crowd.

"In exchange, her father, Lord Balor has agreed to join his forces with ours against the Summer Court," Midhir said. "We will waste no more time. The union will occur on the eve of the Winter Solstice. Then, we shall bathe in the blood of lesser fae, and once more, the Otherworld will be whole."

The crowd roared with approval, and Vetus felt his last shred of hope for peace shrivel inside his chest.

The tea in her cup was cold when Freydis remembered to take a sip. Marcus had left, but his display of jealousy toward Rowan lingered in her mind. Freydis did not welcome the unspoken accusations indicated by Marcus's reaction. Rowan was a friend. A friend of a friend, really. She could have tea with whomever she pleased, even if that person were an unfathomably gorgeous non-human being.

Admittedly, Freydis liked that Marcus was jealous. She could not remember the last time anyone bothered enough to get jealous. It was never like that with Astrid, and she never really had any other meaningful or committed relationships that would warrant it otherwise.

She'd been too busy hiding and seeking vengeance for her mother, filling the emptiness she felt with whatever man or woman piqued her curiosity at the time. But she had never cheated, not even when the opportunity presented itself. That was not about to change, even if she felt confused about her feelings.

As if thinking of him had somehow summoned him to her, Rowan knocked at her door.

"Is he gone?" he asked.

"Marcus left, yes," Freydis confirmed. Rowan seemed anxious or agitated—she couldn't tell. His cheeks were flushed, and he was twisting the ring on his finger. "Is something wrong?"

"I know we've only just met, but I feel like I have known you for years. Vetus is like an older brother to me—a father even, and I have spent many years listening to him talk about you. He cares deeply about you, you know."

Freydis nodded, though she had no idea where this was going.

"Freydis," he paused, reaching to tuck that stray strand of hair behind her ear again, "*Fierce One*. You are so much more than whatever human part you cling to. *Why* do you try so hard to be one of them?"

Freydis, feeling the heat start to rise in her face, stared at her cold cup of tea. No one had ever asked her that question, and she was not sure she even knew the answer. Apart from Vetus, she'd never spoken to someone who shared her immortality. Freydis sat at the table, closed her eyes, and breathed deeply. Rowan's sweet, earthy scent calmed her.

"When they executed my mother, my human father just left. No explanation. I fled Norway and went to Scotland, where I met Vetus. I spent the next century trying to drown my grief in the blood of humanity. I changed my face, my name, and lived many different lives. I fought in every war someone would pay me to fight in." Freydis paused and drew in a long, steadying breath. Rowan sat at the table across from her and gave her a gentle and encouraging smile.

"I killed without conscience, and I became *exceptionally* good at it—but no amount of blood or death could ease my pain. I think part of me had hoped I would die." She looked up, fighting the tears forming in her eyes. "I don't know who I am. Perhaps because I am partly human, when I am with humans, at least I feel like I belong somewhere."

Tears continued to fill her stormy eyes, but they did not dare to fall. She let her eyes hold Rowan's gaze and swallowed down the sob wanting desperately to escape. He stayed silent as if he knew the words pouring from her lips needed to be spoken.

"Then I met Astrid, a beautiful human woman who knew my truth, and I finally belonged. I struggled for a long time—nightmares, flashbacks. There was a drug called Librium." She closed her eyes, remembering, "It helped...but once in its grasp, I couldn't get out, but Vetus came to my rescue, again—he is always saving me."

He reached across the table to where she was still holding the cold cup of tea and put his hands over hers. "When I was a boy, my mother always said everything happens for a reason," Rowan swallowed deeply. "And I struggled for a long time to keep believing that after she died in my arms."

Freydis couldn't hold her tears any longer, and as they spilled over her cheeks, Rowan continued, "I can still remember how the sword I raised to defend her felt in my small hands. It was so heavy I couldn't even swing it, and I was struck down. All I remember after that was Vetus's face. I thought he was the angel of death."

Rowan reached to wipe away her tears. Her cheeks didn't flush, and she didn't balk at the intimacy.

"Freydis, I don't know how we ended up here, in this moment. And I don't know why we had to suffer, but more than ever before, I believe that everything happens for a reason. *We* are here for a reason."

Freydis closed her eyes and leaned her cheek into the warmth of his palm against her face.

A knock at the door made them both jump, and Rowan pulled his hand away as Freydis frantically wiped the remaining tears from her face. When she reached the door, she turned to look at him, eyebrows raised, her expression a silent question.

"You look wonderful," he answered.

She rolled her eyes and opened the door.

"Cass?"

"Why do you look surprised to see me? We have a dress fitting today," Cass paused, "for my wedding. Remember?"

"Oh! Oh Gods, Cass, I completely forgot," Freydis cringed. "Give me five minutes."

Freydis dashed toward her bedroom, leaving Cass and Rowan in awkward silence.

Chapter Ten

Engagement festivities continued through the night at the Winter Palace, and in his quarters in the southern tower, Vetus lay awake, listening to the revelry. He spent little time in the Otherworld, preferring his castle on Loch Cé. The Winter Court had not been home for centuries, but he couldn't help wondering if his absence had led to his hopeless predicament.

A large family portrait hung on the wall at the far side of the chamber. He stared impassively, trying to recall if there had ever been a time when they were happy, as the image made them appear. He had not been there when his mother left, and now, more than ever, he wished he could speak to her. A daughter of Summer, Maeve had always been able to temper the Winter King in a way that no other could. The king would not have dared to challenge the Summer Court if she were still by his side.

Suddenly, the portrait slid to the side, and the Winter King entered from a secret passageway. Vetus leaped up from the bed, his heart racing. He had forgotten about the hidden door. The king returned the portrait to its original position and stood, his back to Vetus, silent as a statue, gazing at his family.

"I miss her every day," he said, "and I would gladly rip this world apart to have her back." He turned his dark eyes to Vetus, and a chill crawled up Vetus's spine like a spider. "You betrayed me."

"You speak of my betrayal as if I didn't experience yours earlier," Vetus stood tall, defiant. "You know Petra longs for vengeance. She held an iron blade to *my* throat, and yet, *you* welcome her into our home and place her on a pedestal?"

Midhir's onyx eyes burned with fury. "*My* home. You made it clear centuries ago that you had no place here. And then to sneak behind my back to conspire with that Summer witch."

"Father," Vetus huffed, relenting, "I tried to prevent war—"

"No, Vetus," Midhir growled, "you tried to undermine my efforts to reunite the Otherworld. The realm has been too long divided. I will humble Tarynn and those Summer fools as soon as I unite the four treasures."

"She doesn't have Nuada's sword," Vetus said. "It's with the elves."

The fair folk were incapable of outright lies, so Vetus knew Midhir would not question the truth of his words.

"To redeem yourself from your treason, you will retrieve it for me," Midhir said. "And you will leave immediately following your brother's union to the Fomorian princess."

The air pulsed with energy; the combined threat of each one's magic lingered dangerously close to the surface of their silent struggle for dominance. Midhir's magic was well practised and drew on the strength of Winter itself. If it came to magic, Vetus would not win. Not yet.

He would obey his father, the king, regardless of the hatred he held for him in his heart. But he wouldn't hesitate to use the opportunity as a means to further his own ends.

"As you command, *Ard Ri*." Vetus bowed, and Midhir left the way he came. Vetus was not sure how he would be received in Alfheim. He would need to return to Loch Cé first and ensure Freydis was safe before he left.

To mortal eyes, Arbor Castle on Loch Cé was a sad ruin on a lonely island, but that was nothing more than a masterfully crafted glamour. It had belonged to Vetus for centuries. The ancient stone keep was well hidden amongst the trees on the island, but a tall lookout tower afforded an unobstructed view of the loch and surrounding Irish landscape.

The castle and grounds were elegantly decorated for the Yuletide season. Large, sweeping garlands of evergreen hung everywhere, interspersed with simple arrangements of holly berries. The light from a multitude of candles made the castle feel cozy and warm.

Vetus loved when the castle was bustling with activity. He was heartsick to think he had been away longer than he had planned and would be leaving again so soon. He bypassed the main entrance to the keep, preferring a hidden passage that led directly to his private quarters. He could hear the faint echo of voices from above.

Two women were waiting for him in his study when he arrived. Ophelia, a nereid, had been a loyal and trusted friend and the head of Vetus's household for over eight centuries. She reminded Vetus of a water goddess. She wore her cerulean hair in a fishtail braid, wrapped around her head like a crown. It suited her.

The second woman bore a striking resemblance to Vetus's mother. His younger sister, Princess Kerridwen, Ruler of Autumn, was sitting at his desk, twirling a strand of her long chestnut hair between her fingers. She had dressed for travel in an earth-toned cloak and forest-green surcoat. Her brown leather riding boots were speckled with mud that was starting to dry.

"I see you finally found your way home," Ophelia said, greeting him with a warm embrace. She held his shoulders, taking him all in, as was her way. He noticed her eyes linger on the healing wound Petra had given him, and then she met his gaze. "We've been expecting you."

"Big Brother!" Kerridwen beamed. "I had hoped to see you before I turned in for the night!" She stood on her tiptoes and wrapped her arms around him. Though she was a foot shorter than him, Vetus could feel her warrior's strength in her embrace. She smelled of cinnamon and woodsmoke.

"Kerri, your presence here is a salve for my disconsolate spirit." He smiled ruefully, "How are Leila and the children?"

"They are hardly children anymore, Vetus, but they are well, and you know my wife; she would rather be lonely than have anything to do with our father. This wedding idea of his is insane." She smiled wickedly, "Besides, I had hoped Rowan would be with you."

Vetus shook his head and laughed despite himself at her mischievous grin. "Leila would kill you if she heard that come from your lips."

"She knows my heart will always be hers. I just love the way Rowan squirms when I'm around and looks at me like a lovestruck child," she laughed.

"You are cruel to exploit his infatuation for your own vanity," he chastised, "but he will be sorry he missed you."

Ophelia poured them each a glass of dark Irish whiskey and made her way to the large hearth to light that evening's fire. When she'd finished, she sat beside the hearth, sipping her whiskey, giving the siblings privacy. Vetus winked at her.

"Ophelia tells me you visited the Winter Palace willingly," Kerridwen said. It was more of a question than a statement. She knew better than anyone how Vetus hated his father.

"Yes, and then I saw Tarynn."

"Planning a family reunion?" she teased.

"I went to ask for help and to try to prevent a war." He swallowed a large mouthful of whiskey and grimaced. "Alas, I failed on both accounts."

Vetus met his sister's gaze; a reflection of the newly lit flames flickered in her onyx eyes. She took his face in her hands.

"Vetus, I have never known you to accept defeat," she smiled. "You will find a way."

"Midhir demands I go to Alfheim after Lir's wedding," Vetus said. "I am to retrieve Nuada's sword."

"Then you must let me come with you," Kerri grinned. "I haven't visited the elves in an age. I'm overdue."

Vetus took both her hands in his own. "I do not deserve your loyalty, but still, you give it. Alas, this is something I must do alone."

Kerri shrugged and stood on her tiptoes, placing a kiss on his forehead before moving to gather her cloak. "I must be off to bed if I am to tolerate father's wedding charade."

"Let me see you out, Your Highness," Ophelia offered.

Kerridwen waved at her dismissively and smiled, "I know the way."

Once she had departed, Vetus moved toward the hearth and collapsed into an antique wing-backed chair across from where Ophelia sat. She remained silent, watching him as he sipped from his glass and stared into the fire.

Vetus was weary, and the weight of all his worries seemed heavier now that he was home. He wanted nothing more than to rest and warm himself by the hearth and tell Ophelia all about his trip to the Otherworld. His life, however, had never been so simple.

Ophelia nodded, a dark expression clouding her face as she appeared to consider his news. He was surprised at her lack of retort. She never had a kind word or thought for the Winter King.

"What aren't you telling me?" he asked.

"A Fomorian assassin attacked Freydis. Rowan intervened, and she killed it...," she paused. He could tell she chose her next words carefully. "I do not think it is a coincidence that he bid you go now."

"I know," Vetus sighed, rising from his seat, "but I cannot refuse him. He is the king. And I need more time to find Lugh's spear. At least this should keep him off my back for a while."

"It is a fool's errand he sends you on. The elves may not welcome a Prince of Winter."

"I will take Freyr's Path," Vetus said, pointing at the ancient map on the desk now in front of him, "under Vøringfossen in Norway."

"And what of Freydis and Rowan?" Ophelia asked him, worrying at her bottom lip.

"Rowan needs to stay focused, so he needn't know; else he'd try to come with me." Vetus smiled to himself, his heart swelling with pride for the loyal warrior Rowan had become. "Freydis ."

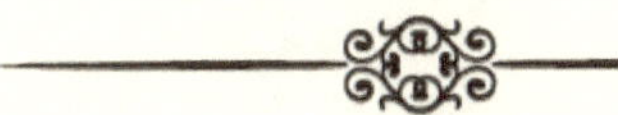

Vetus stayed up long after Ophelia had left him alone in his study, contemplating her words of warning. It was true; the elves were not on friendly terms with the Winter Court, and the possibility of trouble loomed. He would need to be prepared for any eventuality. Norway in midwinter meant the waterfall would be frozen, so he would need to break through it. His Winter blood might be useful for a change, though he would also need speed and secrecy to be his allies.

He stood up from the desk and stretched his arms above his head as he turned to face the hearth. A wedding portrait hung above it. It was the only picture he had of his late wife, other than in his mind's eye. Her raven hair and stormy grey eyes were life-like in the dancing shadows cast from the flames beneath.

"I may be walking into a trap, my love, but what other choice do I have?" he sighed, raking his fingers through his hair. "I am afraid that I may fail and lose everything I have left. I wish I had your courage. Watch over me, will you?"

He spoke to her, as he often did, in the quiet, in the dark. It was when he felt her presence the most. Travelling to Norway made the ache in his heart almost unbearable, but she would be with him. She always was.

Chapter Eleven

The tires chirped as the plane touched down on the tarmac at Reagan National Airport in Virginia. Tina watched Marcus as he sat, eyes closed, jaw clenched, and gripped the armrests of his seat. A sheen of sweat made his pale brow gleam. Tina was accompanying him on his trip to finalize the contract with DARPA for the AI enhancement project they agreed to fund.

"Thank you for coming with me; I didn't want to come alone," he said to her.

"Of course! We make a wonderful team," she smiled, then added, "I kinda thought you would have brought Freydis with you."

"I suppose maybe I should have," he said. "I am still getting used to the idea of a serious relationship. She is so independent, even distant sometimes. And then there are moments where it's like I am the only thing she sees, and only she and I exist. It's terrifying."

"It sounds amazing," Tina said.

"I haven't said this to anyone," Marcus paused, "but I think she might be the one. Once everything is in place with this project, I think I might be ready to take things further."

Tina forced a smile, hoping it would hide her disappointment, and hurriedly turned to look out the window as they taxied to their gate.

Marcus did not notice what lay beneath her smile.

If he had, he would have seen longing in her eyes when she looked at him. He might have noticed how she hung on to every word he said, laughed at all his jokes, and spoke his name like it was the sweetest thing she'd ever tasted. He would have seen her heartbreak when he confirmed he would never be hers.

The plane arrived at their gate, and they departed among a mass of bodies to find a man with a sign bearing **Dr. Wolfe** waiting for them.

When Marcus and Tina arrived at the headquarters of the Defense Advanced Research Projects Agency, they were greeted by the familiar face of Deputy Chief Scientist, Dr. Claire Ellis.

"Welcome to DARPA, Dr. Wolfe," she smiled. "Here are your guest passes. Please follow me."

Marcus and Tina followed Dr. Ellis through a series of security checkpoints to a set of elevator doors. Marcus wasn't sure what he had expected DARPA headquarters to look like, but he was surprised by how plain and unassuming it was. If he were to judge by the entrance and foyer, it could have been any old office building. Their destination was an unremarkable boardroom on the tenth floor.

Seated at the table in the poorly lit room were more scientists, obvious in their white lab jackets, and at least a dozen people in military uniforms. A single empty seat with a small stack of papers in front of it waited for Marcus. No one seemed to notice or even care that there weren't enough chairs for everyone. Tina stood behind Marcus at the table.

"Dr. Wolfe, the document in front of you is the contract, with all the discussed changes, only missing your signature. Please take a moment to ensure everything is in order before you sign," Dr. Ellis said. She didn't even bother to make any introductions.

Marcus reviewed the document briefly. This was it. All that stood between him and everything he had worked so hard for. He turned to look at Tina, who gave him a reassuring smile. Marcus breathed deeply, willing his hands to stop trembling. He picked up the pen and, swallowing any reservations he had, signed his name on the dotted line. He would finally have the resources to make his dreams a reality, even if they now looked a little different.

Chapter Twelve

A colourful, brightly lit evergreen filled Cass and Ethan's apartment with its sharp, sweet smell. Cass would keep it up all year round if it wouldn't slowly dry out and die, leaving endless pieces of itself scattered all over the place. Not to mention the fire hazard.

She supposed, if it were artificial, none of those concerns would exist, but a real Christmas tree was a non-negotiable necessity. Its full, deep-green branches were a welcome reminder that life not only endures but can thrive even in the coldest and darkest of times.

"I invited Freydis to spend Christmas with us," Cass said casually, earning her a knowing smile from Ethan. "She would be alone if I didn't."

"And?"

"She said no—at first," Cass smiled mischievously. "Then I insisted, and she said yes."

Ethan laughed and kissed her on the forehead, "Of course you did."

She looked up at him, the lights from their tree reflecting in his brown eyes. He always accepted her every want and whim. He never judged her. How had she been lucky enough to find such unconditional love?

Vetus had expected a far larger ceremony for his brother's union with Petra, the Fomorian princess and his ex-fiancée. The great hall in the Winter Palace was barely half full. A small delegation of Fomorian nobility stood huddled together, and the remaining guests were high fae of the Winter Court. The Fomorian King, Petra's father, was notably absent, which Vetus knew was likely a subtle insult toward his father.

He had forgotten how grotesque most of the Fomor were. Dwelling in the depths beneath the human realms, many were translucent, and their bodies were often deformed. Missing limbs were common. Most looked as though they'd slithered out from a swamp or lurked in the deepest depths of the ocean. Creatures of nightmares. Petra was one of the very few exceptions.

Standing on the dais with Vetus and the king was Vetus's sister, Kerridwen, the Ruler of Autumn. He was grateful for her presence.

The hall had been elegantly decorated for Winter Solstice, with the addition of subtle oceanic accents meant to represent Petra's Fomorian descent. Vetus couldn't help but wonder why Midhir had not made more of a spectacle.

"I expected a bigger crowd," Vetus murmured to Kerri.

"The idea of tainting his sacred bloodline must be killing him," Kerridwen mused. "No doubt he is ashamed that it has come to this."

"Just enough effort to make it believable," Vetus nodded.

The large obsidian doors groaned as they opened wide to reveal Petra, dressed in an antique midnight-blue satin gown adorned with tiny diamonds that, in the candlelight, looked as though she was wearing the night sky. A small, inconspicuous silver circlet sat neatly upon her head.

"I never imagined our baby brother would settle down," Kerridwen whispered.

Vetus scoffed, "Ha. We both know he won't. This whole farce is a pathetic attempt to win favour with Father."

"To think it could have been you standing there with her."

"I thank the Gods for missing that...opportunity," Vetus sighed. "Father has never forgiven me."

"Of course not," she agreed. "Midhir only allows what benefits him. So, the real question, then, is what does Father stand to gain?"

Vetus hushed his sister as Midhir glared in their direction. His brother Lir, wearing his ceremonial general's uniform, escorted Petra through their guests, stopping before the dais where the Winter King waited to perform the ceremony.

Petra turned her head slightly toward Vetus and sneered, her eyes gleaming. Vetus knew she would count their union as a victory over him, but even this would not settle the debt she believed he owed her.

The couple performed a handfasting ritual and exchanged their words of commitment to each other. Midhir then proceeded to speak ancient words, affirming their union. Vetus managed to remain stoic until the ceremony finished and the celebration began. He couldn't get out of there fast enough and excused himself at the first opportunity.

As he was about to slip out, Kerridwen grabbed him by his arm, turning him to face her.

"Please be careful on your trip, Big Brother," she smiled sadly. "I wish you would let me come with you."

"Your wife would kill me, and I have more than enough enemies already," Vetus laughed. "I love you, Kerri. Don't worry about me."

"I will always worry about you, Vetus. You have done this alone for so long." She looked up directly into his emerald-green eyes, "All you need to do is ask for help."

Vetus bent to kiss her on the forehead. "Say hi to Leila and the children for me?"

She nodded, and without another word, he left, apprehension and uncertainty gnawing at his core.

Christmas Eve arrived, and Freydis stood reluctantly outside Cass and Ethan's apartment building. A light snow was falling. It reminded her of Vetus, which inevitably made her think about Rowan and if he had someone to spend the holiday with. She wasn't sure why the thought of him being alone bothered her so much.

Freydis had to admit there was something magical about this time of year, but she didn't usually celebrate Christmas. Sure, she had participated in the festivities with Astrid during all those years, but she was merely going through the motions because it was important to Astrid. Freydis could remember celebrating the Winter Solstice with her mother and father as a child, but that was several lifetimes ago.

She breathed in deeply, filling her lungs with the cool evening air. She could do this. She could put on a brave face and get through one night. Marcus was back from Virginia, so he would be there. He had called when he got home to say he accepted the counter-offer from the government for his funding. He was over the moon, and she was happy for him. She wished he would have asked her to go with him on the trip, but Marcus did not need the distraction.

With a final steadying breath, she entered the building. Marcus greeted her and hung her coat as Cass piled delicious treats on the table around a red poinsettia. The apartment was decorated beautifully. Evergreen garlands draped the windows, adorned with pinecones, red ribbon, and holly berries. Cream and golden candles of various sizes sat on the windowsills. In the doorway, between the kitchen and living room, hung mistletoe.

The food was delicious. Freydis filled her plate with shortbread cookies and gingerbread and poured herself a cup of eggnog. She watched as the others laughed until their sides ached. She tried her best to join them, but it felt superficial and hollow.

Cass ensured everyone's cups remained full as Marcus filled them in on the last few changes that had to be made to finalize the contract. He spoke at length about all the new resources the partnership would give him access to. He was sure, with DARPA's support, the six-month deadline for human clinical trials would be easy to meet. Freydis tried to appear interested in everything he said, nodding here and commenting there, as appropriate.

"We have some news as well," Cass interrupted, earning a relieved smile from Freydis. She would never get used to how much Marcus liked to talk.

"We are having a baby!" Cass and Ethan exclaimed.

Their unbridled joy was palpable, and Freydis immediately moved to hug her friend. A pang of guilt went through her as she realized she hadn't noticed the now-obvious changes in Cass. She looked radiant, and a slight bump was visible beneath her shirt. Ethan had also been coddling her incessantly. Freydis knew they would make wonderful parents. Their child would have a loving, stable family, something Freydis had always dreamed of.

"So, what does that mean for the wedding?" Marcus asked. Freydis nudged him, a scowl of disapproval on her face. She was relieved when Cass laughed.

"We will move up the date," Cass looked at Ethan for confirmation. "We are thinking mid-May now. Baby is due early June."

The rest of the evening was spent celebrating not only Christmas but Marcus's success and Cass and Ethan's baby news. Freydis watched them, feeling somehow apart from it all. This was human life: surprising, simple, and beautiful. thing she always wanted. So, why did she feel so empty?

When the night finally ended, Marcus insisted on walking Freydis home despite her protests. He had so much to drink, more than she had ever seen him drink before. She wished she felt as intoxicated; maybe then his presence would have been tolerable.

Once inside her apartment, he wouldn't keep his hands to himself. She tried to encourage him to go to sleep, but she knew what he really wanted. They hadn't been intimate or had any time together in nearly two weeks. So, despite the emptiness she still felt, she tried to lose herself in the physicality of it all.

His kisses were slobbery, and the smell of liquor on his breath made her stomach roil. It became obvious quickly that this would be all about him. His pleasure.

No gentle caresses or affectionate words.

No intimate connection.

She had known many men like that, so she did what she always had and let her mind drift while her body endured, wishing she was anywhere else.

Once Marcus was finally snoring loudly beside her, she crept out of bed and ran herself a bubble bath to try and soak away the discomfort and disgust she now felt.

Chapter Thirteen

Freydis spent the weeks following Christmas in the library, trying without success to find evidence of her mother's people or anything about the deadly magic she seemed to possess. It felt like a hopeless search. There had been countless leads and just as many dead ends. Whoever her mother's people were, they didn't want to be found.

So instead of chasing shadows, she accepted Rowan's offer to give her some hand-to-hand combat training. She needed a refresher after her two-hundred-year sabbatical from fighting. Martial arts, yoga, and any basic self-defence tips that popped into his head.

"The key to hand-to-hand combat...," Rowan grunted as he blocked a well-placed knee to his groin.

"I know how to fight," Freydis snarled and threw a right hook. Rowan blocked it. "I'm just rusty."

"Okay," Rowan smiled. "Well, don't forget to keep moving and don't be afraid to fight dirty. Honour is a thing of the past."

"I don't believe that," Freydis said. "There are still those who stand up for what is right, even if they stand all alone. Vetus is one of them."

Rowan nodded and threw a jab. Freydis dodged easily. She knew he wasn't giving everything he had. Her competitiveness flared.

"You're not even trying," Freydis glared at Rowan. "Stop pulling your punches. The people trying to kill me won't."

Rowan inclined his head and pressed forward with a jab-cross-hook combination punch, and Freydis parried, but barely. She stepped back slightly and lost her balance, falling on her behind. Her face flushed immediately when Rowan miserably attempted to hide his grin.

"It's hard to fight on your ass," Rowan taunted, extending a hand. "Better work on your balance."

Freydis swatted his hand away and stood up. She walked by him and, before he could turn, jabbed him in the back of his knee with her foot. He dropped to one knee and turned to look at her just in time for her to tackle him.

He managed to twist but was too slow to avoid her. He landed on his back, and she landed directly on top of him. He felt enormous beneath her. She didn't know how she expected him to react, but he burst out laughing. The sound was contagious, and she couldn't hold in her own laughter. She laid her head on his chest as she laughed, and he instantly quieted.

Freydis became hyper-aware of the warmth of his body beneath her and the sound of his heartbeat where she rested her head. It felt good. But guilt bubbled to the surface as she thought of Marcus, and she rolled off Rowan, getting back to her feet.

"I think I'm done for the day," she said, avoiding eye contact.

"You worked hard today," Rowan said. "Same time tomorrow?"

"I can't," Freydis said brusquely. "Cass needs me for wedding stuff."

Rowan nodded and gathered his things. "You ladies have fun."

Freydis smiled sadly and wished she didn't have to watch him walk away. She was slowly beginning to realize that Rowan was becoming her anchor, in the same way Astrid had been for all those years. But Astrid was safe, and their life together was peaceful, and here and now with Rowan was anything but safe. Yet she felt more real and alive than ever before, and that was a different kind of peace.

The sky was a bright, cloudless sapphire blue, and Vetus could see the waterfall from where he lay in the snow. It was one of the only times he could remember being grateful for his Winter blood. The ambush had come from every direction, happening faster than what he had time to react to. It did not surprise him when they left without killing him. A slow and painful death would suit their purpose.

He was certain at least one of his legs had broken, considering the angle at which it now lay. He had left the bolt in his chest to prevent further blood loss, but if the crimson snow was any indication, it did not matter.

Though, it was not his blood only that stained the snow around him. He managed to take down several attackers before he fell, their foul black ichor confirming their Fomorian identity.

His heart was beating rapidly, and his breathing was becoming increasingly laboured and shallow, but at least the pain had stopped. It was fitting he should die here, poetic even. Norway had taken her from him and now would reunite them once more. He wondered if Midhir would mourn him. Would his mother find out about his death? Who would protect Freydis?

A wave of pure exhaustion swept over him. His heart slowed.

None of it mattered now. He was ready. He closed his eyes, and for a moment, he was sure he heard a voice speak his name.

"Solveig," he whispered her name. He wanted to let go, to be with her at last.

He heard the voice a second time and opened his eyes. A beautiful woman stood over him, fully clad in armour, wings outstretched like an eagle in flight. She bent down and smiled.

"Vetus Mac Midhir, you will not journey to Valhalla today. This life is not finished with you yet."

Gently, she placed an arm around his back and under his legs and lifted him. Gods, she was strong. His eyes closed again, and he thought for sure he was dead despite her words. She carried him effortlessly. He felt weightless.

"Who—who are you?" he asked. "Where are you taking me?"

"We go to Alfheim. You may call me Val."

Every moment apart, Rowan thought about her. Her stormy eyes, the way she spoke his name, the pain hidden behind every laugh—all of it. Every messy, broken, extraordinary piece of her. Especially the way she'd pretend to be annoyed by his shameless flirting. He never missed the sparkle in her eyes or the pink hue of her cheeks.

Rowan didn't know at which point the flirting changed from mindless chatter to the utterings of his heart. *Gods be damned*, he had fallen harder for Freydis than any other in more than two millennia.

He needed to speak with Vetus, but Vetus had been unreachable. Ophelia said he had gone to see the elves at the behest of the Winter King. Rowan knew Vetus hadn't told him because he would have demanded to go with him. Ophelia also informed Rowan that Midhir had sent a messenger to Loch Cé requesting Rowan return to court. His presence was required at once, but he'd made a vow. He could not leave Freydis without saying goodbye.

Freydis arrived late to meet Cass. She hadn't even bothered to change. Cass was waiting outside Freydis's apartment when she arrived.

"Oh, Cass, I'm so sorry I'm late," Freydis huffed. Cass eyed her outfit suspiciously.

"Red cheeks, out of breath, hair a mess...were you with Marcus?" Cass smirked.

Freydis chuckled, "Please, lately I'm a little more than an afterthought for him."

Cass's smile faltered. "Yikes. I had a feeling something was up with you two. You've been spending less and less time together."

"I get that he's busy, but it's getting harder and harder to pretend I'm satisfied with our relationship. I'm happy for all his successes, but it's hard to feel committed when you barely see each other." Freydis let her hair down and brushed her fingers through it.

"It'll get better, Freydis. Marcus cares about you. Ethan and I both see it. Anyway, enough about them. Today is about us. Well, me really, but there isn't anyone else I'd rather plan a wedding with."

Freydis forced herself to smile at Cass, the eternal optimist.

Chapter Fourteen

Alfheim was gifted to Freyr, the Norse God of peace, fertility, rain, and sunshine, from the rest of the Norse pantheon. The last time Vetus visited Alfheim, Freyr still sat upon its glorious throne. A castle of polished white stone carved into the mountains shone like a beacon above the lush green valley below. The enormous branches of Yggdrasil, the world tree, were visible in the sky. The view stole his breath.

If humans were correct about heaven, Vetus was sure they described Alfheim when they spoke of it. Even the Otherworld could not compare to its beauty and magnificence. The division between the courts was like poison, corrupting them slowly from within.

Vetus's leg had been set and bound, and he could already feel it beginning to mend, though he still needed a walking stick for support. His leisurely pace along the winding road toward the castle belied the coiling anxiety in his gut.

He'd received a summons from the castle now that he was rested and recovering. Vetus was surprised they allowed him to move about freely without an escort, though his injuries made him significantly less threatening.

Vetus approached the open portcullis that led to the grand courtyard below the castle. Inside, a small gathering of elves sat at a stone table. Only one stood to greet him.

"Welcome, Winter Prince, we are pleased to see you on your feet," spoke an elf; his voice was a deep rumble, like distant thunder. He stood tall as a tree, and his golden robes reminded Vetus of morning sunshine, a clear mark of honour from the Gods. "My name is Sigurd, and I am the steward of this realm."

Vetus bowed as deeply as his injuries allowed. "Well met, Sigurd, Steward of Alfheim, though I am surprised to learn Lord Freyr is absent."

A rush of whispers went around the table, and Vetus sensed he had missed something.

"My Lord Freyr departed, not yet to return," Sigurd frowned. "We have not seen or heard from him for half an age."

"How can that be?" Vetus asked. "He was here when last I visited." *Why hadn't Tarynn mentioned it?*

"We remember. You came with your lovely wife," Sigurd paused, his face softening. "We grieved to hear of her passing. It was shortly after when Lord Freyr left us."

Sigurd looked weary and troubled. Vetus hoped he would be open to what he had come to ask.

"I am humbled by your hospitality and care, but I am here at the behest of Midhir, King of Winter." Using the walking stick for support, Vetus stood at his full height. "I have come for Nuada's sword, that it might be returned to its proper place among my kin."

"And here we thought you'd come seeking information about the Oraculians," Sigurd mused. "Why else would your father send his assassins after you?"

Vetus felt as though the air had been sucked out of his lungs. His legs went weak beneath his weight, forcing him to sit. A knowing grin spread over Sigurd's face. Elves were not known for their cruelty, but the implications of Sigurd's accusation were astronomical. He would have to unpack Sigurd's words later. He couldn't afford the distraction.

"You are not the first to come in search of that ancient race, and we can tell you where to find them, but we have already given you much with naught but gratitude in return." Sigurd's grin vanished, "We require more."

Vetus forced the words from his mouth, "Anything. I will do anything."

"A sword and information you seek, equally valued and likewise dangerous. We will give them to you if you agree to our terms."

Vetus nodded, and Sigurd continued, "First, none but you can wield the sword."

"Done."

Vetus would have agreed to anything, but he had blurted out his answer before his mind had registered what Sigurd had said. His father sought the sword. He would be murderous when he found out that only Vetus could wield it. *Situation: No change.*

"Though, I may have another solution," Vetus added.

Sigurd nodded in acknowledgement. "And secondly, you will help us solve the riddle of our missing Gods."

"I can't imagine what help I could offer, but you have my word, as Prince of Winter."

Vetus sensed a wave of relief pass over the elves upon his agreement. And although he now had more questions than answers, for the first time in a long while, Vetus had hope.

Rowan had never experienced Arbor Castle as anything other than busy, so the quiet and sombre atmosphere unnerved him. The castle attendants spoke with hushed voices and kept their distance as if they had a secret they were desperate to keep.

No smiles or happy voices greeted him.

Ophelia appeared from the corridor that led to the undercroft, where access to the water and the Otherworld were located. Her usually tidy hair hung in disarray around her shoulders, and her eyes were sunken and dark from lack of sleep.

Rowan worried about her. She was the closest person to a mother figure for him. She had been for many years, and he'd never seen her look so flustered. His concern must've been clear on his face because she gave him her best reassuring smile.

"Ah, you are a pleasant sight in this desolate place," she cupped his cheek affectionately. "I thought you would head straight to the Winter Court."

"*Aintín*, I need to speak with Vetus before I see the king. Has he returned?"

"Oh, dear boy, I didn't have the heart to tell you." She paused.

Panic spread through Rowan as quick and searing as lightning.

"He was attacked on his way to the elves and gravely injured."

"Where is he?" He turned to leave, but Ophelia grabbed his hand. "I must go to him."

"He lives, and as far as I know, he is safe in Alfheim," she swallowed. "But I do not know the extent of his injuries."

"I will go to him and bring him home. The king can wait."

"I believe he is betrayed by the king," she whispered.

"I will kill him if that's true," Rowan snarled.

"Kill the Winter King?" Ophelia scoffed. "You wouldn't be the first to try, and despite your courage, you would not survive."

Rowan scowled, but in his heart, he knew the truth of her words. Midhir was formidable, having ruled Winter for thousands of years. There were very few who stood a chance, and he was not counted among them.

"Vetus must be our priority," Ophelia said. "Everything else will wait."

By the following morning, Rowan had made his preparations and begrudgingly agreed to take a small retinue of the castle guard with him. Soldiers loyal only to Vetus would be smart insurance, Ophelia had insisted.

He followed the smell of freshly baked bread to the kitchen, where Ophelia sat, chatting with the cook. She turned to him, her face tight with anticipation.

"I have written to Princess Kerridwen and told her of Vetus's attack. I also sent word to Freydis. She deserves to know," Rowan said. Ophelia nodded her approval.

Vetus was just as important to Freydis, and Rowan didn't want her to find out from someone else and worry. He would retrieve Vetus for them both.

Time flowed fluidly and freely as water in the hidden places beyond the human realm—winding and wending ever onward of its own accord. Vetus knew he had been in Alfheim far longer than he'd intended. The elves were preparing for the spring feast of Ostara, marking the renewal and return of fertility to the land, by the time he'd healed enough to move on.

He took advantage of the extra time in Alfheim. He visited the legendary dwarven smiths who had forged Thor's mighty hammer. Their craftsmanship was legendary, and he had the perfect task for them.

The elves stayed on top of everything of note occurring in the hidden places of the world. The Oraculians, though tricky to find, were still scattered about the human realm. Fortunately for Vetus, he'd discovered the location of Freydis's family. It troubled him greatly to learn that he was not alone in searching for them.

Most importantly, Vetus had acquired Nuada's sword, and with it, a warning that his attack may have been orchestrated and an indication that his father wanted him dead. He could understand why, but that didn't lessen the sting.

Sigurd's revelation about their missing God was deeply concerning. As if he didn't have enough on his plate. He'd gather what knowledge he could and investigate as circumstances allowed. Vetus intended to honour his word. If the Gods were truly disappearing, it would explain many things not only in the Otherworld but in the human realm as well. Long had humanity been teetering toward the precipice of oblivion, and Vetus couldn't shake the feeling that his father had something to do with it.

Once he regained his strength and ensured Freydis was beyond the king's reach, there would be a reckoning; he would see to that.

Freydis tried to ignore the nauseating feeling lingering in her gut. Rowan stopped by to tell her he was called away on urgent business and would be gone for several days. Maybe weeks. It should not bother her as much as it did.

She had Marcus and his project to focus on. Cass's wedding. The baby.

Finding her mother's people, Gods willing.

Rowan was only a friend.

He was just her bodyguard.

Freydis shouldn't ache like a piece of herself was missing. It shouldn't be Rowan she wanted to tell that she found the book series she'd been eyeing on sale or that the price of her favourite tea had gone up.

It shouldn't be him...but it was.

Chapter Fifteen

Cass and Freydis spent the past few weeks in wedding-planning mode. Viewing venues, sampling caterers, and dress fittings filled their schedule. Freydis hated every minute of it. But it made Cass happy, so it was worth every agonizing second.

After tasting cakes at bakeries around Boston, they ended up at Cass and Ethan's apartment, with Freydis acting as wine sampler while Cass surfed the internet for more ideas.

"I didn't realize how much is involved," Freydis groaned, "and Gods, the cost."

Cass laughed, "Well, good thing I'll only have to do it all once."

Freydis raised her wine glass in a mock toast, downing what was left.

"Have you decided on the wine?" Cass asked.

"I'll probably need to sample a few more before I decide."

Freydis and Cass laughed until their sides hurt.

When the wine was gone, and they'd had their fill of wedding nonsense, Freydis was more than a little tipsy. Cass graciously offered her their spare room and a change of clothes for the night. Grateful, Freydis sauntered to the spare room, where she clumsily removed her clothes and stood looking into the mirror that hung from the closet door.

She traced the faded, barely visible marks that covered her body—the ones that told the story of her violent past. She thought those days were long behind her, but she knew the attack before Christmas was not random, and she could no longer go about as usual. It's not like she could call the police. What would she say? *Please help; an assassin from a mythical race is trying to kill me.*

She pulled on one of Ethan's baggy t-shirts that Cass had loaned her and crawled into bed. As she adjusted the pillow, she noticed a small cream-coloured envelope lying underneath. Inside was a handwritten note that read,

Freydis,
Vetus has been gravely injured.
I go to bring him home. I will send word when we arrive.
Arbor Castle, Loch Cé, Ireland
—R

Through the window, lightning flashed, and thunder shook the building. Heart racing, Freydis sprang out of bed, knocking the note to the floor. Fighting against the dizziness from the wine, she frantically grabbed her discarded clothes, fumbling as she tried to dress again. Cass came in with a candle in time to witness the frenzy.

"Freydis, what are you doing? I brought this in...," she held up the candle, "in case we lost power...Freydis?"

"I have to go," Freydis snapped. "Can you drive me to the airport?"

"I don't understand," Cass sat on Freydis's bed, hands absentmindedly on her belly. "What happened?"

Without breaking stride, Freydis answered, "A friend needs me. It can't wait."

"It's late. There won't be any flights until morning," Cass moved toward her. "Shouldn't you tell Marcus you're leaving? Or pack? Just wait until morning."

"Cass," Freydis stopped moving and looked directly into her eyes, "It's Vetus. It can't wait."

Without saying anything, Cass left the room and returned a moment later with a folded piece of paper. She handed it to Freydis.

"I was given this number before we met by the Crown Prince of Winter," she said, "in case of an emergency."

Freydis hugged Cass and grabbed her cell to dial the number. It rang only once.

"Hello, Freydis," a woman's voice answered, "I've been expecting your call."

The hidden entrance to Alfheim, Freyr's Path, was the rendezvous point. Vetus, Sigurd, and a small contingent of elven guards waited for the escort that would accompany Vetus home. It was nearly Beltane, so the melting snow and ice made Vøringfossen a sight to behold. Winter's grip was fading, surrendering to the warmth of Spring.

Vetus's extended stay in Alfheim meant that Midhir remained without Nuada's sword, and therefore, would not have gone to war with the Summer Court in his absence. He was grateful in that regard.

They didn't have to wait long before a small group, on horseback, rounded the bend on the canyon floor before them. Vetus was relieved to see Rowan leading the entourage. Pride filled Vetus's heart. The boy he rescued had grown to be a formidable and honourable man.

Rowan leapt from his saddle, and after a few short strides, he knelt before Vetus, head bowed, "My Prince. Forgive me. I should have been with you."

Vetus motioned for Rowan to stand, "Dear boy, you have nothing to apologize for."

"I do, my Lord. I have failed you—more than once." Rowan stood, and Vetus waited for him to continue.

"I have betrayed your confidence," he continued, losing all composure. "I don't know how, I—I didn't mean for it to happen. I think I love her—the Gods know I do, and I truly didn't mean for it to happen. I've never let my guard down for anyone like that before, and I—"

"Be silent," Vetus commanded. "You love her...you mean Freydis?"

Rowan nodded but didn't meet Vetus's glare.

"Does she know?" Vetus tried to keep his voice even, fighting to overcome the anger broiling in his guts.

"No, my Lord, I don't believe so," Rowan met his gaze.

Vetus's eyes darkened, "Where is she, Rowan?"

"I didn't leave her alone. She has been busy wedding planning with her human friend, Cass."

"Half-human," Vetus corrected. "Cassandra Walsh is my brother's daughter."

Rowan looked up. Vetus could see his wide eyes holding a mixture of pain and realization.

Vetus continued, "If she is there, she will be safe for now."

"Ophelia has eyes on her as well, I insisted," Rowan added.

"Walk with me," Vetus said.

Vetus explained everything that happened leading up to the ambush and attack, beginning with Petra at the Summer Court, then Lir's wedding, and ending with his near death at the hands of the Fomor.

He explained what he had learned from the elves about the location of Freydis's family and how he had successfully retrieved Nuada's sword. He prodded Rowan about everything that had happened since he saw Freydis last, careful to avoid any mention of the feelings Rowan claimed to have for her. That would be a matter for Vetus to deal with later.

They talked for a long while before returning to the waterfall, where a handful of elves stood waiting expectantly. Vetus turned toward Rowan and squeezed his shoulder.

"I have a gift for you." Vetus smiled, then chuckled at the confusion on Rowan's face, "Kneel once more."

Rowan knelt, and a tall elf wearing silver robes handed Vetus a magnificent sword. Vetus laid the sword blade across his hands, holding it out over Rowan's bowed head.

"Commander Rowan MacArtur, I bestow this sword upon you in recognition of your unwavering fealty and devotion. Let it be a reminder of the greatness within you. With this blade, may you defend the vulnerable, and may it strike fear in the hearts of your enemies."

Rowan stood, taking the hilt of the sword. And holding it over his heart, he pledged, "My life and sword are yours. All that I am, I owe you. Though I am unworthy, I will serve you with honour until my dying breath."

"I have no doubts." Vetus pulled Rowan into his embrace. "Now, let's go home."

When she finished the telephone call, Freydis left her room to find Cass still waiting up. Her eyes seemed to search Freydis's face for clues.

"Well?" Cass asked.

"I am much calmer than I was before the call," Freydis said, flopping down on the sofa beside Cass. Freydis leaned and rested her head on Cass's shoulder.

"So, you aren't leaving in the morning?"

Freydis twinged at the hopeful tone in Cass's voice.

"No, the woman on the phone told me that Vetus is alive, and Rowan has gone to bring him home." Freydis sighed, relief spilling over her. "She told me I would be notified when Vetus was home, and if I wish to see him, arrangements will be made for me to go to Ireland."

"Ireland? What about Marcus?" Cass asked, rubbing her swollen belly.

The weight of those words slammed into Freydis like arrows piercing her chest. She hadn't even considered Marcus. Not for a moment. Not even for a breath.

"I forgot about Marcus." Freydis's cheeks were on fire as she covered her face in her hands. "I'm a terrible person."

"No, you're not," Cass said, pulling Freydis's hands away from her face. "Things still aren't better with you and Marcus?"

"I don't know," Freydis sighed and shook her head. "I can't be myself around him. I can't confide in him. Everything is superficial with us. I'm exhausted after spending time with him."

"You shouldn't have to pretend to be someone you aren't, Freydis," Cass said.

"I know, but I can't tell him what I truly am. He wouldn't understand."

"Are you sure?" Cass picked at her nails. "What's the worst that could happen?"

Freydis gaped at her, "You would ask me that? You who visits the witch trial memorial every year? You heard what he said about magic. He might not burn me at the stake, but he'd definitely think I'm nuts."

"I'm sorry," Cass blushed. "You're right. So, what are you going to do?"

Freydis shrugged and laid her head back on Cass's shoulder.

Chapter Sixteen

T he journey from Alfheim was arduous. The guards who had travelled with Rowan to retrieve Vetus returned the way they had come. Vetus and Rowan stayed in the human realm to avoid any potential ambush that might be lying in wait. That meant car rentals, flights, delays, and all the other joys associated with travel in the human realm.

When the plane landed in Ireland, Vetus was exhausted, but he had to get Nuada's sword to the Winter Court, and he wanted to look his father in the eyes when the king tried to deny the attack. Confronting his father would be drawing a line in the sand, but he had been an obedient son and the crown prince for centuries. It had nearly cost him everything.

One of Vetus's drivers was waiting for them outside the terminal. Rowan secured what little belongings they'd travelled with and joined Vetus in the limo.

"Once you are securely back at Arbor Castle, I will answer the Winter King's summons," Rowan said.

"I'm not going to Arbor Castle," Vetus said. "I am coming with you to see the king. I will present Nuada's sword and confront him about these attacks."

Vetus watched Rowan swallow whatever protest he wanted to make. He knew Rowan only wanted to protect him, but Vetus was done tolerating his father's antics.

"Also," Vetus continued, "I am appointing you the captain of my personal guard. I will inform the king. He wouldn't dare deny me after all that has happened. He might wish me dead, but he would never do so blatantly. There is a reason why he enlisted the Fomor. No doubt, he intended to blame my brother's wife if he had succeeded."

"I am glad I'm just a soldier. I would not wish to belong as a member of the court, not even on my worst enemy." Rowan laughed.

"Well, they are no doubt already members," Vetus grinned.

The courtyard of the Winter Palace was desolate, but that wasn't entirely unusual. Winter fae were significantly less social, as the warmer seasons meant the waning of their power. Many preferred to torment humans during this time of year. They hadn't gone to battle as Midhir had promised, so there would be an abundance of mischief and even violence that had to go somewhere. Humans were an easy and enjoyable target.

Vetus did not share his Winter brethren's pleasure in torturing humans. He supposed he was more like his mother in that regard.

The few fae who did linger were mainly those in the service of the king, and as Vetus and Rowan approached the palace, the hushed voices and averted eyes made Vetus uneasy.

"It would seem that I am the last person they expected to see," Vetus said.

The obsidian doors to the great hall were ajar, and from inside Vetus could hear raised voices. Holding up a hand to signal Rowan to stop and stay silent, Vetus approached the opening and listened.

"I demand you hold her accountable," a female voice said. "He is the Gods-damned crown prince, Father." Vetus knew that voice. *Kerri.*

"Princess Petra is blameless," Midhir's icy voice replied. "She has assured me she knew nothing of the attack."

"She's lying!" Kerridwen yelled.

The pain and frustration in her voice made Vetus's blood boil. He'd heard enough. He hauled open the heavy door and marched through with Rowan tight at his heels. It took every ounce of his will to hide his exhaustion and the pain that lingered from the injuries. Vetus didn't dare come before the king with his walking stick.

Kerridwen spun around toward the sound, and Vetus watched as recognition and relief spread across her face. He barely had time to steady himself before she wrapped her arms around him. Her tear-stained cheeks were cool against his neck, where she buried her face.

"I thought you were...," unable to say the word, she shook her head as more tears fell.

Vetus murmured words of comfort to his younger sister and wiped her tears with his gentle hands. When he had calmed her, together, Vetus, Kerridwen, and Rowan approached the king.

"You are late," Midhir's words echoed through the hall.

"Forgive me, Father, I was delayed," Vetus knelt before his father.

"Did you get it?"

Vetus reached for the weapon strapped to his back. From the plain leather scabbard, Vetus drew Fragarach, Nuada's legendary sword, and held it across his hands before the king.

Midhir gripped the sword and inspected it.

"Your delay has interfered with our plans for war. Our power wanes, and even with our Fomorian allies, we cannot hope to seize the Summer Court until the seasons change."

Midhir turned his focus to Rowan, and Vetus could sense Rowan tense beside him.

"Commander," Midhir growled, "you will remain at court when the prince departs. We have preparations to make, and your service is required here."

Rowan bowed his head to the king, but it was Vetus who spoke.

"No."

"What?" Midhir glared at Vetus, "What did you say?"

A deadly cold filled the room as Vetus said, "He is not staying here. I have appointed him the captain of my personal guard."

Vetus placed a reassuring hand on Rowan's shoulder as Midhir seethed.

Vetus continued, "Since the well-being of your crown prince doesn't seem to concern you, or worse, you actively work to undermine it, I am forced to ensure my own safety."

Frost spread over the floor around where they knelt.

"If I wanted you dead, my son, you would still be lying in that snow," Midhir snarled.

Vetus inclined his head to the king but held his gaze, "As you say, *Ard Ri*, but the commander is still coming with me."

"You dare to defy me, Vetus Mac Midhir," the king hissed. The temperature in the room continued to plummet as father and son argued.

"Your Majesty," Rowan interrupted, his breath visible in the air, "once I have seen the prince safely home and coordinated his security needs, with his permission, I will return to aid you."

Vetus frowned at Rowan's words but could not begrudge him for his honourable heart.

"I accept your offer, Commander," Midhir said, glowering at his children. "At least there are some who understand loyalty left in my court. Now get out."

Rowan, Vetus, and Kerridwen left the great hall and made their way to The Lusty Leprechaun. They hadn't eaten in hours, and Rowan could sense Vetus's strength faltering after the exchange with the king. Despite the crown prince's bravado, he was still recovering.

"Do you believe the king?" Rowan asked.

"Our father would never admit outright that he tried to have my brother killed. Nor would he admit his failure if he had," Kerridwen replied.

Rowan looked at Vetus, who despite his immortality, looked as though he had aged greatly since their visit to the lands of Summer some months before. It seemed so long ago.

"My prince," Rowan pleaded, "I know how much Freydis means to you...and what she means to me...but is it worth all this? Worth your life? Surely, there is another way to keep her safe. Swear to the king you will leave your friendship behind. Something. Anything."

Rowan watched a look of shock followed by an understanding settle on Kerridwen's face.

"Vetus...he doesn't know?" she whispered.

Vetus shook his head and rubbed his face with his hands.

Rowan looked from brother to sister, waiting for answers. "What don't I know?"

"I can't just leave Freydis behind," Vetus sighed. "I made a promise to her mother that I would keep her safe."

"I know you and her mother were close, but surely, after all this time, your debt is filled."

"No, boy, the debt will never be filled," Vetus swallowed. "I will never abandon our daughter."

"Her daughter," Rowan corrected. "You mean 'her daughter.' Freydis's father is human."

Vetus gave Kerridwen an exasperated look. "Magnus was a construct, a ruse. Another way to keep her safe. When we found out that we were with child, we fled Ireland and went to Norway. We sought sanctuary from the elves and decided that I would be Magnus when I was at home to protect her identity, and Solveig would stay there as I did Midhir's bidding, safe with our child."

Kerridwen took her brother's hand as he continued, "When they started hunting witches, fearing for Solveig and Freydis's safety, I went to my mother and father for help. The king refused, calling our daughter an abomination. He said, if he ever found her or if I tried to claim her as my child and heir, he would kill her. That is why my mother left. Everything I have done has been to keep her safe."

"All these years," Rowan couldn't hide the pain in his voice, "you listened as she raged and hated her father...all these years?"

"And it will all be for naught if the king gets his way. He seems hell-bent on killing her." Vetus's eyes darkened. "But I will destroy *him* before I let that happen."

Rowan felt a chill move through him all the way to his bones.

"She mustn't know," Kerridwen added. "Rowan, you cannot tell Freydis what you have learned. It's for her safety. You are the only one outside our family, save Ophelia, who knows the truth."

Rowan nodded his understanding as memories from the past several months came flooding back to haunt him.

The blustery weather of early spring had finally given way to milder May days. Peonies, rhododendrons, and the odd early rose were blooming, adding a touch of colour around the city.

Marcus finally found time to invite Freydis to dinner, so she wanted to make an effort to look half-decent. She chose a midnight-blue bodycon dress that hid nearly all her scars. The rest she could glamour easily. Cass lent her a pair of silver ankle-strap heels. Her long brown hair, which was usually tied up in a messy bun, hung down in waves, covering her shoulders. Cass did her makeup.

Freydis never liked going out, and she hadn't since she arrived in Boston. If she was being truthful, she didn't feel like doing anything that night either. But once she was ready, she felt beautiful for the first time in a long while.

She arrived at dinner with no time to spare. Marcus was already there, waiting for her. Seeing him in his simple button-up shirt and jeans made her feel overdressed, but his reaction to her appearance eased the initial self-consciousness she felt. He rose from the table to greet her and pulled her to him, kissing her tenderly.

"You are stunning," Marcus smiled, taking her all in. "It hasn't been that long since I've seen you, has it?"

Freydis smiled weakly, "Long enough."

Marcus pulled out her chair and poured her a glass of red wine. Freydis winced but hastily schooled her expression, hoping he hadn't noticed. She preferred white.

"I ordered for you," Marcus declared, making her temper flare briefly.

"How did you know what I want?"

He laughed off her comment, and before she could say anything else, the waiter arrived with their meals. It was clear that Marcus had spared no expense. The spread of food on the table was more than just dinner. It was like a celebration feast. Freydis felt the heat in her cheeks when she realized that he didn't really pick something for her, but merely ordered a bit of everything.

Freydis looked at him across the table, his warm, dark eyes meeting hers. They sparkled, full of barely contained excitement. He pulled his chair over closer to her.

"I'm going to be the first recipient," Marcus blurted. His words crashed down on her like a waterfall.

"I'm sorry, what?" Freydis paused, waiting for him to clarify.

"We are starting human trials next week, and I have volunteered to go first."

He did what?

"Marcus, are you sure that's a good idea? I mean, there has got to be someone else who'll volunteer," Freydis pleaded. "What if something goes wrong?"

There were too many unknowns, and Freydis cared deeply about Marcus. He would be risking everything. She knew what his work meant to him, but she couldn't suppress the nagging feeling that this was a terrible idea.

"I know it's new, and maybe this decision seems rash to you," Marcus said, "but I trust my research and my team. I have spent my whole life working for this, Freydis."

Her eyes fell to where he now held her hands in his, and a twinge of shame rippled through her. Marcus leaned closer and tucked an unruly wisp of hair behind her ear. She thought of Rowan.

Meeting his gaze, Freydis could see the vulnerability in his eyes. The hope.

"I need you to do this with me," Marcus said.

The temperature in the room dropped as though a ripple of Arctic wind had swept through, and his words immediately sucked all the air from her lungs. *What was he asking her?* She inhaled deeply, forcing herself to calm down enough to speak. Fear threatened to steal her voice.

"I know this is important to you, Marcus. I know it's your dream come true," Freydis caressed the back of his hands with her thumbs. "I care about you, and if this is what you really want, you have my support."

"No, Freydis," Marcus laughed, "I don't mean your support. I want you to be a participant in the clinical trial. We can do it together."

His words kept coming. Freydis was lightheaded and felt as though someone had pulled her chair out from under her.

"Marcus, I can't."

He kept talking.

"Marcus. Stop." She pulled her hands away. "I can't do this. I won't."

In that moment, it no longer mattered to her how much she cared for him; she knew she could never bring herself to tell him who or what she was. She didn't even know herself, and several lifetimes of experience told her that humans fear what they do not understand, and fear leads to destruction. Panic rushed through her.

Freydis couldn't bear the thought of looking into his eyes and seeing fear there. He was asking her the impossible, and yet for all the stars in the sky, she couldn't come up with an excuse or reason that he might accept. Truth was not an option. If she allowed them to cut into her, they would discover she was more than human.

"Freydis," Marcus pleaded, taking her trembling hands in his own, "please. You have been with me through these past difficult months. This is everything we have sacrificed our time together for. All the days apart. All of it. This is a dream come true. Our dream. It will change everything. It will mean longer, healthier lives for us and the people we love. It will change the world. I am giving you the chance to be part of something bigger than us."

Freydis sat there, silence filling the space between them. Closing her eyes, she willed with everything she had to just disappear.

"Please, Freydis...I love you."

She pulled her hands away. It was the first time he'd spoken those words to her.

Rising from the table, Freydis said, "I'm so sorry, Marcus. I can't do this anymore."

Freydis wouldn't make eye contact. Couldn't. But she could feel his eyes on her. He didn't speak and he didn't rise from the table. Perhaps he was waiting for an explanation, but it would never come. So, Freydis walked away, leaving him there, without looking back.

Outside, a warm late-spring rain started to fall, and as Freydis walked in the direction of Cass's apartment, thunder rumbled in the distance.

Freydis just walked out. He should have stopped her.

No, if she loved him, she would have done this with him.

Marcus stood in his office. Work would ease his mind, distract him. He would do this procedure with or without her. *Damn her.*

"Marcus?" Tina's quiet voice called from the doorway. "What are you doing here so late? I thought you had a date with Freydis tonight?"

"It's over."

Tina came into his office, still wearing the pretty blouse and black skirt she wore earlier in the day. She must not have left work yet. Marcus was sure her eyes brightened at his news.

"That wasn't a very long date," Tina teased, but her tone held more cautious hope than humour.

"I asked her to be part of the clinical trial. With me." He swallowed.

Tina's vanilla coconut smell filled his nostrils. She had moved close enough that he could almost touch her.

Marcus sighed, "She freaked out and refused. And then she broke up with me."

Tina's expression softened, and for the first time, Marcus noticed how lovely she was.

"I'm sorry, Marcus," she murmured, closing the distance between them. "It seems so sudden. Did she explain?"

Marcus shook his head. "She said something like, 'I can't do this,' and left me sitting there, stunned."

"What do you think she meant? The clinical trial? That seems like a bit of an overreaction."

"I don't know what she meant, honestly. I guess she has kinda been off the last couple of times I've seen her."

"So, what are you doing here if your heart's broken?" Tina murmured.

"Looking for a distraction. Work never walks out on me," Marcus chuckled.

Tina's expression changed, and the way she now looked at him made his entire body tense. "I would have said yes to the trial. To you."

She had barely finished speaking, and they were face to face. Close enough to feel her sweet breath as he asked her, "Really?"

Her gaze moved to his lips as she murmured, "Yes."

Marcus lowered his mouth to hers as she pressed herself against him, frantic and hungry. He felt the warmth of her fingers slide under the lower hem of his shirt, and she pulled it over his head. His heart was racing.

This was wrong, wasn't it?

Their hands roamed over each other, discarding clothing as they went.

She left. Freydis just left him, but Tina never had.

He opened his mouth slightly as her tongue traced the opening, and he moaned as the kiss deepened and intensified. Her skin was soft and smooth under his hands, and her body responded to his touch.

He whispered against her mouth, "Are you sure?"

She nodded, and he lifted her into his arms. Her legs wrapped around him as he pressed her against the wall. He had wanted a distraction.

He found one.

Chapter Seventeen

In the courtyard at Arbor Castle, Vetus waited, leaning on the ornate oak cane he had brought with him from Alfheim. Before him, several ranks of his newly trained personal guard stood, being inspected by Rowan. Security had increased tenfold at the castle since Vetus returned home. While he appreciated Rowan's concern, it felt excessive.

"An impressive group," Ophelia said, coming up behind him. "The boy has been busy."

Vetus nodded his agreement and noticed her silent assessment of the cane, which he seemed to need more and more the past few weeks.

Keeping his eyes focused on the courtyard, he raised the cane slightly. "The damp Irish weather."

The corner of her mouth turned upward in a slight smirk, "Mhmm."

He knew she didn't buy it, but he was grateful for her indulgence.

"I'm tired, Rowan," Vetus announced. "Meet me in my study when you're finished."

Rowan gave a sharp nod of acknowledgement, and Vetus turned to Ophelia. "Walk with me?"

Once they'd entered the keep, Vetus asked, "When was the last time you spoke to the Gods?"

Ophelia stopped dead. "Which Gods?"

"Any of them."

He watched her consider the question and added, "When I returned for Lir's wedding, Lord Balor, Petra's father, did not attend. At first, I hadn't thought much of it, but then in Alfheim, the steward said Lord Freyr had not been seen or heard from in an age. I hadn't really noticed until recently, but I can't remember the last time I saw or spoke to any of the ancient ones."

"Well, that is not entirely unheard of. Even the humans haven't commmuned directly with the Gods in thousands of years," Ophelia didn't hide her disdain. "The Gods are fickle."

Vetus gave her a warning glance. "You haven't answered my question, My Lady."

"I have no time for the Gods," she answered. "Why do you dwell on them?"

"It might be nothing, but the steward of Alfheim gave me the impression that Lord Freyr's disappearance was uncharacteristic, and as much as Balor and my father hate each other, his absence from Petra and Lir's wedding was unsettling. What if there are more who have disappeared?"

Ophelia snorted, "Good riddance."

Vetus couldn't keep the smile from spreading across his face, "Can you just look further into it for me? I'll owe you."

She waved at him dismissively, leaving him to climb the stairs toward his study alone.

Vetus lounged in the wingback chair by the hearth, sipping whiskey, when Rowan's voice broke the silence.

"I see it now." Rowan stared at the portrait of Solveig, Vetus's wife and Freydis's mother, hanging above the mantel. "She looks just like her."

Vetus silently watched him from across the room and could still picture the boy he carried in his arms, bloody and dying, before Solveig saved him. Long before Freydis was born, an eternity ago.

"I don't know how I missed it," Rowan said, pouring himself a glass of whiskey. "I still remember the day you saved me. I thought you'd brought me to an angel."

Vetus closed his eyes and smiled, "I did."

"You never told me she was your wife," Rowan murmured. "And Freydis—why had I not met her before?"

"It's complicated, Rowan," Vetus levelled his gaze. "Everything I have ever done was to protect Freydis. I couldn't risk provoking my father. He blamed Solveig and Freydis for everything that has befallen my family. No one could know except those who already did. Midhir wouldn't help me protect them, and it cost me Solveig."

"I could have helped," Rowan whispered. "I would have helped you."

Vetus stood and moved to place his hand tenderly on Rowan's shoulder. "You have, and you will. Before you return to the Winter Palace, I need you to go to Freydis until I can find a more permanent way to keep her from harm. If Marcus is in the picture, she will not leave Boston."

Vetus watched something close to anger flicker across Rowan's face at the mention of Marcus. No, not anger. Jealousy.

"I understand," Rowan said.

"It's only temporary," Vetus added. "And I need you to leave tonight."

Rowan stood and finished his whiskey before inclining his head to Vetus, "As you command."

Cass was already asleep when Freydis arrived at her apartment. Freydis had hoped she would be. Ethan answered the door and offered to wake her, but Freydis declined, asking instead if she could crash at their place for the night. She didn't want to be alone.

Freydis knew the conversation she didn't want to have would come in the morning. She hoped Cass and Ethan would understand. Freydis didn't sleep, and when the morning finally came, she was sitting at the table with her second cup of tea when Cass woke up and joined her.

"I can't believe he'd ask you that," Cass scowled. "Although, breaking up with him might have been a little excessive."

Freydis sighed, "It's more than that. It's been coming for a while, I think. I'm sorry it had to happen right before your wedding. I promise I won't make it awkward."

Cass waved off her comment, "We're all grown-ups. Marcus will get over it."

Freydis continued, "I will never be able to be who I am with him, and I don't want to lie to him."

Cass nodded and shifted in her seat, rubbing her round belly. "This baby hardly stays still. I will be glad when she arrives."

"Wait," Freydis held up her hand. "*She?*"

A baby girl.

Cass's smile lit up her entire face, "We found out yesterday!"

"Ethan must be so excited," Freydis beamed, grateful for the change of subject.

"He is," Cass giggled, "and terrified."

Freydis reached for Cass, taking her hand. "He will be the most wonderful father."

Cass's eyes welled up slightly at Freydis's words. Freydis understood. The concept of a "father" was foreign to them both.

"I'm leaving for Ireland right after the wedding," Freydis said. "Vetus should be back, and I need to go to him. He has always been there for me."

"How long will you be gone?" Cass's nervous laughter made Freydis's stomach lurch.

"I won't be gone too long, Cass. I need to be here for when our baby arrives."

Cass beamed again at the mention of the baby and pulled Freydis in for a hug.

Chapter Eighteen

The Verb Hotel held a special place in Cass's heart. Located near Fenway Park, it had been an obvious choice for Ethan when he'd planned their first anniversary. They'd watched the Red Sox beat the Yankees that day, and afterwards, Ethan had arranged for the LOVE package at the hotel. It seemed fitting that she now stood in the same room as Freydis laced up her wedding dress.

"Tell me if it feels too tight," Freydis said. "I don't want to squish the baby."

Cass smiled, "Thank you for helping with everything, Freydis. I don't think I could have done it without your help."

"Of course, you would have, and besides, I'm sure Marcus would have just hired someone. He is taking his best man role very seriously." Freydis gave Cass's back a quick, gentle rub, "All done. Ready to see?"

Cass swallowed deeply and turned to face the full-length mirror. Her empire-wasted ivory beaded lace gown hung elegantly to the floor, covering the lavender-coloured flats she wore. Freydis fixed Cass's court-length train and stood beaming behind her.

"You look like a goddess," Freydis murmured.

Cass ran her hands over her belly and met Freydis's gaze in the mirror. "Ethan's parents have decided not to come."

"What?" Freydis scowled, "Why?"

"They send their 'congratulations' but refused to attend since we aren't being married by a priest. I think that's why Marcus is making such a fuss. Trying to compensate."

Freydis nodded, "He would do that."

"Are you sure it won't be awkward between you two?" Cass asked.

"Stop worrying about me and enjoy your day." Freydis checked her watch. "It's time to go."

Freydis handed Cass her bouquet of purple hydrangeas and white roses, and they made their way to the limo waiting for them.

Ramler Park was a small, yet beautiful place for an intimate wedding. That's why Cass chose it. The officiant stood with Ethan and Marcus in front of the white-columned pergola. A small group of Cass and Ethan's acquaintances stood on either side, and Cass and Freydis began their approach from behind the small fountain at the opposite end of the tiny courtyard.

Cass could hardly feel her legs moving beneath her, and if Freydis hadn't been walking with her, she wasn't sure she would have been steady enough to make it. She fought a pang of grief as she made eye contact with their guests. She had no family in the crowd.

She finally worked up the courage to look at Ethan and saw his whole face light up with wonder. A string trio played *Canon in D*, and the sun had just set below the horizon. Strings of white fairy lights twinkled in the twilight as the first stars began to appear in the darkening sky.

As Cass and Freydis approached, Ethan stepped forward to meet them and took Cass by the hand.

"I'm sorry they're clammy," Ethan whispered before kissing the back of her hand. "You are so beautiful."

Cass felt her cheeks redden.

Their guests formed a circle around them and the officiant. Cass noticed that Marcus couldn't seem to take his eyes off Freydis, who seemed oblivious to it.

The officiant moved through the ceremony to the point where Cass and Ethan would exchange their vows. They had each written their own.

"Ethan Wolfe," the officiant stated, "you may now recite the vows you have prepared."

Ethan held both Cass's hands in his. They were no longer clammy.

"Cass, I had stopped believing in magic until I met you," Ethan's voice shook. Cass gently squeezed his hands. He smiled. "You are the sun in my cloudy sky, and there isn't a day that passes that I am not in awe of you. You bring joy to everyone you meet. From the first moment you said my name, it was the sweetest sound I'd ever heard. And the first time I heard you laugh, I wanted to do everything I could to keep you happy. The first time I kissed you, I knew I wanted to marry you." Ethan swallowed deeply.

"When you are sad, I will hold you and wipe away your tears. When you are weary or sick, I will care for you. I will remember all our firsts and be with you for all of our lasts. I will honour you and love you above all others from this moment on."

Cass's hand was shaking as Ethan slid the ring onto her finger. Then he wiped away her tears.

She glanced at Freydis, who gave her an encouraging smile.

"Cassandra Walsh," the officiant continued, "you may now recite your vows."

"Ethan, you are the rock that I have built my life on. You've been my strength through my darkest days. I didn't know what a good man was until I met you. You've never held me back or been afraid to let me be true to myself. You've made me feel more loved than I ever thought possible. I couldn't've dreamed up a better husband, and I am honoured to be your wife. I will spend all my days loving you. From this day on." Cass placed Ethan's ring onto his finger.

"By the power vested in me by the State of Massachusetts," the officiant declared, "I pronounce you husband and wife. You may—"

Ethan didn't wait. He took Cass's face into his hands and kissed her deeply. He still took her breath away.

Nearly two hundred years had passed since Freydis visited Ireland to fight in one of their rebellions against British rule. She hadn't had time to visit Arbor Castle. Her stomach was a twisted ball of knots as she waited for her luggage. Ophelia, whom Freydis had never met, planned every step of her trip. Apparently, a car had been arranged to take her from Ireland West Airport to Loch Cé.

The lack of control over the situation was excruciating, but Vetus had regularly relied on Ophelia to make his arrangements. If Vetus trusted her, Freydis decided she could too.

A familiar sweet, earthy smell wrapped around her, standing at the luggage carousel, only moments before he whispered in her ear, "Hello, my Fierce One."

His husky tone and warm breath on her neck made her toes curl, and she turned to face Rowan, who stood behind her with a childlike mischievous grin on his face. She hadn't seen him in a few months, and it hit her hard how much she'd missed him. The look he was giving her made her cheeks warm and her mind go blank. It took every ounce of her will not to lunge for him and jump into his arms.

"I have come to retrieve you, My Lady." Rowan gave her an exaggerated, almost theatrical bow and reached for her luggage. Gesturing toward the exit, he smiled, "Shall we?"

The drive flew by. They had a lot to catch up on. As their car pulled into Loch Cé Forest Park, Freydis kept her eyes peeled out the window.

"He lives in a public park?"

"Hiding in plain sight, yes," Rowan murmured, pointing to the public jetty. "We have to go by boat to the island."

When they exited the car, Freydis could see the island with the ruined castle out on the lake from where she stood on the dock. "That can't be it," she said, meeting his gaze.

He wasn't looking at the castle, though. He looked at her like she was the first light he had seen after days of wandering in the dark. The butterflies in her stomach danced with delight.

"That," Rowan said, pointing to the ruined castle, "is the ruins of McDermott's Castle. It has a very interesting history."

"Oooh, talk dirty to me," Freydis purred. Rowan laughed.

"Local legend says that an obligation of perpetual hospitality had been laid upon the McDermott family by the Hag of Lough Key," Rowan said. "Vetus made an agreement with Cormac McDermott to break the curse in exchange for ownership of the island."

"So, you are asking me to believe that Vetus lives in that old ruin?" Freydis scoffed.

"You aren't looking at it correctly," Rowan laughed, pulling her toward him. "As someone who can craft glamours, have you never learned to see through them?"

Freydis shook her head and frowned, "No. Never."

Rowan placed his hands on her shoulders, pointing her toward the castle, and gave her a gentle squeeze. "Okay, first lesson. Close your eyes and try to forget about the ruin you saw. Got it?"

Freydis gave him a skeptical look, but she obeyed, leaning into him, trying to ignore the feeling of their bodies pressed together. "Done."

He brought his lips near to her ear and whispered, "Now, breathe in deeply and try to feel as present as possible. Feel your toes and follow that feeling up your body; notice every part, all the way to the top of your head."

Freydis opened one eye, turning her head slightly to glare at him. Gods, he drove her crazy, but if this was what madness felt like, she wanted to drown in it.

"No peeking!" He poked her, and again she closed her eyes. "Keep breathing."

Freydis sighed impatiently, "Why am I doing this?"

"Most people spend all their time either thinking about the past or worrying about the future, so they often fail to see what is right in front of them," Rowan explained. "To see through the glamour, you need to be present and have a little magic in your blood. You meet the second requirement, so you just need to be here, in this moment with me, and nowhere else."

Freydis swallowed, inhaled deeply, and opened her eyes.

"Oh, *Gods*," she gasped. "It's incredible."

Vetus's home, Arbor Castle, stood proudly on the island, its tall tower like a spear thrust toward the clouds. Even from the opposite shore, Freydis could see movement outside the castle. When she'd finished gaping, she noticed Rowan had left her and was now standing in a small wooden boat with two wooden oars. She couldn't contain her laughter.

"You've got to be joking!" She shook her head. "Is this how everyone visits the castle?"

Rowan smiled wickedly.

"No. Only you." He winked, "The rest of us use magic, and we keep those ways secret."

Freydis stuck out her tongue, which earned her a laugh. She grabbed Rowan's outstretched hand and stepped carefully into the boat.

Watching as he loaded her belongings into the little boat, Freydis blurted, "I ended things with Marcus."

She didn't know why she said it, but she didn't miss the grin Rowan tried to hide. He turned his silver eyes toward her. His face was a mask of concern.

"I'm sorry. Are you alright?"

"No, you're not," she grinned at him.

"No. I'm not." He returned her smile. "But I do want to know if you're alright. I know how much he meant to you."

"I'm alright," she said, more to herself than to Rowan.

"Good," he winked and handed her an oar. "Hope you're feeling strong today."

Marcus arrived back in Virginia a day before the procedure for last-minute tests and pre-operative preparations. Tomorrow, they would shave a small patch on his head, and he would go to sleep while members of his team supervised. They would drill a few small holes and thread the device into his head, placing the neural implant onto the surface of his brain. It would be among the greatest scientific medical breakthroughs of the twenty-first century.

Even though it would be an easy recovery, Tina promised to help him through it, and once he was feeling well enough, she would undergo the procedure. Just as she'd said she would.

"Are you nervous?" Tina asked, gently caressing his tense shoulders.

"I'd be a fool not to be," Marcus laughed, "but I trust the research and our team."

Marcus reached for her hand and gave it a squeeze.

"Promise me everything will go according to plan," Tina's voice was barely a whisper. "Even if it's not true, promise me."

Marcus held her gaze, pulling her toward him to kiss her gently, "I promise."

The next morning, the entire team wished him luck, and Tina stayed with him until it was time. The cool saline they used to flush his IV left a salty taste in his mouth. He closed his eyes and counted backward from ten. All the way to his lifelong dream.

Chapter Nineteen

Vetus and Ophelia chatted over tea and a late lunch in the castle's kitchen. Rowan would be arriving any moment with Freydis, whom Vetus hadn't seen since before her trip to Salem. So many things had happened since then. He wasn't sure where to begin. He wanted to tell her everything about who he was and what he'd discovered in Alfheim. All of it. He wanted her to know the truth, but it terrified him to think of the dangers she would face once she knew.

"What is happening in that princely head of yours?" Ophelia asked. "You need to stop worrying. She's a grown woman. You do her an injustice by not letting her have the truth so she can learn to navigate it."

Vetus raked a hand through his hair, "Yes, but *how* do I tell her?"

"Tell me what?" Freydis's question echoed through him. He turned toward her, and she hurried into his arms. He grimaced as pain shot through his leg from his bracing himself under her assault. She didn't miss a thing.

"Oh Gods, I hurt you," Freydis winced, and she searched his face. "How bad is it?"

"It gets better every day," he lied.

"So, what do you want to tell me?"

"I found them," Vetus said. "I found your mother's people."

Vetus watched as the world came crashing down on her. She swayed, unsteady on her feet, but Rowan was there with a supportive hand on the small of her back before Vetus could move.

"Where?" the word tore from her throat.

"South America. Belize, specifically." Vetus cleared his throat, "I don't know how many are left, but at least now you can decide what comes next."

Tears pooled in her eyes. "I'm afraid."

Vetus pulled her into his embrace, "I know, Dea, but you are not alone."

She leaned her head against his chest, and Vetus fought against the urge to remain silent.

"There is more I need to tell you." He patted the chair beside him, "You should sit."

Freydis glanced around the room at those gathered, then did as he commanded. He turned his chair so that he was facing her and took one of her hands in his.

"In all the years we've known each other, you have never once pried or asked about my heritage, but I can hide it no longer. For your safety." Vetus swallowed deeply and looked briefly at Ophelia, who only smiled.

"My name is Vetus Mac Midhir, and I am the Crown Prince of the Winter Court. I am a descendant of the Tuatha Dé Danann, and yes, I am the lord of this castle. My father is Midhir, the King of Winter and son of the God Dagda and Goddess Morrigan. My mother was a princess of Summer, daughter of the God Manannan Mac Lir and the Goddess Áine. I have lived for thousands of years."

"You," Freydis glared at him. "*You* had Cass spy on me? Told her my secrets?"

"I did it to protect you," Vetus held up his hands. "I believe my father wants to harm you to get to me."

"Why would he...," Freydis paused, as though she'd remembered something, and Vetus watched as several emotions passed over her face. "Are you Cass's father?"

Vetus sighed, "No, she is my brother Lir's child."

An invisible weight seemed to lift from her shoulders. "You have a brother?"

Vetus nodded, "And a sister."

"Let me get this straight: your father, who happens to be the King of Winter, wants me dead to what, punish you? And you—you are a fairy prince?" She didn't hide her disbelief, "Don't expect me to bow to you or call you 'your highness.'"

Everyone laughed, and Freydis turned to Ophelia, "And who are you?"

"A friend," Ophelia smiled.

"I have a thousand questions," Freydis sighed.

"There will be time for all that, but first there is one other matter I want to discuss with you, Dea, before we get you settled in." Vetus drew a steadying breath, and Freydis visibly stiffened. "The elves told me about a memorial that's been built in Vardø, Norway. For those who lost their lives during the witch trials."

Freydis closed her eyes and clenched her fists, but Vetus didn't miss her lip tremble.

"The dedication will take place a week from tomorrow," Vetus continued. "I think it is important that you go. It will help you heal."

Freydis shook her head as tears silently stained her cheeks.

"I will go with you," Rowan murmured, "if you'd rather not go alone."

Freydis opened her eyes toward Rowan and nodded.

Vetus gave him a grateful smile, "Ophelia will make the arrangements."

After everything that had occurred earlier in the day, Freydis was surprised by how energized she felt. Too overwhelmed to sleep, with so many thoughts running through her mind and her body still on Boston time, she made her way to the castle's library. Many of the books were older than Freydis herself, but she was pleasantly surprised to find more modern works as well.

Row upon row of dusty wooden shelves overflowed with treasures, lovingly collected through the centuries by Vetus, her dearest friend. As she did whenever she found herself among so many books, she walked silently along the shelves, hand trailing across the bindings, waiting for that quiet invitation to enter into a sacred bond between a book and its reader.

There were too many for her to select them all, so with a stack of intriguing titles, she sat at the big stone table in the centre of the room. She pulled out one of the ornate but comfortable chairs and dove in. Original works by Dante Alighieri, Chaucer, and Dickens and personalized handwritten works by Aristotle, Marcus Aurelius, and St. Thomas Aquinas filled the table before her.

Vetus had possibly known them all. He was far older than she ever could have imagined. What else didn't she know about him? To think of the stories he could tell. The historian in her wanted to pick his brain for hours.

Gently flipping through her treasures, careful to touch each page as little as possible, she didn't notice that Ophelia had slipped in until she cleared her throat. Freydis's head snapped up, her gaze locked onto where Ophelia stood.

"I hope I'm allowed to be in here," Freydis smiled sheepishly. "I couldn't resist."

Ophelia's eyes sparkled mischievously, "What else is a library for if not for reading?"

Ophelia was beautiful the way the moon's reflection on a calm sea was beautiful. Her very presence was soothing. Freydis wondered if she was also fae. She closed the well-read pages of Marcus Aurelius's *Meditations*.

"So, do you live here...*with* Vetus?" Freydis drawled, trying to make small talk.

Ophelia laughed, "Not like *that*, but yes, I run the prince's household for him."

"Are you a fairy, like Vetus?"

"No. And of all the monikers, I would suggest you choose another. The term 'fairy' is discourteous," Ophelia corrected. "I am a nereid. We're like a water spirit, minus the spirit part."

"Are you immortal too?" Freydis had so many questions.

"I do not age, but I suppose I can be killed." Ophelia paused, her brow furrowed. "That seems to be the way with most of the immortals I have known."

"Most, but not all? What about the Gods? Vetus said his grandparents were actual *Gods* and *Goddesses*."

"Yes, he did," Ophelia smiled knowingly.

"I have heard of the ones he mentioned. Does that mean that the Celtic deities are the real ones?" Freydis was bursting with excitement. There was so much she wanted to know. To learn.

"They are all real," Ophelia said. "All the Gods from all human religions of the world."

Ophelia moved toward the bookshelf, where she pulled out a small leather-bound text and set it on the table beside Freydis.

"Seriously?! That's incredible!" Freydis felt a tightening in her chest as she reached for the ancient tome. "But if that's true, then why don't they intervene or answer prayers?"

Ophelia snorted, "Because they don't care. Not like humans do. In truth, they are rather capricious."

"Can I meet them?" Freydis was on the edge of her chair.

"I'm sure you will, at some point, though none have been seen in a very long time. Perhaps you should talk to Vetus about it."

Ophelia turned as though to walk toward the door, but there was one other question that Freydis wanted to ask.

"Why serve Vetus when you could be free? Surely, he would let you go."

Ophelia's face softened, "I owe him and his late wife a life debt—"

The words were barely out of her mouth when she pinched her lips together, giving Freydis the impression she had said too much.

"Vetus was married?" Freydis couldn't believe it. She didn't know Vetus at all. "Does he have any children?"

"I think," Ophelia said, "these are not my tales to tell, but I would be happy to show you around the castle and grounds tomorrow. I just stopped by to make sure you had everything you need before I went to bed."

"May I stay and continue reading for a while?" Freydis asked.

Ophelia nodded and made her way to the door. Before exiting, she turned to Freydis, "I'm so happy to have finally met you, Freydis."

Maybe it was a trick of the dim lighting, but Freydis was sure she saw tears in Ophelia's eyes.

Rowan stood on the battlements under the stars, listening to the water lap against the shore. Freydis had reacted surprisingly well to everything that was unloaded on her earlier. Gods, she *was* fierce. Unflinching. He was not having as simple a time in processing everything he had learned over the past several days.

He admitted his love for her to Vetus, only to find out later that Vetus was her father, not just a long-time friend. That made her a princess. If she was unavailable before, this made her untouchable.

Rowan paced, trying to calm the thoughts racing in his head. There was no way he'd sleep.

"I've always loved this view," Vetus's voice pierced the night. "Especially for brooding."

Rowan stopped pacing and looked out over the lake. "I feel off-kilter, like I can't get my footing. When Ophelia told me you'd been attacked, it brought everything back from when I was a child. Everything."

Vetus nodded.

"And then Freydis…," Rowan continued, raking his hands through his hair, "I thought I was content as a soldier. I would've lived an honourable life, happy to serve the Winter Court…until I met her. And now?"

Rowan turned to face Vetus, but Vetus only gazed toward the horizon. His courage faltered. Rowan cleared his throat and continued, "I do not intend to tell her…how I feel. There is no good that can come of it."

Rowan wanted Vetus to tell him differently, wanted him to give his blessing, as silly as it was to hope. Vetus met his eyes with a level gaze. "Be on your guard in Norway. Midhir is beyond all reason, and I'm sure he is planning another attack."

There it was. No blessing, not even an acknowledgement. It stung more than Rowan cared to admit.

"I will never let any harm come to her, Vetus," Rowan swallowed deeply. "Even if she can never be mine, I will protect her as if she were. I swear it."

Vetus knocked his knuckles on the crenellated wall and nodded, leaving as abruptly as he'd appeared.

Rowan blew out the breath he hadn't realized he'd been holding and continued pacing.

Chapter Twenty

Everything hurt.

Cass opened her eyes to flashing lights and raised voices. She lifted a hand to wipe her hair from her face and caught a glimpse of her arm, which was covered in blood. Blood. She could smell the coppery tang mixed with something else. *Gasoline, maybe?*

Why was there so much blood?

And then it hit her. Last she remembered, she and Ethan were on their way back from supper. An animal, no wait, a man on a horse sprung out in front of them. Ethan swerved, and then everything went black.

She tried to move, but her body had been strapped to a stretcher. Where was Ethan? Her first attempt at calling to him was lost in the noise from the emergency workers.

"ETHAN!" she yelled again. "Where is Ethan? Where is he?"

Panic started to flood her body, and she began trembling furiously. *And the pain, oh God, so much pain.*

"Ma'am, it's okay. We are gonna look after you. Everything will be okay," a young paramedic spoke to her, then listened to her belly. *Oh God, the baby.*

"My baby! Is my baby okay?" she cried. This couldn't be happening. Where was Ethan?

"Ma'am, you are leaking some amniotic fluid, so we are gonna get you to the hospital and get you and your baby looked after, okay?"

"Please, where is Ethan?"

"Ethan, is that his name?" the paramedic asked. "He has already gone ahead in the other ambulance, okay? We will be right behind him."

No, this couldn't be happening. What was a man on a horse doing on the road at that time of night?

"What about the other man? The one on the horse?"

"What other man?" the paramedic froze. "Was there someone else in the vehicle with you?"

"No," Cass winced as pain shot through her body. "No, the man on the horse. The one we swerved to miss."

"The witnesses said there was nothing on the road when your vehicle swerved."

The paramedic took out a pen light and shone it into her eyes and then spoke into the radio, something about head trauma, and then looked back at Cass. "No one else was hurt."

How could that be? She saw it. She was sure. Ethan saw it too. Then he reached his arm in front of her before swerving.

"We are just going to give you something for the pain," the paramedic said. "The hospital isn't far. You're gonna be okay."

Cass fought to stay awake, but as a flood of calm washed over her, she surrendered to it.

"I'd forgotten how bare the land is."

Freydis stood looking out to the Barents Sea. How had her parents survived in such a place? Only the strong could survive in a place like Vardø. Had she been strong once? She didn't remember the emptiness. Freydis remembered the majesty of the aurora borealis—the reflection of the Valkyries' armour, her mother had told her. She had wanted to be a Valkyrie—what girl didn't?

Freydis remembered her home as a place of life, bursting with wild animals, cold winds, and midnight sun. It was a magical place to grow up in as a child.

"Your mother must've been an incredible woman," Rowan smiled and winked at Freydis. "Only the most formidable could survive this place."

He zipped up his lightweight jacket and gestured toward their destination. He followed a step behind her as Freydis approached the first small building of the Steilneset Memorial. He didn't try to speak, which she was grateful for. His presence steadied her, but she had no words. Over 350 years had passed since she was there last.

Her feet grew heavier with every step toward the square building. It was covered in reflective panels, which mirrored the bleak landscape and churning waters of the Barents Sea. The sky was overcast, and Freydis pulled her jacket tight around her against the wind off the water. She stopped at the entrance and stood silently. She could sense Rowan behind her.

"I don't think I can do this," she whispered, turning her stormy eyes toward him. He was stoic. His eyes seemed to search her face.

"You can, Fierce One, I am with you. You don't have to face this alone." He placed his warm hand on her shoulder and gave it a squeeze.

Freydis stepped inside the little building and choked back a sob. In the centre of the building sat a lone chair, a flame burning brightly from the seat. Around the perimeter were oval mirrors that cast varying reflections inside the structure. The work had been titled *The Damned, the Possessed and the Beloved.* It was hauntingly beautiful in its simplicity.

Freydis breathed deeply as she stared into the flame. This would be the easy part, she knew, because inside the other long building, called Memory Hall, along the walls, were ninety-one windows at irregular heights, each with a solitary light to represent a victim of the witch trials. Each window was also accompanied by a hanging black silk sheet inscribed with white letters, identifying the victim and the details of their ordeal.

There she would find her mother's name written on black silk, her memory reduced to a small window and lonely light overlooking the sea.

Entering the second building, Freydis walked slowly down the long hall, passing each window and light, until she felt a pull as if she knew exactly which window and light belonged to her mother. Freydis turned to face the plaque and traced the words with her trembling fingers. The lights in the hallway flickered.

Falling to her knees, she sobbed uncontrollably. She didn't care that the memorial was packed with people for the unveiling or that Rowan saw her fall apart. Three centuries' worth of grief came flooding back, and all she wanted was to let it drown her.

The sobs wracked her body. She couldn't even catch her breath as her heart shattered all over again.

Seeing Freydis fall to her knees and fall apart was the worst thing Rowan had experienced since he lost his mother. He couldn't help her. He couldn't pick up her broken pieces or take away her pain.

He couldn't bear it.

He knelt beside her and pulled her close, holding her as she cried against his chest. He ran his fingers through her long, silky hair, murmuring meaningless words of comfort. He would hold her forever if that's what she needed, *Vetus be damned*.

When her sobbing quieted and he felt her body relax, he helped her to her feet. Her head still against him, she whispered, "Please don't let me go."

He held her tighter, and despite everything that warned him against it, he placed a gentle kiss on top of her head and whispered, "Never."

Her body stilled and she looked up at him.

Her gaze was penetrating but he held it. That damned wisp of hair was in her face again, so he gently tucked it behind her ear, careful not to break eye contact. She opened her mouth slightly as though about to speak.

"Freydis, I...," Rowan tried to say something. Maybe he was going to apologize for the kiss, but before he could finish the sentence, she placed a finger over his lips to silence him, tracing them gently. His breath hitched as he leaned into her touch. She raised herself up on her tiptoes and placed a gentle kiss where her finger had been seconds before.

Lighting forked through his veins at the feel of her soft lips.

After the kiss, she stayed on her tiptoes, her lips still close enough that he could feel her breath, waiting.

"*Freydis.*"

Her name escaped his lips like a desperate plea. Their lips pressed together once more, and she relaxed into his arms. He pulled her close, helping support her weight to take some of the pressure off her tiptoes, and the kiss deepened. He parted his lips slightly and felt a flicker of her tongue. It made his knees quake.

A flash of guilt moved through him. She was upset, vulnerable. This might not be real. And she was Vetus's daughter. He tried to lean away, get her to look at him, but she moved with him.

If this was what she needed, if it would help in this awful moment, consequences be damned, he would give it to her. Rowan slid his hand up her back, tangling his fingers in her soft hair. Her body pressed against him, and they fit perfectly, as though they were two halves of the same whole.

A cellphone rang somewhere in the distance.

No. It was her phone.

When she looked at the call display, her face reddened, and she held up the phone for him to read it.

Marcus Wolfe.

Rowan cleared his throat, but his voice was raspy, "Are you going to answer it?"

"I should," her voice sounded apologetic.

Rowan felt his jaw clench slightly. He nodded.

"Hello?" she answered the phone, still in his arms. For a heartbeat, she listened, and as he watched her, all the colour drained from her cheeks. Slowly, she stepped away from him, looking at him wide-eyed.

When she hung up, she stood, unmoving.

"What is it?" Rowan asked, reaching for her. He cupped her cheek, "What's wrong?"

Freydis swallowed, "There's been an accident. We need to leave."

The antiseptic smell was the first thing Cass noticed when she woke up. Her mind was fuzzy, and her body felt heavy as she tried to move. Pain shot through her, clearing away the haze, and her hands flew instinctively to her abdomen. The familiar bump was gone, replaced by a squishy emptiness. A panicked whimper was all she could manage. *Where was her baby?* Her throat burned, and her mouth was incredibly dry.

"Cass! You're awake!" Freydis's voice cut through her panic.

"What...What happened?" Cass croaked. "Where is my baby?"

Tears filled Freydis's eyes, and Cass fought the urge to vomit.

"She's okay, she's perfect," Freydis reached for Cass's hand. "They had to do a C-section. Your placenta ruptured during the accident, and the doctors had to deliver her to save you both."

"She's alright?" Cass repeated. Freydis nodded and squeezed her hand. Panic seized her again.

"I need Ethan. Where is he? We need to choose a name." Cass looked expectantly around the room.

Freydis's face softened, but Cass could see the pain underneath. "Ethan hasn't woken up yet."

"But he's okay too?" Cass pleaded. "Freydis?"

"The doctors are giving him the very best care. Marcus has barely left his side," Freydis paused. "There was a lot of damage, Cass."

Cass squeezed her eyes shut, shaking her head as if trying to convince herself it wasn't real. A small sob escaped her lips.

"I should get the nurse," Freydis said gently. "And once they check you over, I will get them to bring her to you, okay?"

Cass nodded weakly but kept her eyes squeezed shut. This wasn't happening. She was dreaming. She had to be dreaming.

Chapter Twenty-One

"Ethan," Cass sobbed quietly, "*please* wake up."

She held his cool, clammy hand against her cheek. A crown of white bandages covered his dark hair and stood in stark contrast to the deep purple bruises on his face. His chapped lips were parted slightly by the tube currently breathing for him. She wanted to scream, rip the tube out, feel his lips against hers, hear him utter her name again.

Instead, he lay there like an empty shell. *No progress.* The doctor had whispered those two words to Freydis before he'd left only moments before. They were the worst words she'd ever heard.

"Cass," Freydis cooed, rocking the sleeping baby in her arms, "do you want to hold her?"

Cass reached out for the baby and turned to face Ethan once more. "You need to wake up, Ethan. There is someone you need to meet."

Cass twisted her body in the chair so that, if Ethan had been awake, he would see his daughter.

"Aoife, this is Daddy," Cass's voice faltered. "Isn't she beautiful, Ethan? She has your dark eyes."

Sobs wracked her body once more, and when Freydis appeared at her side to take Aoife, Cass could barely even say thank you.

"I can't live without him, Freydis. This wasn't supposed to happen."

Cass held Ethan's hand against her face again, kissing it between every plea for him to hear her and wake up. She didn't even notice when Marcus came into the room.

"Any change?" Marcus whispered. Cass only shook her head.

"Freydis, will you give us a moment?" Marcus asked. Freydis nodded and bounced and swayed with the baby out the door, closing it behind her.

Cass did not want to speak, but she knew Marcus understood her grief better than anyone. He pulled a chair over and sat beside her.

"I keep waiting for this nightmare to end, Marcus. I keep begging him to wake up." She turned her tear-filled eyes toward him. "Why won't he just wake up?"

Cass flinched at the warmth of Marcus's hand as he gripped her free hand. "I will do whatever I can to help, Cass, I promise."

Cass nodded absently.

"I've spoken to my team and the board at DARPA. They said, with your permission, we could enter Ethan as a participant in my clinical trial."

She shot him a glare, but he continued, "It would be a chip, just like the one I received. It might help restore some functionality. It's a chance at least."

Cass let his hand go and turned away from Marcus, refusing to speak.

"You don't have to decide right now, Cass." Marcus rubbed her shoulder, and it took every ounce of her willpower not to shrug him off. "This isn't for me or my research. It's for Ethan. And for you and the baby. Just think about it."

As if she sensed Cass's distress, Freydis came back into the room, and Cass heaved a sigh of relief. Freydis hadn't left her. Not once since she woke up and found her waiting at her bedside.

"Freydis," Cass murmured, "you should go home, eat, get some rest or something. Aoife and I will be okay until tomorrow."

"Let me take you for supper," Marcus chimed in. "It's the least I can do."

"Alright," Freydis said, "I'll make sure the nurses check in regularly, okay?"

Cass nodded, and Freydis placed Aoife into her arms. Cass did her best to smile at Freydis as they left. When they were finally alone, Cass inhaled deeply and began humming a lullaby to her beautiful baby girl.

Vetus seethed as Rowan explained why he had returned without Freydis and what his contact in the Winter Court had risked his life to tell him.

"You are sure it was Dullahan?" Vetus cursed. Rowan nodded.

"What about Cass and the baby?" Vetus asked.

"They live," Rowan's face tightened as he continued, "but Ethan hasn't woken."

Vetus sighed deeply, "Midhir has truly gone mad. No one is safe."

A familiar scent of cinnamon and woodsmoke entered the room only a heartbeat before Kerridwen appeared.

"You speak a heavy truth, Big Brother, but it's worse than you could ever imagine." Her eyes locked on to his and she swallowed.

"Tell me, Kerri," Vetus squeezed his eyes shut as though to brace for a blow.

"Petra is pregnant, and Midhir has stripped you of your position as crown prince and appointed Lir in your place. He has denounced you as a traitor of the Winter Court."

"Is that all?" Vetus said dryly, scrubbing his hands over his face.

"How can the court allow him to do that?" Rowan groaned.

"Those high fae bastards are too cowardly to stand up to him," Kerridwen hissed.

Vetus paled as the reality of his sister's words hit him.

"Rowan, you must get to Freydis. Midhir will be arrogant after attacking Cass, even if it wasn't entirely successful. Leave right away."

Frost crept up the walls as Vetus turned to his sister, "I'm going to do something stupid, Kerri. Are you with me?"

A wicked smile spread across her face, "Always."

"Where do you want to eat?" Marcus asked.

"Honestly, Marcus, I'm too tired to go out for supper. Just take me to my apartment, and I'll find something there." Freydis leaned her head against the car window.

"Come to my place. I'll order in, and we can just relax."

Freydis felt a flicker in her gut, but her exhaustion made it impossible to think about what it meant. She hadn't really slept since Rowan sent her through that magic door. She'd been in Norway one minute and Rowan's apartment the next. He hadn't come with her, and they hadn't talked about what happened. Everything stopped when Marcus called about the accident. There would be time later to figure out everything with Rowan.

"That sounds great," she gave him a lazy smile.

Freydis had forgotten the incredible view of the harbour from Marcus's condo. She stood on the balcony, letting the warm summer breeze tousle her hair and caress her skin. Marcus would be back soon from meeting the delivery guy with their food. He'd ordered Italian.

"Freydis? Food is here," Marcus's voice called from inside. Freydis made her way to the galley-style kitchen, where he had laid everything out and poured two glasses of wine.

"Bon appétit."

His smile was exactly how she remembered it. A pang of longing moved through her. Freydis picked up the nearest glass of wine and downed it in one big gulp. She wiped her lips with the back of her hand and held the empty glass out to Marcus for a refill. He laughed and began to pour, but the glass slipped from Freydis's hand and shattered on the countertop.

"Oh Marcus, I'm so sorry." Freydis moved quickly to clean up the mess and hissed as a piece of the glass sliced her finger. "Ow, damn it."

Marcus chuckled, "Stop, you'll cut yourself worse. Here."

He handed her a tissue and cleaned the rest of the broken glass and spilled wine. She watched him take another glass from the cabinet and fill it with wine before handing it to her.

Freydis blushed, "Thank you."

He gave her a dismissive wave, "Don't mention it."

Freydis set the glass down and searched his face. "How are you holding up, Marcus?" She didn't know how he could be so calm, given Ethan's situation.

Marcus only shrugged in reply.

"How's work?" Maybe that would get him talking. For the briefest moment, something flickered on Marcus's face. Too quickly for Freydis to place the emotion.

"Well," Marcus grinned, "you are looking at the first of several successful human trials."

Success. Freydis forced a smile, "That's great news. I'm happy for you. Do you notice a difference?"

"Not much...not yet anyway. I'm still in the recovery phase." He smiled, "Next, I will participate in the analysis phase, where we will compare my data from before the procedure to the data now. Once that is complete, we'll move into the programming phase, which is where the big improvements or changes will become noticeable."

Freydis swallowed as the words *programming phase* echoed inside her head. They sounded so inhuman, so artificial, like he was no more than a computer. She forced a smile onto her face, though it didn't reach her eyes. She took another gulp of wine.

Marcus continued, "And you? What have you been up to?" His voice was tight.

"I was in Ireland for a bit, visiting family."

"I thought you were from Iceland and an only child," his tone was accusatory.

"I am," she admitted, "I have cousins in Ireland." Freydis wasn't sure why she lied, but Marcus seemed to buy it.

"Let me have a look at that cut," Marcus said, reaching for her hand. He removed the tissue and held her finger close to his face. "It doesn't look like it'll need stitches, but we can have someone look at it if you're worried." His dark eyes stared at her.

She pulled her hand away as subtly as she could and smiled, "I'm fine, Marcus. I heal quickly, remember?"

"Right, well, let's eat before it gets cold."

While they ate, Freydis avoided any further questions about her, or her family, and tried to keep the focus on Marcus. After dinner they moved into the sitting room, where they talked and drank and kept drinking until their words slurred as they spoke.

Maybe it was the stress of everything that had happened, or maybe it was the wine, but when Marcus looked at her, his eyes hungry and dark, her body felt electric. Freydis was tired of worrying, tired of grieving, tired of thinking straight, so she stood up from where she sat across from Marcus, walked to him, and lowered herself into his lap.

Freydis pushed her fingers into his hair, and he pulled her close, nuzzling his face into her neck, breathing her in deeply. His lips traced a path down her neck to her collarbone as his hands moved up her back beneath her shirt. Her body relaxed under his touch, and she shifted her hips, adjusting her position to feel him warm and hard beneath her.

"Mmm, I've missed you," his voice was breathy as he kissed her. Slowly, deeply, he explored her mouth with his own. "I haven't stopped thinking about you."

Freydis leaned away just enough to pull his shirt over his head in one fluid motion. His chest and arms were more defined than the last time she'd seen him without a shirt. She rubbed her hands against his bare skin, admiring the change.

He tried to speak again, but she silenced him with a kiss. She didn't want to talk. She didn't want to hear him say he missed her; she didn't want to explain why she'd left him. She just wanted to forget and be lost in this moment with him.

Marcus shifted slightly and stood, holding her in his arms. His strength was another new development. Freydis wrapped her legs around his waist and pulled her shirt over her head as he carried her to his bedroom and laid her onto his bed.

She knew he wanted this, even needed it, as much as she did. It was written all over his face. This was the mind-numbing bliss she craved, so she let herself be consumed by it.

It was after midnight when Freydis left Marcus's condo and got a cab back to her apartment. She would have preferred to walk, but she was intoxicated, and Marcus insisted on making sure she arrived home safely. It wasn't until she was nearly at her door that she wondered why he hadn't asked her to stay, not that it mattered.

Rowan's sweet, earthy smell reached her at the same time as she grabbed the doorknob to her apartment. It was unlocked, and she knew he would be waiting inside before she finished opening the door.

Freydis closed the door and leaned against it, facing Rowan, who sat at the table.

"I've been here all night," Rowan's voice was low and full of restraint. "First, I checked the hospital, and Cass said you went home to eat and get some rest. When I arrived here, your door was locked. You were supposed to be here, so when you didn't answer the door, I couldn't not check on you."

Freydis's stomach twisted at the look on his face. Regret mixed with relief and something she couldn't quite place. She watched him inhale deeply.

"I'm sorry, Rowan, I was with—"

"You were with Marcus. I can smell him on you, though I'm surprised I can with the sour stench of wine pouring off you." His eyes bore into her, "Did you share his bed?"

Freydis scoffed, "Share his bed? That's none of your business."

Rowan slammed a hand down on the table, and Freydis jumped. Rowan flinched at her reaction and the realization that he'd scared her. He swallowed. "Isn't it? Isn't it my business, Freydis? Or was what happened in Norway just because you were sad? Is that all I was, a distraction?"

Her cheeks instantly felt like they were on fire.

"I don't know." She pressed the palms of her hands into her eyes and whispered, "I don't know what happened in Norway."

Rowan's silver eyes were icy as they searched her face. She could see the muscle in his jaw feather as he seemed to contemplate his words. He stood abruptly.

"Vetus believes that his father is responsible for Cass and Ethan's accident. He sent me here to keep you safe, and I thought…"

Rowan turned his face away from her, but his anger was palpable, and she watched him clench and unclench his jaw a few times before facing her again.

"I'm so sorry, Rowan." Freydis moved toward him. "I wasn't thinking, and I'm drunk. It was stupid, but it didn't mean anything. I just wanted to forget."

He smiled sadly at her, "Mission accomplished. But I guess that's what you do, isn't it?"

"What?" Her mind was fuzzy, and she felt like she might vomit.

"You run, distract yourself, and never face anything. You let other people clean up your messes because someone always has. You are over three hundred years old, Freydis. It's time to grow up."

His words slammed into her. Fine, if he wanted to fight, she would fight.

"I don't *need* you here to protect me. I've spent my whole life until you waltzed in taking care of myself." Maybe it was the wine, but the tears started falling. "I'm sorry if I am broken and too fucking damaged for you, Rowan."

Rowan moved so he stood mere inches from her, so close she had to look up to meet his gaze. The warmth of his body and the way he smelled made her skin prickle.

"That's just it, Freydis," Rowan laughed softly, not breaking eye contact. "You have always been perfect in my eyes. Marcus? This human world? They aren't worthy of you."

"You don't even know him...you barely know me. A few stories don't make you an expert, Rowan."

He held up his hands in surrender, "You're right, Freydis. You're right." Rowan moved toward the door. "Get some rest."

"That's it? You're just going to walk away?" Freydis hissed.

Rowan didn't say anything.

"Good, go!" Freydis yelled at him, "Get out, Rowan. I don't need or want your protection."

Rowan shook his head and left, closing the door silently behind him.

Freydis leaned against the door and slid to the floor. Tears flowed freely as she curled unto her side and pulled her knees into her chest. She lay there until she cried herself to sleep.

The next day, Freydis's head felt like someone had tightened a vise around it. *Too much wine.* The bright LED lights in the hospital were unbearable. *Definitely, too much wine.* Cass was fastening Aoife into her car seat when Freydis walked in.

"You look like you didn't sleep at all," Cass laughed. "You almost look worse than you did when you left yesterday."

"Well, you look wonderful." Freydis hugged her and helped gather the few belongings she had left to pack.

"I'm afraid to go home without him," Cass whispered.

Freydis turned toward her friend, fighting the tears that threatened to fall at the brokenness in Cass's voice.

"I can stay with you as long as you need," Freydis smiled. "That way you can visit Ethan every day if you want."

"Okay," Cass nodded.

As they were about to leave the room, Marcus walked in. Freydis couldn't even look at him. The shame she felt at Rowan's words, the look on Rowan's face, made it impossible.

"Cass, before you go, did you make a decision about my offer?" Marcus asked. He didn't look at Freydis either.

"Fine, Marcus," Cass sighed. "Go ahead."

Marcus reached into his pocket and pulled out a piece of paper. He unfolded it, handing it to Cass with a pen. "This is a consent and release form. You just need to sign this, and I can take care of everything else."

Cass nodded, "When?"

"First thing next week." He kissed her cheek and gave her a wide smile. "Thank you, Cass."

Freydis didn't ask Cass what she was consenting to. She wasn't sure she wanted to know. Ethan was their family, not hers. She wouldn't judge them for whatever ways they tried to cope with the horrible situation they faced.

Chapter Twenty-Two

Marcus didn't get hungover anymore. Another benefit of the implant. He was feeling sharp and focused as he walked into Anderson Technology and Robotics. Tina was waiting for him at the security desk.

"Did you get it?" she asked.

He noticed her subconsciously move her hair to cover the shaved spot that remained from her implant procedure. Marcus handed her the consent and release form that Cass had signed earlier in the day.

"Excellent!" She clapped her hands together. "If this can help Ethan, just think of how many others we can save."

Marcus kissed her on the cheek, but his mind was elsewhere. He watched her waltz away to process the form as he entered the elevator. He wasn't headed to his office on the third floor. Instead, he instructed ALI, the Automated Lift Interface, to take him to the fourth floor. The laboratory.

People in white lab coats sat at various stations, elbows deep in research. Only one non-descript woman bothered to look up when Marcus entered.

"Dr. Wolfe?" She smiled. "To what do we owe the pleasure?"

Marcus reached into his pocket and withdrew a small plastic bag containing a bloody tissue and handed it to her.

"Can you run some tests on this? Specifically, an NIR spectroscopy. Maybe also test for antibodies, anomalies, or anything out of the ordinary."

"That's an odd request." She held up the plastic bag and squinted at the tissue; Marcus tensed. The researcher shrugged, "But anything in the name of science."

He let out a long breath and smiled, "I appreciate your help. Send the results to my assistant, okay?"

The woman nodded and went back to her station. Marcus had expected more questions or at least a little pushback. Marcus shoved the sliver of doubt he was feeling deep inside him and left the lab on the fourth floor to go visit Ethan at the hospital.

Ethan's room was quiet except for the whirr from the electronic machines breathing for him and monitoring his heart. And the too-loud tick of the clock. Marcus tried to ignore all the wires and hoses as he sat beside his brother.

"The procedure will take place tomorrow," he spoke softly. "Cass gave consent if you can believe it. I always thought she was skeptical of my research, but we both just want you to wake up."

Marcus laid his hand over his brother's, mindful of the IV line attached to it.

"I had the same procedure a couple of weeks ago, and I know it sounds scary, but you don't have to worry. I trust my team. You're in good hands."

A nurse quietly entered the room and checked Ethan's vitals. Her voice was soft as she said, "We are going to do some blood work to keep an eye on his liver and kidney function. The lab tech should be in shortly."

Marcus nodded and the nurse left.

"I can't wait until you meet your daughter," Marcus whispered. "She looks just like Cass, only she has our eyes."

A notification chimed on Marcus's cell, and when he pulled it out, a message from Tina read: *Urgent. Call me ASAP.*

Marcus stepped out into the hall as he dialled her number.

"Hello?" her voice sounded anxious.

"What is it? What's happened?" Marcus wasn't sure he could handle any more bad news.

"The results from the lab are in. From the sample you dropped off," Tina paused.

"Well?" Marcus said impatiently. "What did they say?"

"Marcus...are you sure the blood belonged to Freydis," Tina asked.

"Yes, of course, I'm sure. Why?"

"The results weren't human, Marcus. The researcher I spoke with said the blood belonged to no known species on this planet and—"

Before Tina had finished speaking, the phone fell from Marcus's hand and shattered on the floor.

Freydis encouraged Cass to visit Ethan and leave Aoife home with her, exactly as she'd promised. Cass was a shell since the accident. Her beautiful optimism was all but gone. It broke Freydis's heart to see her friend in pain, and even though the baby was perfect, it seemed difficult for Cass to truly connect with Aoife.

Freydis stepped in to help as often as she could, especially on days when Cass just couldn't function as a mom because she was too busy surviving the hell she now found herself living in. Freydis didn't mind.

Cass made sure that Aoife was sleeping before she'd left for the hospital and left a bottle for her in the refrigerator. She promised not to be long, but Freydis told her not to rush. The relief and gratitude on Cass's face nearly brought Freydis to tears. Besides, Aoife would make a wonderful distraction from thoughts of Marcus or Rowan.

Gods, how she had messed that up. The hurt and betrayal on Rowan's face broke her heart every time she thought about it. But then she'd remember the things he'd said. She didn't owe him an explanation. She was a grown woman, despite his comment that it was time to grow up, and she could do whoever and whatever she wanted. It didn't matter that some of what he'd said was true, did it? He still shouldn't have said it.

Gods, Freydis hoped Rowan apologized soon though, because ever since Norway, apart from the drunken night at Marcus's, all she thought about was kissing him. The feel of his strong hands tangled in her hair, the taste of his lips—it was magic in every sense of the word. He was another piece of her puzzle that had been missing.

She realized after their fight that he was exactly what she'd looked for in every relationship she ever had. None came close. The way Rowan held her, his arms felt like home. Kissing him had changed everything. She knew it the moment she'd walked into her apartment that night and found him waiting. The feelings terrified her.

Freydis had never loved an immortal or anyone else in that way. Not after her father had abandoned her and let her mother die. And what would Vetus think? Would he be happy? Did Rowan even feel the same?

An almost imperceptible thrum of magic pulsed through Cass and Ethan's apartment as though someone had left a window open just a crack, and a breeze slipped through. The tiny hairs on the back of Freydis's neck stood on end. She had felt something like it before, she realized, and her instincts had her moving quickly and quietly toward where the baby slept.

Peeking through the barely open door, Freydis watched as a creature of nightmares hunched over a small bundle, whispering words in a tongue Freydis had never heard. The bundle began to cry.

Freydis threw open the door and lunged at the creature, who moved away quicker than she had anticipated. Freydis's movements felt slow and clumsy. The creature snatched the bundle from the floor and bolted toward the window.

"Stop!" Freydis shouted, reaching toward the creature, and as if she had snared it with some invisible force, it froze. The bundle howled. Frost appeared on the windowpane.

Freydis glanced into the crib and heaved a sigh of relief as Aoife, quiet as a mouse, stared up at her with Ethan's dark eyes. Pure, unadulterated rage flooded into Freydis as she turned on the creature who remained frozen.

"Who sent you?" Freydis snarled, and the creature merely cackled. Freydis carefully pulled aside part of the cloth the creature carried, revealing the bundle to be a sickly and deformed-looking baby that half resembled Aoife and half something so grotesque Freydis couldn't describe it if she'd tried.

"Tell me who sent you," Freydis commanded, and the creature writhed against the invisible bonds.

"The Winter King," the creature hissed; its confirmation of her suspicion was all Freydis needed to hear. "He is coming for you too, girl."

Freydis became fury and vengeance, like destruction incarnate, and with barely any effort, merely a thought, the creature and the bundle it carried turned to dust.

Freydis's chest heaved as she gulped down air to slow her racing heart. She turned back to the crib for Aoife. Undiluted power surged through her veins. She felt so *alive*.

"Come here, sweetheart," Freydis cooed. "You are safe."

Aoife remained in Freydis's arms until Cass returned home. Freydis explained what happened as tears poured down Cass's cheeks. Once she had calmed down, Cass explained that Freydis had probably stopped Aoife from being replaced by a changeling—the typically deformed offspring of the fae, who is left in place of a human child, altered to appear in every way identical to its human counterpart. The changeling would grow up sickly or otherwise troubled, while the human child was taken to the Otherworld to dwell among the fae.

Freydis didn't mention, however, how she had turned the changeling and would-be kidnapper into dust that remained on the nursery floor. So, as Cass cuddled and fed the baby, Freydis nonchalantly grabbed the broom and dustpan and went to clean up the residue.

Vetus and Kerridwen arrived on the border between the Autumn and Summer Courts.

"So, what exactly is your plan?" Kerri asked.

"I am going to make Tarynn an offer that will help her against our father."

"You have nothing to bargain with. You are no longer recognized as crown prince." Kerridwen grabbed his arm, forcing him to stop walking and face her. "She is just as likely to hand you over to him in exchange for peace as she is to help you."

"I know, but I have to try," Vetus said. "She is our only hope. I can do this alone, Kerri, if you would rather stay neutral."

Vetus watched Kerridwen contemplate his words. She reminded him so much of his mother. She had Maeve's fiercely protective nature and warm heart.

"Fuck Midhir," she grinned wickedly. "Leila is going to kill me...and you if this goes badly."

Vetus laughed, "I don't know why she puts up with you, Kerri."

"If you knew what I can do with these hands and this mouth," she winked at him, "you wouldn't need to ask."

Vetus shook his head.

They hadn't made it far into the Summer realm when a patrol of Summer cavalry surrounded them. Vetus raised his hands but didn't miss Kerridwen reaching for the blade at her side.

"We are here to see Her Majesty on personal business," Vetus said.

"Do forgive me, Your Highnesses, but we are required to escort all visitors." The patrol commander swallowed. "Her Majesty is taking no chances where Winter is concerned."

"Lead the way," Kerridwen drawled, rolling her eyes.

The Summer Palace was crawling with fae armed to the teeth. The escort wasted no time depositing Vetus and Kerridwen before the queen. She lounged across her throne with her feet draped over its armrest as pixies braided a crown of yellow buttercups and purple wild clary into her hair.

"Someone's been naughty," Tarynn purred.

The prince and princess knelt before the ancient throne. Tarynn turned her gaze to Kerridwen.

"Kerri, if you didn't have Midhir's abysmally dark eyes, you would be the picture of your mother."

Vetus cringed, and without looking, he could feel Kerri tense beside him. Kerridwen's eyes were the only aspect of herself she loathed. Tarynn was in a mood today.

"Your Majesty," Vetus dared to speak, "I come before you, stripped of my title and an enemy of my court. I am here only as your nephew, and for the love you bore my mother, I beg you to help me."

"Not so insolent this time, Nephew?" Tarynn's eyes narrowed at him. "I should have you pay for your disrespect with your Winter blood."

With a flick of Tarynn's wrist, vines covered in thorns surged from the ground, winding around Vetus's arms and legs, keeping him on his knees before her.

Kerridwen gasped, "Your Grace, please, have mercy. I'm sure my brother regrets any offence. You know how our father can get under one's skin."

Vetus did not move. He barely breathed, as doing so caused the vines to tighten around him. Tarynn tilted her head, looking at the siblings like a predator assessing its prey.

"Did you have anything else you'd like to say, Nephew?" Tarynn crooned.

Careful not to disturb the vines, Vetus whispered, "Midhir believes he has recovered Nuada's sword. What he doesn't know is that it is a forgery. I am willing to act on behalf of the Summer Court until I take the wretched throne of Winter for myself."

Kerridwen gaped at the words he had spoken. Tarynn steepled her fingers and seemed to consider his confession.

"Three days," Tarynn murmured. "In three days will be the new moon. I will give you my answer then."

Kerridwen sighed, "Thank you, Your Majesty."

"Don't thank me yet, girl," the Summer Queen sneered. "Vetus will remain in this room, wrapped in those vines, until the sun sets on the third day. If he tries to flee or you try to free him, I will tie a garland of flowers around his neck and send him to his father."

From the corner of his eye, Vetus watched Kerridwen's face contort with rage. She opened her mouth as if to speak, and Tarynn lifted a finger.

"Tsk, tsk, Kerri, I would keep your thoughts to yourself," Tarynn grinned. "You are welcome to stay as my guest, or you may return to your court."

"I will stay," Kerridwen scowled. "Thank you for your hospitality, Your Majesty."

Vetus closed his eyes and focused on his shallow breath.

He'd endured worse.

Chapter Twenty-Three

Freydis was grateful for a decent sleep in her own bed.

When she woke the next morning, she poured the steaming hot water into her mug, the tea infusing and transforming it into a nectar fit for the Gods. Rowan had not come for tea or their morning conversation in days. She was still angry with him, but his absence felt like a growing abyss that threatened to swallow her whole.

She missed how good it felt to hide nothing about herself. With Rowan, she could just be Freydis. Sure, she had Cass and Vetus, when he wasn't doing princely things, but it was not the same. The connection with Rowan was undeniable. His presence soothed the storm that raged within her. No one else had made her feel safe the way he had in his arms that day in Norway.

Freydis removed the used teabag from her favourite mug and added just a splash of milk when there was a knock on the door. She was surprised to see Rowan waiting on the other side. She stepped aside, still holding her mug, and gestured for him to come in. Freydis closed the door behind him and sighed, "So, did you come to—"

Before Freydis could finish speaking, Rowan grabbed her by the throat, lifting her into the air. A surge of panic rushed through her as she struggled in his iron grip. Her wide eyes searched his emotionless face.

She kicked and thrashed wildly, but he did not falter. In a split second of clarity, Freydis remembered the mug in her hand and smashed it against the side of his head.

Rowan howled with rage and threw her across the kitchen. She landed on her hands and knees, springing up instantly. Freydis grabbed a knife from the countertop and turned with it held out to face Rowan.

"Rowan, stop! Why are you doing this?"

He crossed the room in two large strides and grabbed the wrist of the hand holding the knife. Freydis shrieked with pain as she felt the bones shatter. The knife fell to the floor. Rowan did not answer and, with his free arm, backhanded her across the face.

As she fell, a blinding pain shot through her head, and she could feel her face swell instantly. Tears poured from her eyes, blurring her vision. With her undamaged hand, she frantically tried to wipe her face and focus long enough to do something, anything.

"Please," she sobbed, "you don't want to do this."

She could taste the coppery tang of blood from the split in her lip as she begged him. Heat rose into her cheeks as shame filled her from the weakness she was showing.

He grabbed her hair, pulling her to her feet, and seized her by the throat again. This time she was empty-handed. She clawed at his hands and face, thrashing about helplessly, trying to free herself. Rowan slammed her hard against the wall, knocking what little breath she had left clean out of her.

Her lungs ached, desperate for air, but Rowan's hand was a vise around her neck. As she struggled against him, she couldn't think straight. She tried to reach inside and find the magic. Nothing. Not even a whisper of it. She pleaded with her eyes, but seeing Rowan's vacant, dark expression, she knew her situation was hopeless.

Like a shadow, Death had always followed her. They had danced together many times, so she had learned to recognize the familiar steps. She had even longed for it and came close to dying before, but she was unprepared for the calm sensation that flooded her, relaxing her body as her vision dimmed and went dark.

Marcus had repeatedly reassured her that everything would be fine, but Cass couldn't shake the feeling of dread roiling around inside her. Ethan had been prepped for the procedure, and Marcus had explained in detail what the procedure entailed and what Ethan's recovery would look like.

Cass gently kissed Ethan, "I love you, and I will be waiting for you on the other side of this. Aoife and I will be waiting."

Marcus's team wheeled Ethan into the operating room.

"Everything will be okay, Cass. I promise," Marcus said. "I will call you as soon as it's over."

Cass could only nod. She would never feel truly comfortable with the idea, but as the days continued to pass and Ethan's condition remained unchanged, desperation had overruled reason.

"So, where is Freydis? I haven't seen her in a few days," Marcus asked.

"Probably at her apartment," Cass muttered. "I had to push her out the door to recharge and change her clothes. But I haven't heard from her today."

The clinical trial liaison for the hospital led Marcus into the viewing gallery for surgical suite number three, where Ethan's experimental procedure would soon take place. Marcus had already vomited twice before arriving at the hospital, but he had a few saltine crackers in his briefcase just in case.

"Our hospital is thrilled you've chosen to partner with us to conduct these clinical trials. Innovations like yours are the future of modern medicine," the liaison nattered on.

Marcus smiled politely and continued to watch the surgical team as they finished preparing the operating room. Marcus was used to the cold, clean look of a well-kept laboratory, but something about the suite below made his blood run cold.

"If you like, I can stay and keep you company," the liaison offered. "I—"

"No. Thank you, but my assistant should be along shortly. And this isn't a random patient, but my own brother, and his life depends on this, so I'd really like to watch it on my own."

"I understand completely, Doctor Wolfe. Your brother is in excellent hands. Some of the country's finest surgeons are in that room, and—"

"Thank you," Marcus cut the man off, "really."

Marcus tried not to scowl. The man was only doing his job.

The liaison left only moments before a gurney with Ethan lying on top, dressed for surgery, was wheeled into the surgical suite. A hollow-sounding voice erupted from the two-way speaker on the wall of the viewing gallery.

"Dr. Wolfe, my name is Dr. Julian Carr, and I am the head of neurosurgery here at the hospital. It is a pleasure to meet the mind behind this technology, and I am honoured to be leading this procedure today. I will try to talk my way through the process as we go, but there will be the occasional time when communication will not be possible, given the nature of what we are doing. However, for the most part, I am happy to answer your questions as we go along."

Marcus didn't trust his voice not to falter if he spoke, so he only nodded and gave the surgeon a weak thumbs-up.

Dr. Carr's scratchy voice came through once more, "Okay, folks. Let's begin."

"Due to the nature of Mr. Wolfe's injuries, his brain has suffered some trauma, which has caused a fair bit of swelling. We have opted for a craniectomy instead of the more common craniotomy, which means we will not immediately replace the portion of the skull we remove, to help alleviate the pressure from the current swelling and any other inflammation that might occur because of this procedure," Dr. Carr explained.

Marcus could hear the surgeon's voice, but his mind kept flashing back to memories from his and Ethan's childhood. Ethan's first touchdown, his first time catching a fish, even the first time he introduced Cass to family, all paraded through Marcus's head like a family home movie. How could his little brother be the person lying on that table? Ethan had always been stronger, faster, and better with women. He didn't deserve this.

"We will be attaching the neural implant post-laterally to the cerebral cortex." Dr. Carr began to cut into Ethan's head, and Marcus immediately felt lightheaded. He sat where he couldn't see into the theatre. He was grateful for Dr. Carr's steady voice as he continued to explain the procedure, step-by-step.

Hours had passed, and Marcus marvelled that the surgeon was still speaking after all this time. He must be exhausted. Marcus was beyond exhausted. When he wasn't focused on Ethan, he thought about Freydis.

Marcus had hoped Freydis would have been there at the hospital earlier to support Cass. He wanted to confront her but had no idea what he would say. His skin crawled at the thought of every time they had been intimate. He didn't even know what she was.

Only Tina knew that the lab results were for Freydis and not some random undiscovered species he had stumbled across. He was certain if he told anyone, they would think he had lost his mind.

Freydis looked human. Maybe the results had been wrong. Maybe he was crazy. And why hadn't Tina arrived yet? He decided to call her.

"Hello, doll," he crooned into the telephone. "I'm just sitting here in the gallery, waiting for you. Listen, I need you to reach out to our government contact at DARPA and find out who handles the discovery of new species. I mean, unless you think this is more of an area 51-type situation."

Tina didn't laugh at his attempt at humour. "Marcus, are you sure you want to do this? You cared about Freydis once, even talked about her being the one. You will not be able to come back from this."

"She lied to me, Tina. Hid what she is," Marcus seethed. "Her DNA could hold clues that humanity has long searched for. We know she heals quickly, but who knows what else. This discovery could be bigger than the implant technology."

Tina sighed, "Okay, Marcus. I am almost at the hospital. I will do some digging later and find out who we call."

Marcus hung up the phone and realized that Dr. Carr had gone silent. He walked to where he could see down into the surgical suite and paled. The surgical team was in a frenzy, and though he couldn't hear it, Marcus could tell the head surgeon was barking orders. A crash cart had been wheeled in, and Marcus knew from the from the monitor he could see that they had lost him.

The scientist in him knew what the probability of success had been, going into the surgery, but the big brother in him was frantic. Time slowed down. He tried desperately to holler through the two-way speaker, "He's dying, do something. DO SOMETHING!"

But the familiar crackle was painfully absent. Marcus began banging both fists on the laminated glass, but the surgical team below had already stopped their attempt to resuscitate his brother. Dr. Carr ripped off his surgical mask and cap, looked at his watch, and stormed out of the suite.

"Marcus?" Tina's quiet voice was deafeningly loud in the silence. "How's it going?"

The words no sooner left her mouth than her face contorted with the realization of what had occurred. The next several moments were a blur. Tina was still holding him when Dr. Carr entered the gallery.

"The implant didn't work," Marcus stated robotically.

"I'm so sorry, Dr. Wolfe, we did everything we could," the surgeon murmured. "There was simply too much inflammation."

Marcus knew Dr. Carr was still speaking, but he ceased being able to hear the words. Gone, Ethan was gone. But he'd promised Cass. He *promised* everything would be fine.

"Dr. Wolfe?" the surgeon placed his hand on Marcus's shoulder, "Is Ethan's wife still here? I can give her the news if you'd prefer."

"No—no, I sent her home to rest," Marcus knew he was speaking, but he didn't recognize his voice. "I—I said I would call her with an update."

The surgeon nodded, "Again, I'm very sorry for your loss."

Vetus lay limp in the clutches of the vines, and just as Tarynn promised, at sunset on the third day, they retracted into the ground. Vetus collapsed onto the throne room floor. For three days and two nights, no one had bothered to check on him.

His mouth was so dry, and hunger clawed inside his stomach. The thorns had allowed a small but steady trickle of blood. Though not enough to kill him, it certainly contributed to his thirst and exhaustion. He lacked the ability to even sit up on his own.

He wasn't sure how long he had laid free on the floor when hurried footfalls approached him.

"Oh, Big Brother," Kerridwen's pained voice was followed by her tiny, strong hands under his arms. "Let's get you up. The queen should be here with her decision soon; then we will get you cleaned up."

"*Water,*" Vetus croaked, "I just need water."

Kerridwen conjured a small glass of water for him, and he would have sworn on his immortal soul that it was the best thing he had ever tasted.

"Still alive, Nephew?" Tarynn's singsong voice echoed through the chamber. As she approached him, all the tiny pinpricks from where the thorns had pierced him vanished, taking the stinging pain they'd left with them.

She looked him over from head to toe, "Better?"

"Yes, My Queen," he murmured. "Thank you."

Vetus and Kerridwen watched as the queen ascended her throne. Tarynn was an apex predator with feline grace. Vetus was relieved she didn't decide to kill him. Relative or not, she had murdered for much less. But Vetus knew before he came up with his plan to seek her aid that it wouldn't be easy to convince her to help. As he awaited her decision, he hoped that her hatred of Midhir and his act of contrition with the thorny vines would be enough.

"It pleases me greatly to hear that Midhir does not possess Nuada's sword, but that does not lower the risks facing my court. Midhir will be wroth when he finds out I am appointing you my emissary to the Winter Court," Tarynn preened.

"You are most gracious, Your Majesty," Vetus swallowed. "I am honoured."

He might as well have promised her his soul.

"Indeed. And of course, you understand, as the official emissary, you will be protected from any harm your father might attempt against you by ancient laws."

"I understand," Vetus bowed deeply.

"In exchange for my gift," Tarynn continued, "when the time does come for war, you will fight on behalf of the Summer Court *with* Nuada's sword and any other little tricks you have up those clever sleeves of yours."

"I am yours to command."

The Summer Queen dismissed the siblings from her presence, and once they were safely outside, Vetus looked at Kerridwen, who looked as though she might explode.

"What?" Vetus asked.

"You are out of your damned mind," Kerridwen shook her head. "But I have never known anyone braver."

Vetus only smiled.

Watching the clock was excruciating, and when she wasn't watching the clock, she was checking her cellphone for notifications. The surgery should have been done by now. Why had Marcus not called? It took every bit of restraint that Cass could muster not to pack Aoife up and have a cab take them back to the hospital.

A knock on the door made Cass leap from the sofa and dash to unlock it. *Perhaps Marcus wanted to give the good news in person.* Upon opening the door, Cass found herself face to face with a beautiful woman with long wavy chestnut hair who looked to be in her thirties. Her emerald-green eyes were a striking reflection of Cass's own, but she had never seen this woman before.

"Hello, can I help you?" Cass asked.

"Hello, Cassandra," the woman's silvery voice crooned. "My name is Maeve."

Cass was dumbfounded. How did this woman know who she was?

"May I come in?" Maeve asked.

"Yes, of course," Cass offered, "I'm sorry, how rude of me. I thought you were someone else."

Maeve's movement was light and lithe as she brushed into Cass's apartment.

"Yes, I had hoped to be here before he'd arrived."

Cass gaped as the woman continued, "I will explain after he leaves."

As though her words spoke it into being, there was another knock on the door. Maeve dismissively gestured for Cass to answer it.

"Marcus!" Cass scolded. "I have been going practically out of my mind waiting for your call."

"Sorry, Cass," Marcus's throat bobbed. "I...I wanted to be the one to, ah, tell you."

Cass's heart stopped. Everything stopped. *No,* she begged, *no no no no...*

Cass shook her head from side to side as she frantically whispered, "Don't say it, Marcus...you can't say it."

Tears poured down her cheeks as Marcus nodded his head sadly.

"I'm so so sorry, Cass."

"YOU PROMISED!" she screamed, breaking down into sobs as she collapsed onto the floor. She couldn't even look at him. "YOU KILLED HIM, MARCUS! YOU AND YOUR FUCKING EXPERIMENT!"

Through her tears, Cass watched as Maeve escorted Marcus out and closed the door. She screamed after him, "I hate you, Marcus, I HATE YOU!! And I will never forgive you."

The strange woman bent down to wipe a tear from Cass's cheek with her cold hand. "Cassandra Lilith Walsh, my name is Queen Maeve of the Winter Court, and I am your grandmother."

Cass sniffled, "What?"

She is fae.

"I am heartbroken at the news of your loss. We tried to help, but he was gone before he ever reached your healers," Maeve's features softened. "I can befuddle your senses until you have accepted your new reality?"

Cass managed a tiny laugh, "I do not wish for you to befuddle my senses, but it was a generous offer."

Maeve inclined her head, no doubt in approval over their exchanged pleasantries. *Definitely fae.*

"Now that's out of the way," Maeve clucked, "let's get down to business. When are you and my great-granddaughter moving to the Otherworld?"

Cass balked, "With respect, Your Majesty, I just found out the love of my life is—"

Cass couldn't say the word. *Gone. Ethan was gone.*

"I cannot possibly go...I—I need to make arrangements...and find someone to look after the bookstore."

Another fit of sobs ripped through her body. This couldn't be happening. Maeve just stood watching. Stoic.

Cass tried not to let Maeve's cold and uncaring demeanour shake her. She was a Fae Queen. She didn't feel emotions like humans do, even if she was her grandmother.

"I understand," the queen nodded. "Take your time. May I see Aoife?"

The request stunned her, but Cass nodded and led the Queen of Winter to where Aoife lay in her bassinet.

"I remember when you were this small," Maeve murmured. "I used to watch you sleep."

Cass didn't have any words. She was overwhelmed with everything she felt. If she were honest with herself, she would say she was in shock, and *the only person other than Ethan that she wanted to talk to in that moment was Freydis.*

: Chapter Twenty-Four

Rowan was still furious with himself for what happened with Freydis. He replayed the events of that night repeatedly in his mind. He got so worried when she hadn't been home, and then for her to waltz in reeking of alcohol and *Marcus*, he stopped thinking clearly. The thought of anyone else's hands on her—Gods, he was out of his mind, but she didn't belong to him, or anyone else for that matter. He had no right to speak the way he did, and now she wanted nothing to do with him.

Midhir was expecting him now that he'd arranged Vetus's personal guard and Freydis made it quite clear she didn't want him around. He had no reason to keep the Winter King waiting.

Rowan stalked around his apartment, gathering things into his travel bag while working up the courage to stop by and say goodbye to Freydis before he left. Hopefully, he would not be gone too long. Hopefully, she would be safe without him there.

He closed his door, and the sound of the bolt sliding into place as he locked it seemed to echo through the hallway. As he turned to leave, the strong scent of sulphur filled his nostrils. *Demons.*

He broke into a run toward Freydis's door. The smell was overbearing. He threw his shoulder at the closed door, bursting it open in time to see his exact likeness kneeling over Freydis's lifeless, blood-covered body sprawled upon the floor.

Her clothing was torn, and the demon held a kitchen knife in its hands. It had begun to carve symbols into her skin. In a heartbeat, Rowan hurled himself at the attacker. Their bodies collided, tumbling away from Freydis. The jolt caused the creature to reveal its true self.

"You are too late, little half-breed," the demon hissed.

Rowan sprung to his feet, drawing his dagger from his belt in a fluid motion. The demon howled with rage and locked eyes on Rowan.

Time slowed as Rowan drew in a deep, steadying breath, drawing back the blade for the throw, releasing it as he exhaled. The dagger found its mark in the centre of what Rowan assumed was the demon's forehead. Upon contact with the blade, the demon disintegrated, leaving a scorch mark on the carpeted floor.

Rowan rushed to where Freydis lay, broken and bloody, on the floor. "Freydis—Freydis wake up!"

Kneeling beside her, he could see one side of her face was swollen and badly bruised. Her lips were sticky with drying blood that had dripped down to her chin. Purple marks encircled her neck, where the demon had stolen her breath, and more blood seeped from the shallow etchings on her skin.

No, please, no.

Her chest did not visibly move, but he thought he could feel a faint heartbeat under his trembling fingers.

Please wake up.

The angle of her hand and discoloured wrist indicated that it was broken. He adjusted her position as gently as he could and attempted to give her a few breaths.

Stay with me.

Though she would not wake, he could see her chest begin to rise and fall with shallow breaths. He thought his own heart was going to beat out of his chest. Gently, he cradled her limp body in his arms, as tightly as he dared, but careful not to hurt her. He was startled by how tiny she felt in his arms.

"Fierce One, please...please wake up," he whispered to her as he held her against his chest. She smelled like lavender and copper. He would not forgive himself if she did not make it. His mind was racing. She needed help. He laid her gently in her bed and tried to think. His blood-covered hands trembled as he caressed her face.

Sitting on the edge of her bed, he felt movement at the same time as he heard her gasp. She had propped herself up enough to grab the Scottish dirk she kept by her bed. She glared, her one good eye wide with fear, the blade in her hand barely raised toward Rowan in defence.

"Stay away from me," she rasped, "or I will kill you."

Rowan stood, his bloody hands splayed wide. "It's me...It's me, Freydis. I won't hurt you."

"You just attacked me!" she snarled, tears streaking her bloody cheeks.

"That wasn't me!" he said. "It was a demon wearing my face."

"You're lying," her voice wavered. "Do not come any closer. I will kill you, Rowan."

Her spark of strength died out, and she collapsed back, still feebly holding the knife as it lay on the bed.

Rowan knelt beside her and slowly reached for her, gently wrapping his trembling hands around the hand that held the blade. He slowly guided her hand and the blade to his throat, maintaining eye contact.

"I swear to you, it's me, My Fierce One. I swear it."

She dropped the knife. Tears continued to stream down her face as Rowan climbed up beside her, wrapping his arms around her as if his arms could keep her from breaking apart. She cried, tears and blood staining his shirt. He ran his fingers gently through her hair, trying to soothe her.

Once she had calmed, he murmured, "You need a healer, Freydis."

Freydis did not answer as she had fallen asleep, so he reached where her cellphone lay on her bedside table and messaged the only person he could think of. *Cass.*

While Freydis slept and they waited for Cass, Rowan moved through her apartment, attempting to navigate the aftermath of the attack and restore some semblance of order to lessen the blow once Freydis was up and about.

When he reached the kitchen, he filled the kettle with water and plugged it in. He opened the cupboard to retrieve her favourite mug, the one she always used each time he'd visited, but it wasn't there. A quick glance around the room revealed the mug's shattered remains near the door he'd broken down to get in.

Rowan sank to his knees and carefully began to retrieve each tiny piece that lay scattered on the floor. He shoved aside a chunk of the broken door to gather the few remaining pieces of her favourite mug and made a mental note to reimburse Vetus for the damage. *What a ridiculous thing to worry about.*

His hands trembled as he discarded the pieces of broken glass into the trash.

"Good God!" Cass gasped as she stepped through the smashed door. Rowan was about to speak when Maeve, the Queen of Winter, walked in, cuddling an infant in her arms. Rowan instantly lowered himself to the floor before her.

"My Queen," he gasped.

"Hello, Rowan," the queen crooned.

Rowan watched as they surveyed the room, stopping at the pool of blood on the floor.

"Where is she?" Cass whispered.

Rowan pointed toward Freydis's bedroom and watched Cass hurry toward her friend.

"How long has she been sleeping?" Cass asked. "She looks awful."

She watched Rowan place a cup of tea on the bedside table and gently wipe a strand of hair from Freydis's face. After her initial shock at his intimate gesture, her eyes rested on the amethyst ring he wore. It was larger than hers but otherwise identical.

"Not long. Since I messaged you," he answered.

Cass returned her gaze to Freydis, taking a mental inventory of her injuries. Rowan must have helped her change because her pajamas were clean, but her bed and Rowan were covered with drying blood.

Cass grimaced, "What the hell happened?"

"A demon attacked her...wearing my face. She needs a healer." Rowan locked eyes with Cass, "I need you to help her."

Cass could hear the desperation in his voice.

"This is bigger than me. She needs a doctor," she scolded. "You should have called an ambulance."

"No doctors," Freydis croaked, startling Cass and Rowan. "Just do what you can, Cass."

Maeve appeared in the doorway and handed the baby to Rowan. "I will help you, Cassandra."

Cass watched Freydis's eyes widen at the sight of Maeve.

"Who are you?" Freydis whispered.

"Freydis, this is—"

Maeve placed a hand on Cass's shoulder, silencing her.

"I'm a friend," Maeve murmured and nodded at Cass to continue.

Cass silently surveyed Freydis's injuries and looked at Maeve. "She's lost a lot of blood."

Maeve turned to Rowan, "Take the baby out of the room."

Cass shot him a warning glare, and Rowan left the room with Aoife, giving them space. His presence there was very unnerving. She was having trouble coming to terms with everything. Ethan was gone...and she'd almost lost Freydis too. A demon wearing Rowan's face, a ring that looked like hers, and Maeve, the Queen of Winter—her grandmother. All of it was more than she could process, and with her grief, she wasn't sure if she could summon enough healing magic to help Freydis.

"Ethan's gone," Cass blurted, her hands hovering over Freydis's face. Even through the severe injuries, Cass could see the pain of understanding spread through Freydis's features.

"Gods, Cass," Freydis burst into tears.

Cass closed her eyes as her own tears flowed.

"I'm so so sorry," Freydis sobbed.

Cass forced herself to look at Freydis. They had both lost so much.

Freydis winced as Maeve lifted her shirt to reveal the cuts on her skin. Cass paled at the sight of them.

"I think my wrist is broken too," Freydis said, raising her arm slightly.

"I need to be honest with you, Freydis. I feel like I am in way over my head," Cass moved on from Freydis's face to her arm.

Maeve continued to assess the lacerations on Freydis's body. "The demon had begun a ritual of some kind. I am unfamiliar with the symbols. They aren't fae, but they are ancient."

Cass continued, "Demons? I mean, I know there is a whole other world that humans don't believe is real, but...try moving your fingers."

Freydis made a fist and extended her fingers once more. Her wrist was still swollen, but her expression seemed to indicate the pain had eased a little.

"I don't know either. I have lived hundreds of years and haven't been attacked by demons, and now twice in one year," Freydis shrugged. "Can you show me my face?"

Cass retrieved the little mirror from Freydis's bedside table and held it up for her. Cass had cleaned the remaining blood from her face, and the swelling had gone down enough that she could open both eyes.

Cass looked at her apologetically, "I'm not sure I can do much more. I focused mostly on easing the pain."

"It's okay, Cass, I heal fast. There isn't much pain left," Freydis smiled encouragingly, but Cass knew that she was likely trying to spare her feelings.

"The magic wouldn't come when I called for it, Cass. Why can I feel it sometimes, but it abandons me when I need it most?"

Cass looked at Maeve, who remained silent, and she got the sense that Maeve knew something she wasn't willing to say.

Rowan came back into the room with Aoife in his arms. "I have to go. Freydis, I don't know how long I will be gone, but you are not safe here."

Cass took Aoife from Rowan as Maeve spoke, "I will take you all to my son. To Ireland. We will leave as soon as you're packed."

"I can't leave. At least not until after the funeral, but Freydis," Cass gently squeezed Freydis's uninjured hand and met her gaze, "you should go immediately. I will follow after."

Rowan bowed his head to Maeve and moved to kneel beside Freydis. He reached for her hand, taking it in his and placing it over his heart. Cass had to consciously keep her mouth closed as she watched their interaction.

"My Lady, I have failed you. I swear I will never again let my emotions affect my duty. I hope someday you will forgive me." He placed a gentle lingering kiss on her hand before letting go.

They watched as he left the room without another word. Cass could see the pain caused by his departure written all over Freydis's face, and she recognized the loss it conveyed.

Footfalls from Rowan's leather boots echoed through the empty halls as he approached the towering obsidian doors of Midhir's great hall. His palladium cuirass, no longer engraved with Midhir's sigil, now bore Vetus's sigil instead. Rowan had left the ornate sword Vetus had gifted him back at Arbor Castle. It didn't feel right to use it serving the Winter King.

The great doors yawned widely, inviting Rowan inside. Midhir sat tall and rigid on his twisted throne. Lir and Petra stood on his right, and Leannán Sídhe sat on the dais steps to his left.

Rowan bowed before them, "*Ard Rí*, I have come to honour my vow of service."

Before he could look up for a response, four pairs of hands seized him, clamping shackles to his wrists and ankles. It happened so quickly he didn't have a chance to try to fight or flee.

A sudden stench of death and rot filled Rowan's nostrils. He knew the scent and knew without looking that General Dullahan had entered the great hall, interrupting his audience with the king. The general's worn leather boots and bloody spurs echoed as he strolled toward the throne, carrying his head in the crook of his arm. A hideous grin and eyes that burned like the fires of hell looked up at the king.

"It is done, my King," Dullahan's gravelly voice sent shivers down Rowan's spine. Midhir's smile was saccharine as he nodded to Lir.

"Commander Rowan MacArtur," Lir's snivelling voice hissed, "you are hereby accused of high treason against His Majesty, Midhir, King of Winter. Your interference in the king's business and disloyalty will not go unpunished. An assembly of high fae will render judgement in accordance with our laws at a time of their choosing. Ad interim, you will remain beneath this keep."

"Your Majesty," Rowan pleaded, pulling against his captors, "I am no traitor. I have served your house and this realm faithfully for centuries. Have mercy."

The king waved his hand dismissively, and Leannán moved to where Rowan stood bound. Running her slender finger over the shackles on his wrist and up his chest, she raised herself just enough to place a kiss on his cheek. With a sultry and almost serpentine voice, she whispered into his ear, "Looks like we will be getting to know each other better after all."

Chapter Twenty-Five

Maeve created a portal to Arbor Castle in Freydis's apartment. Apparently, whoever Maeve was, she didn't need to find one that already existed or to use a rowboat. Freydis winced as she approached the portal opening. Maeve smiled at her reassuringly.

"Everything is going to be fine, Freydis. I will be able to do more for your pain when we arrive."

Freydis held Maeve's outstretched hand, and instantly everything went dark. Freydis felt as though she were in a cold, pitch-black room, so dense she wasn't even sure she could breathe. In a heartbeat, she could hear familiar voices and feel the warmth of what felt like a fire, and then they appeared in the kitchen of Arbor Castle.

Vetus, Ophelia, and Kerridwen had been in mid-conversation over what Freydis guessed was dinner when they had appeared. Ophelia's face lost all colour, and Vetus, upon seeing her bruised and battered, surged for her. Freydis groaned.

"Freydis, Gods, what's happened?" Vetus looked her over frantically. He only stopped to acknowledge the woman who stood beside Freydis after Kerridwen gasped.

"Mother?" Kerri's voice was childlike. "Mama, is that you?"

Vetus turned toward his sister's voice and then whipped his head back to where Maeve waited silently.

Freydis felt immediately out of place and a bit shocked that she had been in the presence of the Winter Queen and had not known. She also did not know the other woman who called Maeve mother, but the resemblance was profound. They were practically identical except for their eyes.

Maeve had the same emerald-green eyes as Vetus.

"Hello, my children, I have missed you terribly," the Winter Queen crooned.

Freydis fought back tears as she watched mother and daughter embrace. Vetus, however, did not leave Freydis's side.

"Does the Winter King know you've returned?" Vetus asked coldly.

"No, and I should like it to remain that way for now," Maeve answered.

"Terrible things happened when you left," Vetus's voice was tight. Even if she hadn't been beside him, Freydis would have known the expression he now had on his face from his tone.

"Terrible things are still happening, my son. That is why I have returned, and Midhir is only a very small part of a much larger picture."

"We needed you sooner," Vetus hissed, "much sooner."

"I'm sorry, Vetus. I am, but I have my reasons for waiting, and I can explain them another time, but for now, Freydis needs healing and rest."

As if someone had flipped a switch, Vetus turned his wary eyes to Freydis once more. "Ophelia, please get Freydis settled and summon your best healers."

"Of course," Ophelia said.

"Ophelia," Freydis called after her, "Cass will be coming too. After Ethan's funeral."

Freydis met Vetus's horrified gaze and nodded in confirmation. Ethan hadn't recovered.

"Prepare a room for her and the baby also," Vetus added.

Ophelia nodded and breezed from the room.

Vetus held out his hand toward the woman Freydis assumed was his sister.

"Freydis, may I present my little sister, Princess Kerridwen, Lady and Ruler of Autumn." Vetus then turned toward Maeve. "And you've already met my mother."

Marcus's guilt was all-consuming. He threw himself into planning the funeral. He had failed Ethan. He had failed Cass and their baby. It was the least he could do.

The service was small and intimate, as Cass had requested. After the interment, Marcus swallowed his nervousness and approached her.

"I have no words, Cass, except to say once more how sorry I am."

"I'm sorry too, Marcus. Ethan is...*was* your brother. He loved you so much. He was so proud of the work you do. He would want you to know that."

Marcus fought against the tears that threatened to fall, and his lips quivered as he spoke, "Thank you, Cass. That means everything. We will get through this together."

"No, we won't," Cass's voice was cold and matter-of-fact. "I am taking Aoife to Ireland. Freydis has family there and has invited us to move there with her."

"Is Freydis here?" Marcus looked around expectantly. "I thought she'd be with you."

"She went on ahead," Cass answered. "We are to meet her there."

Marcus tried to think of a way to get more information, details, or something he could use. His meeting with the government representative that Tina tracked down was that evening. "Where—"

Cass interrupted him before he could finish asking.

"Goodbye, Marcus."

All he could do was watch as she turned her back and walked away.

Later that evening, the government representative sat across from Marcus and Tina at the conference table on the third floor of Anderson Robotics and Technology. Marcus watched as he read the lab results, then read them a second time.

"This is remarkable," the man gaped. "You're sure this is legitimate?"

Marcus nodded, "I collected the sample myself."

"Extraordinary," the man shook his head. "I would like to see this specimen for myself."

"Of course," Marcus said, "but unfortunately, it...well, *she* is currently in Ireland."

"What?" Shock appeared on the man's face. "You let it out of your sight? Are you insane? What if something happens to it or someone else discovers it before it's contained?"

Marcus looked at Tina, who had an expression of pure disgust on her face.

"I don't think that will be an issue, sir," Marcus paused. "Her name is Freydis, and she looks and behaves completely human. No one would be able to tell what she is just by looking at her."

"Interesting," the man muttered. "Well, it looks like we will have to send a recovery team to secure and extract the specimen. I want to begin testing immediately."

Somewhere inside, a flicker of regret whispered to Marcus, but he quickly smothered it with the anger that had been festering since Ethan died. There was one thing Marcus knew for sure, and that was that Freydis had advanced healing capabilities. If she hadn't kept her identity a secret, she may have been able to save Ethan, and if that turned out to be the case, Marcus would never forgive her. He would do whatever it took to make her pay for it so no one else would ever suffer because of her selfishness.

The healers had visited Freydis every day, twice a day, for the past week. Most of her physical injuries were healed. She still had some tenderness in her wrist, and the markings from the incomplete ritual were not healing as quickly due to their infernal nature.

Cass was set to arrive next week. Freydis would be grateful to have another familiar face around, not to mention baby snuggles. Ophelia had received word from Rowan at the Winter Palace indicating he was required to remain at court to oversee a special mission for the king. He didn't know when he'd return.

Freydis had hoped to see him once more if only to thank him again for saving her, but also to try and stop the nightmares she had each night where she died at his hands...over and over again.

The dreams weren't real, and she knew in her heart that it was a demon and not Rowan who had attacked her, but she relived it every day—every time she closed her eyes. When she was awake, though, she spent most of her free time in the castle library.

It was there that Vetus found her.

"Dea, I wanted to discuss something with you."

Freydis looked up at her friend.

"Sophia, Mattias, and Isabella are the names of the three members of your mother's family that I found," Vetus paused. "I think you should meet them. Sophia is your mother's sister."

Freydis couldn't fight back the tears, "Her sister?"

Vetus nodded, "Mattias is her mate. Isabella is their daughter, your cousin."

"I would like that," she wiped the tears from her eyes with her sleeve. "Do they know about me?"

"I've sent word to them, so they know. Ophelia will make the arrangements as soon as you're ready," Vetus offered.

"I don't want to wait."

Everything that had happened with Cass and Ethan, her and Rowan, the attack—she didn't want to put it off any longer. She may be immortal, but life could be cruel, and anything could happen tomorrow. It was time to finally embrace that hidden part of herself. It was time to fill in the missing pieces and figure out who she truly was.

A thick morning fog covered the lake, and from where Freydis stood on the battlements, she felt like she was on a castle floating in the clouds. Thoughts galloped through her head. Ophelia had made flight arrangements for her to go to Belize. After years of searching, meeting her mother's sister, meeting family, was a dream come true, the final piece of the puzzle that was her true self.

"It's normally Vetus I find up here brooding," Kerridwen's voice floated from behind her. "Thinking about your trip?"

"Yes, and so much more," Freydis breathed in the damp air. "I've been trying to sort through everything I've learned these past few weeks."

Kerridwen nodded, "It's a lot to digest. Give yourself time."

"I asked Ophelia why someone couldn't just use magic to take me to Belize; she said by plane is safer." Freydis assumed magic would be safer and faster.

"If you are caught in the Otherworld or any of the other hidden places of the world, they will take you to my father," Kerridwen swallowed. "He will torture and kill you on sight."

"Why does he hate me so much?"

"It's a very long and complicated story," Kerridwen nudged her. "But, Vetus would be the best one to tell it."

Freydis rolled her eyes, "Everyone keeps telling me that."

What secrets had he still not told her? She would now have to wait until after Belize, and she had no idea how long she would stay there.

"I had hoped to see Rowan before I left," Freydis said. "I wanted to thank him again for saving my life. I owe him."

"Be careful, girl," Kerri smiled. "Life debts are serious business to fae."

Freydis nodded and Kerridwen continued, "He will be upset to have missed you too. Anyhow, Ophelia sent me up to get you. The car has arrived over on the other side of the loch, and since I haven't travelled in the human realm in a while, I am to escort you to the airport."

Kerridwen wrapped her arm around Freydis's shoulder as they descended from the battlements. Instantly, Freydis felt like a weight had been lifted off her shoulders, as if by magic. She gave Kerri a grateful smile, which she returned with a wink.

"Everything will be alright, Freydis."

Chapter Twenty-Six

Getting to Belize proved to be more complicated than Freydis had expected. With no direct flight from Ireland, Freydis flew to Canada, changed aircraft, and finally arrived in the southern United States, where she would connect with yet another aircraft to take her on the final leg of her journey.

Upon checking in, the ticket agent informed her of a three-hour delay affecting her flight. At least she would have time to grab something to eat. She hadn't eaten breakfast due to her nervous stomach, and the gurgling noises it was making were loud enough to wake the dead.

The airport was relatively small compared to some of the others she'd gone through, but she still needed to look at the visitor map she'd received upon arrival. To her surprise, a familiar voice called her name.

"Freydis?" Marcus smiled as he approached her. "I don't believe it. What are you doing in Texas?"

Freydis hugged him tightly, "I'm so sorry to hear about Ethan. I wish I could have been there to support you and Cass."

She felt him tense in her arms.

"It still doesn't feel real," Marcus murmured, stepping away. "How is Cass? She said she was going to Ireland to live with you and your family."

"I didn't get a chance to see her before I left. I am heading to Belize to meet some long-lost relatives," Freydis pointed to the yellow line indicating her delayed flight on the departures board. "I have a bit of time to wait...wanna join me for supper?"

Freydis was shocked that Marcus approached her at all after their complicated past. She hoped he wouldn't bring it up, but it felt rude not to extend the invitation.

"Sure," Marcus grinned. "There is a lovely place about ten minutes from the airport. We can eat and have you back in plenty of time to catch your flight. I just need to make a quick phone call."

"Sounds wonderful," Freydis agreed.

After Marcus finished his call, she followed him to where a driver and car were waiting for them.

"I'm here on business, so they hired a driver," Marcus shrugged. "Hop in."

The driver placed Freydis's carry-on in the trunk, and Marcus joined her in the backseat. She could sense a change in his demeanour. He sat rigidly, looking straight ahead. A muscle feathered in his jaw. Freydis swallowed the slight surge of panic, but then he turned to face her with dark eyes and a face full of anger.

"What *are* you?" he seethed.

"I don't know what you're talking about," Freydis fought to keep her voice steady.

"Was everything you ever told me a lie?" he asked.

"Marcus, I don't want to argue. Just take me back to the airport." Freydis leaned forward to tap the driver on the shoulder when she felt a sharp pinch in her thigh. She turned quickly to see Marcus depress the plunger on the needle he'd jabbed into her leg.

"You shouldn't have lied to me, Freydis," Marcus said coldly. "This might have gone differently."

"What did you do?" Freydis gaped at him.

"I gave you a sedative. The dose might be a little higher than necessary, but I don't know what you are, so I erred on the side of caution."

Freydis grabbed the handle and tried to open the car door, but it wouldn't budge. A heaviness began to spread through her body and down her limbs as she fought against the fog filling her head.

"Marcus, please," she felt like she was slurring, and her vision began to darken. "Please don't do..."

Everything was bright when Freydis regained consciousness, but she still couldn't move or speak. Her eyes darted around, trying to determine where she was. She could hear voices arguing but was unable to turn her head to see who was speaking. Pure panic raged through her. How could Marcus have done this to her?

She was trapped inside a body that wouldn't respond despite her efforts to will it to obey. All she could do was listen to the discussion being had in the room.

"You effectively gave it an overdose," an unknown male voice spoke. "You're lucky you didn't kill it."

"I didn't know if she'd have any resistance to it or if her abnormal healing would make it wear off faster," Marcus's voice replied. "Just be glad she's here."

"As soon as the specimen is conscious, I want to begin testing," the other man said. "We've done everything we could with it under sedation."

"Marcus are you sure about this?" a female voice pleaded. "This doesn't feel right."

"If you don't like it, Tina, then leave," Marcus growled. "We are going ahead. Can't you give her something to bring her out of it, Doc?"

"No, this sedative has to run its course," the doctor sighed. "We will continue monitoring vitals until it wears off."

Freydis lay awake alone for what felt like hours after Marcus and the others left the room. As the sedative continued to wear off, her ability to move returned, but it didn't matter. They had her strapped to a hospital bed. She was naked underneath the thin white sheet that covered her.

She tried desperately to fight the sobs that clawed to free themselves from her throat. Panic and nausea flooded her at the thought of what they may have done without her knowledge or consent. The feeling of violation was almost more than she could bear.

Looking around, she realized there were no windows, not even on the single door leading out of the room. The walls were a bare, faded grey, and the room was empty except for her bed, two chairs, and the machines monitoring her vitals. Perched on top of one of the monitors appeared to be a camera, about the size of a golf ball, watching her like a tiny cyclops.

I will never get out of this.

"You're awake," Marcus's voice shattered the silence in the room like breaking glass.

Freydis's mouth was so dry she could hardly speak, "Water...please."

He offered her a small sip of water from a Styrofoam cup with a red straw, the colour vivid against the drab surroundings.

"Why are you doing this?" Freydis asked. "What's happened to you, Marcus?"

"You lied to me, Freydis," Marcus hissed. "I offered you everything I had, and you left without an explanation. When I started putting the pieces together, I knew something wasn't right. I had some suspicions and had your blood tested after you cut yourself at my condo that night."

"Why?" Freydis fought to steady her voice. Marcus wouldn't even make eye contact with her.

"You looked like one of us, behaved like one of us...even fucked like we do, but I couldn't shake the feeling that you were hiding something." He pulled the sheet off, exposing her bare skin. "You are covered in scars and all these strange markings. They weren't there before, but some of them are too faded to be new." He covered her back up and pulled one of the chairs over to her bedside and sat. "I thought maybe you had some genetic mutation that helped you heal faster than normal. I thought maybe it could help Ethan."

"Why didn't you just talk to me?" Freydis tried to fight the tears that wanted to fall.

Marcus closed his eyes. Freydis could see him clench and unclench his jaw.

"Marcus, look at me," Freydis pleaded. "Don't do this. This isn't who you are."

Marcus lurched forward and grabbed a fistful of her hair, pulling her to be face to face with him. She forced herself not to cry out.

"I shouldn't have had to ask. You should have come forward right away...if there was a chance you could have helped. That is what a human would have done."

He released her hair and stood up, turning away from her again.

"Since you aren't human, you have none of our rights, but I have asked to be an executor of sorts to act on your behalf. I have authorized a thorough investigation, including a barrage of medical and psychological testing—"

"Marcus, please…," Freydis interrupted.

He ignored her.

"The tests we've completed so far have given us interesting results. You are apparently sterile, as we attempted to locate and harvest your eggs and couldn't find any. We have also done a spinal tap and taken several tissue and blood samples."

Tears fell freely down her cheeks as his words kept spilling from his lips. They had violated her. Taken pieces of her. Perhaps being burned alive was a better alternative to how she now felt. At least eventually, the flames would stop.

"How could you do this, Marcus? I'm still me," she sobbed. "You told me you *loved me.*"

"The thought of everything we did, the way I felt…I am disgusted by it," Marcus hissed. "If I had known then, I never would have said those things. You would have been here a lot sooner."

"You don't mean that, Marcus," Freydis cried. "I know you."

Marcus stood up and looked her in the eyes for the first time since coming into the room. His face was a mix of hate and indifference.

"A psychiatrist will be in later today to begin the psychological evaluation. When you are finished here, you will be turned over to the government, and they will determine what comes next."

"Someone will come looking for me, Marcus," Freydis forced courage into her words. "I have people who care about me and will notice my absence."

"I messaged Cass with your phone," he said matter-of-factly, "told her you arrived safely in Belize and would send an update soon. I will keep providing updates as long as I must. Once you are handed over, nothing Cass or anyone else does will matter."

Marcus returned the chair to its original place and walked out of the room without even looking back.

Unable to wipe her tears with her hands, Freydis screamed and thrashed against her restraints. When she'd exhausted herself, she closed her eyes and prayed to all the Gods to let her die.

Chapter Twenty-Seven

The crushing black of Midhir's dungeons had driven many prisoners mad. If the darkness wasn't enough, the freezing cold was torture. The ceiling was too low for Rowan to stand. He could barely kneel without hunching over. The cells weren't built for the likes of him.

Despite the cold, the dungeon was mercifully damp. The water dripping down the stone walls was the only way to quench one's thirst, but it didn't run fast enough to be collected, so Rowan had to lick the stones themselves. Of course, he had to listen for the sound of it in the inky black and hope his shackles were long enough for him to reach it.

Numerous species of fungi provided the only source of nourishment, and many were highly toxic or possessed hallucinogenic properties. Unable to see, it was safer to avoid eating anything until the sky was clear when the moon reached its apex each night. For those brief moments, enough dim light shining through a small crack in the upper outer wall entered the cell for Rowan to see a few feet in every direction.

His shackles were bolted to the cell wall and were made of cold iron. He wasn't sure how they managed to get them on him, but the iron burned his wrists and ankles, leaving bloody lesions underneath.

He didn't know the extent of his injuries, but if centuries of war taught him anything, the beating the guards had given him before tossing him into the abyss had left him with at least three broken ribs, a split lip, and one hell of a headache.

Deep within the bowels of the Winter Court, Rowan's Summer magic didn't even dare to whisper, and the Winter magic that used to favour him, despite his blood, also remained silent. His only hope was a swift execution handed down from the assembly of high fae that would determine his fate.

Though, they could make him wait centuries for their judgement if they wished.

The alternative would be literal torture. Midhir would likely do it himself, given the chance. Rowan supposed he should be grateful. He had cheated Death for centuries. In all those years, he'd never pieced together how he'd become immortal.

Perhaps it had been only luck that he'd survived an unhealable wound from a legendary sword; perhaps the Gods had a sick sense of humour. It didn't matter. His only regret was never telling Freydis how he felt about her.

Keeping track of time was difficult in the dungeon. Rowan guessed he'd been there for a few days shy of a fortnight. His extreme hunger was altering his perception, so he couldn't be certain. Even the toxic mushrooms began to call to him. At least the fatigue was a small mercy. He slept whenever his mind would cooperate.

Rowan started to doze off when the rattle of a key in the cell door lock roused him. A single silhouette of a guard entered, carrying a lantern. The sudden brightness assaulted his dampened senses.

"Who's there?" Rowan's voice was hoarse and weak.

"Commander," the guard gasped, and Rowan recognized one of the lesser fae soldiers he'd often shared an ale with, "I had them add me to the guard's roster."

The guard approached as swiftly as the cramped space would allow him.

"Here." The guard extended a small pitcher, "Drink."

Rowan drank deeply; the cold, clean water was glorious. He emptied the pitcher. The pity on the guard's face made him bristle, "You'll end up in here too if they catch you."

"Perhaps, but there is a group of us who heard you were locked up, and we joined the guard immediately," he winked at Rowan. "We aren't going to sit idly, Sir. We may not get down here often, but when we do, we'll do what we can."

The guard tossed Rowan an apple, which he devoured in three bites.

"I don't want any of you risking yourself unnecessarily."

The guard gave him another conspiratorial wink and left, locking the cell behind him. Rowan lay back against the wall and listened to the water that endlessly trickled down the stone. Maybe his situation wasn't as desperate as he thought.

A spark of hope had no sooner flickered inside him when the keys rattled the lock again. The ground seemed to fall out from beneath him. If that soldier had been caught for helping him...

When the door to the cell swung open, it revealed something far worse.

Shackled at the hands and feet, gagged, and draped over one of the king's personal guards was a limp figure, bruised and bloody. In the darkness, Rowan couldn't quite see who would be joining him in the abyss until the guard finished bolting the shackles to the wall. The full moon outside shone brightly on the new prisoner through the small crack as though it were a spotlight.

Rowan couldn't stop himself from retching, emptying the meagre contents of his stomach as he gaped at the unconscious woman crumpled against the wall, just within arm's reach. He could barely think straight as her name formed in his mouth, "*Freydis*."

It couldn't be real. He had left her with the Winter Queen. Maeve promised to take her to Arbor Castle—to Vetus.

Maeve lied. She lied to him, and he was fool enough to trust the Winter Queen.

His body ached as he moved toward her, his shackles just long enough to allow him to reach her hand. Gently, he held her hand, stroking the back of it with his thumb.

"Freydis, can you hear me? It's Rowan."

Her eyes fluttered slightly as panic galloped through him. He felt her hand tighten slightly on his. When she opened her eyes, he let go of the breath he didn't know he'd been holding. Her bright blue eyes searched his face. His breath hitched at how, even in this dark place, she was the most beautiful woman he'd ever seen.

"Rowan?" Freydis groaned, "Where am I? What's happened?"

"You're in the dungeon of the Winter Palace, but you shouldn't be here," Rowan swallowed. "You are supposed to be safe with Vetus. What do you remember?"

"As you said, I was with Vetus, and he asked me to go somewhere with him. I can't remember what he called it, but we were attacked, and then I woke up here."

Rowan cursed under his breath, "How could Vetus be so careless?"

"They tortured me, Rowan," tears slid down her cheeks. "It was awful. Please don't let them hurt me again."

Rowan winced at the fear in her voice and watched as she struggled to inch closer to him. He felt so helpless. No matter what he promised or what comforting words he tried to give her, the truth was they would likely both die in Midhir's dungeon.

"I will get you out, Freydis," Rowan lied. He was close enough to feel her warmth. Her shackles were slightly longer than his, allowing her to lean against him.

"Everything hurts," she whispered.

"Try to sleep," Rowan murmured. "You need your strength, and it will help pass the time."

Freydis tucked herself into him as tightly as the shackles would allow. He breathed in deeply, hoping to wrap himself in her lavender scent, but all he could smell was the earthy dampness of the dungeon around them. At least they would keep each other warm as they slept.

Rowan and Freydis stayed close in waking and in sleep, reassured by each other's presence in the endless black of the dungeon. There had been no moon or at least a night clear enough for the light to find the little crack in what felt like days.

Rowan woke to the feeling of Freydis's soft lips on his own. When his eyes adjusted, he could tell she was staring at him with an eerie stillness.

"That is probably my favourite way to be woken up," Rowan murmured, "even if I wake to find myself still imprisoned here."

Freydis smiled, "There are worse fates than being trapped together forever."

Rowan leaned toward her for another kiss when the sound of keys rattling in the door made his heart skip a beat. The door flew open, and four guards entered. They grabbed Freydis, unbolted her shackles from the wall, and began dragging her to the exit.

"Rowan!" Freydis screamed. "Don't let them take me, please don't let them take me."

Rowan roared, pulling with every ounce of strength he could muster, and yanked helplessly on his own chains.

"Let her go, you bastards! Take me!" he bellowed. "I will kill every one of you if you harm her."

Freydis's screams filled the darkness as they hauled her away. Rowan tore at his chains until the cold iron burned and blistered his hands. His whole body trembled with rage.

Then they tortured her.

Rowan knew without seeing it. Knew they'd kept her close enough for him to hear it. The sounds of her wailing and moaning, the screams of pure horror, ripped at his mind and fractured his very being as though he could see it with his own eyes.

Sobs wracked his body. He still had nightmares about finding her barely alive after the demon attack, and now the sounds of her torture would haunt him even when he was awake. Finally, when the silence returned, for the first time since Vetus saved him as a child, Rowan prayed for death.

Chapter Twenty-Eight

The small piece of medical tape holding the feeding tube in place on Freydis's upper lip itched and nearly drove her mad. They'd placed a feeding tube in her mouth after she'd bitten one of the nameless attendants who looked after her basic needs. Feeding tube, catheter, and IV lines meant all she really needed to do was lie in bed and exist, despite how hard she prayed not to. Every day they poked and prodded, taking vials of her blood, pieces of tissue, and her dignity.

Marcus came regularly to interrogate her, yell and rage, or simply stare with disgust. She refused to speak with the psychiatrist. Despite being restrained, she'd assaulted anyone who got close enough, so she was heavily sedated whenever they changed her bedding or untied her for any reason.

Bedsores meant she was sedated more and more often to have wounds tended to. Her body ached from lack of use, and when she wasn't sedated, she could feel weakness creeping in. One doctor cautioned Marcus about muscular atrophy if they didn't find a way to get her moving without endangering anyone.

Whenever she was lucid, she called to the magic in her blood, but the magic wouldn't heed her desperate pleas. If only it would answer, she would use it to end the nightmare that her life had become. It seemed the connection to that part of herself had been severed.

Still, every moment she was lucid, she searched deep for even a thread of it to cling to. The Gods themselves wouldn't stop the destruction she would leave in her wake if she ever found one. These humans wanted to believe she was a creature they could cage and experiment on so she would become the monster Marcus thought she was.

A shuffling and the scrape of chair legs on the floor woke Freydis from the dreamless sleep she'd fallen into. She kept her eyes closed, hoping whoever it was would leave, but Tina's soft voice spoke her name near the foot of her bed.

Without opening her eyes, Freydis responded, "Go away, Tina. I'm not answering any more of Marcus's questions."

"Marcus didn't send me," Tina sighed. "He and all the doctors have left for the day. I offered to lock up after the cleaners were done."

"Well, I won't answer your questions, either." Freydis opened her eyes to glare at Tina. "Go be a good little assistant somewhere else. He must be expecting you back at his place."

"Our place," Tina replied flatly.

Freydis's grin was feral, "How long after I left him? How long until you became his distraction? He did tell you that when I came back after Cass and Ethan's accident, he brought me to his condo and we fucked without a moment's hesitation from him, didn't he?"

The redness in Tina's cheek and the way she clenched her jaw confirmed what Freydis already knew.

"I know you are angry, Freydis," Tina swallowed, "and if I could get you out of here, I would. Marcus isn't acting like the man I fell in love with, but I think it's grief that's making him ignore how awful this is. I have told him more times than I can count."

Heat flooded Freydis's cheeks as she wrestled with the shame of trying to hurt Tina's feelings and the satisfaction of lashing out and not being a victim for a moment.

"You have no idea how I am feeling," Freydis snarled.

"Freydis, if you don't cooperate with the psychiatrist's evaluation tomorrow, they have made arrangements to have you moved to a more permanent government facility," Tina paused, stood up, and moved to be near Freydis's shoulder. "Please tell me how to help you."

"Undo these restraints and open that door," Freydis jerked her chin toward the only exit. "I will go, and they will never find me."

The pitying look Tina gave her made Freydis want to claw Tina's eyes out.

"They will find you, Freydis, they will. Marcus insisted they give you a tracking microchip the moment you arrived here."

The reality of Tina's words crashed down on her like an avalanche.

"Then you can't help me," Freydis said coldly. "No one else knows I'm here. Marcus used my phone to tell Cass I'd arrived where I was going and that all was well. They think I'm in Belize."

"What if I got the phone from Marcus? Is there anyone who could help?" Tina pleaded.

"There is." Freydis looked at Tina as though she was seeing her for the first time, "Why are you willing to risk so much to help me?"

"Because Marcus will never let you go, and when he finally wakes up from whatever madness this is, he will never forgive himself for what he's done," Tina wiped away a tear. "I love him, Freydis, and I want there to be something left of the man I knew before all this. The man who spent his life trying to find a way to help people and make the world a better place. Maybe when you are gone, he will remember."

Freydis wanted to hate Tina, and maybe she did, but all she felt looking at Tina now was sorrow. Tina's willingness to fight for Marcus even if he had become a stranger made Freydis realize she'd never let herself love anyone like that before. Not even Astrid.

"Get a message to Cass, Tina. Tell her whatever you can," Freydis swallowed, "and I will cooperate with the psychiatrist to try and buy some time."

Freydis watched Tina nod and walk quietly out of the room. A flurry of thoughts filled her head as a spark of hope flickered in her gut. Tina was right about Marcus, as much as she hated to admit it. The Marcus she had known and cared so deeply about may not have accepted what she was, but he never would have been this cruel. The question that gnawed at her now was, if this plan worked, would she go in forgiveness or would the vengeance that festered inside her tear its way into the world that deserved her wrath? *Decisions, decisions...*

That night, Freydis dreamt of Rowan. She couldn't see his face, but she recognized his voice calling out her name. She was somewhere dark, a forest maybe, and despite her searching, she couldn't find him. She woke herself yelling his name. Her heart was racing as if she'd been running. Marcus sat at the foot of her bed in one of the uncomfortable-looking plastic chairs that furnished the room.

"I always knew he was more than just a friend," Marcus sneered without looking up from the papers he was reading, "to make you call out his name so desperately."

"Pig," Freydis snorted. "At least Rowan would never do what you have done to me."

"That inadequate, is he?" Marcus quipped. Freydis gritted her teeth.

"What do you want, Marcus?" she hissed.

"The psychiatrist is coming in to see you shortly, but when I received the latest test results, I had to come." Marcus looked up from the paperwork. "How old are you, exactly?"

"Thirty," Freydis replied flatly.

"Don't be coy, Freydis," he grinned. "Your cells show no indication of aging, or at least it's not measurable. The question is, does it have something to do with your ability to heal yourself faster than what humans consider normal, or do you not age."

"You're the scientist," Freydis's smile was saccharine, "you tell me."

She watched Marcus pause as a muscle in his jaw feathered—the only sign of his frustration. *Odd. He must be working on that temper he seemed to acquire with his implant.*

"How many more like you are there, Freydis?" Marcus changed the subject.

"Just me," Freydis glared at him. "The one and only."

"Maybe," Marcus murmured, "maybe not. It doesn't matter if you tell me or not. They won't be able to hide forever. Perhaps we will start our search in Belize."

It took every ounce of Freydis's will not to react to his threat. She hadn't even met her family in Belize, and already she had put them at risk. Tina was wrong about there being any good left in Marcus. That Marcus died with Ethan.

"Good luck with that," Freydis schooled her voice to sound indifferent. "You could search for a thousand years and never find anyone else like me."

"Well, if we can isolate what keeps your cells from aging, perhaps I will use the extra years I gain to hunt down every creature like you, harvest all the usable parts, and make sure humanity thrives." Marcus moved toward her until his face was so close she could smell the stale coffee on his warm breath. "I will make the world a better, healthier place, and it looks like you will be helping me after all."

Freydis spit in his face.

"*Bitch!*" Marcus snarled as he wiped his face. Freydis's chuckle was cut short when he grabbed her chin, forcing her to look at him. "You are never getting out of here. I will make your life a living hell, so you'd better start playing nice."

Freydis hissed, "I have to ask, did you cry for Tina too before you slept with her? Tell her all about your poor sister? Thank the Gods she's not alive to see what you've become."

Freydis hated herself as the words poured from her lips, but that didn't stop her from spewing whatever cruelties she could think of. Marcus squeezed her chin until it hurt to speak but abruptly released her when the door opened, and a sleepy-looking man with a balding pate and sparse grey beard entered.

"Good morning, Dr. Wolfe," the man's voice was quiet and unthreatening as he greeted Marcus. "I see our guest is awake this morning. Is she ready to talk, I wonder?"

"Oh, she's fully lucid this morning, Dr. Bohring," Marcus fiddled with the buttons on his shirt sleeve. "Hopefully, she cooperates."

Dr. Bohring gave Marcus a patronizing smile and sat on the chair at the foot of Freydis's bed. "Good morning, young lady. My name is Dr. Winston Bohring, and I am a cognitive neuropsychiatrist, but I also have some forensic experience as well. I have a few questions for you, and I promise they will be quite painless."

Freydis stared at the colourless walls, listening to Dr. Bohring's monotone voice.

"Please state your full name?" he began.

"Freydis Magnusdottir."

"No middle names?"

Freydis didn't reply.

"So you are originally from Norway, is that correct?"

Freydis nodded.

"And when did you leave Norway?" he asked.

"When I was eighteen years old, after my mother died."

"So, about fifteen years ago?"

"No, in 1662." Freydis sneered and turned to lock her stormy eyes on him.

"I see," he frowned. "And how did your mother die?"

"Burned at the stake."

Dr. Bohring cleared his throat. "This will go better if you just tell the truth, my dear."

Freydis laughed. "Skip the small talk then and ask the real questions."

"From your initial medical assessment, you appear to be in excellent health. Has this always been the case?"

Freydis rolled her eyes, "I am immortal, no health concerns."

"Have you ever experienced anything unusual, heard voices only you can hear or seen something that no one else sees?"

"You mean like the man standing behind you?" Freydis smiled as the doctor quickly turned to look behind him.

"Very amusing. Well, it's clear to me that you are mentally fit, from a medical perspective," Dr. Bohring said, "which will make studying you throughout this process very intriguing. I didn't believe Dr. Wolfe at first, but I am curious enough now that I shall lend my support to this project. I look forward to getting inside that head of yours."

Freydis turned away from his scrutinizing gaze. She would play their games, answer their questions, and hopefully, buy herself enough time for Tina to help.

Chapter Twenty-Nine

R owan lost count of how many times he'd helplessly watched the guards drag her away. Her screams echoed throughout the dungeon, reverberating through him, etching themselves onto his bones. The sound was so primal that he couldn't reconcile it with the image of her he held in his heart.

Each time they'd bring her back to him bloody and unconscious, he'd stretch his chains as far as he could to be near enough to watch her shallow breathing as if his life depended on its continuation. He would whisper all the bright and beautiful stories he could remember his mother telling him as a child, clinging desperately to the ever-shrinking part of him that believed they'd somehow escape the nightmare.

"We will get out of here, Freydis," Rowan murmured into her hair as she slept. Her eyes fluttered open, and she gave him a sad smile. He was struck by how fragile she looked. Her skin hung off her bones, and her eyes were sunken in her skull. He knew in his heart that one of these times they took her away, she wouldn't be coming back.

He brushed her hair from her face and placed a kiss on her forehead. "There are a few guards who are former soldiers who served under my command. They bring water and food when they can. It's been several days, so one of them is due any day. Please hang on, Fierce One. There is no place in this world or any other for me if you aren't in it."

The slight heaviness of her head against his chest told him she'd fallen back to sleep. Despite his own exhaustion, he feared the dreams awaiting him, so he fought to stay awake. Even sleep didn't offer any refuge from his tormented existence, and more than once, he pictured himself gorging on mushrooms to end it all.

But not yet.

Not until he knew Freydis was safe, either in this life or the next.

The next time they hauled her away, the screaming stopped abruptly. She didn't return to the cell. A deep, unrelenting agony flooded him. As he lay on the cold, damp stones, he let go of the last shred of himself and embraced the abyss as it swallowed him whole.

"Commander?" The familiar voice seemed muted or as if it came from another room, but Rowan could see the silhouette of the guard who had brought him water several times before. "I'm sorry I couldn't come sooner. The king has been holding audience after audience with foreign monarchs, and security in the great hall has been tripled. I came as soon as I could."

"Please, what's happened to Freydis?" Rowan pleaded. "I need someone I trust to say it. I need to hear it."

"My Lord Rowan, forgive me, but I don't know what you're talking about."

"The woman who was in here with me, the one they kept torturing, did she—is she?"

He couldn't bring himself to say the words as sobs tried to scurry out in their place. Thankfully, the dehydration prevented any tears. What would this soldier think of the weakness he saw before him?

"Commander, there is no woman. You are alone in this dungeon and have been since they put you in here." Confusion and deep concern painted the soldier's features. "You didn't eat any mushrooms, did you?"

"That's impossible," Rowan murmured. "I saw her with my own eyes, spoke to her, and heard her answer. I felt her with my *own fucking hands.*"

The soldier offered Rowan the pitcher of water, which he swatted away.

"*You,*" Rowan hissed, "you have poisoned me, muddled my senses. I know she was here. I know it."

Rowan repeated the words over and over to himself as the guard set the pitcher of water within arm's reach and retreated from the cell. *Had he lost his damned mind?*

Fever burned inside Rowan, and the scent of infection filled his nostrils. The cold iron shackles had caused blisters that now festered. Barely able to move, Rowan lay in his own filth and prayed to whatever Gods would listen to let him die.

He was so delirious he'd started to hear Freydis calling his name. He covered his ears with his dirty, blood-crusted hands. With a great effort of will, he managed to roll himself over and realized the delusions had spread beyond his hearing to his sight. Before him, Freydis, just as she seemed before the last time she'd been taken, sat against the far wall, illuminated by the momentary sliver of moonlight.

"Rowan, can you hear me?" the voice sounded like her, and he wanted so badly to believe that she was alive, even if it meant she was still a prisoner of the Winter King.

"Be gone, foul spirit," Rowan growled weakly. "I am tormented enough without your presence. Go back to whatever realm you come from and let me die."

"It's me, Rowan. I am no ghost," Freydis moved toward him, her hand outstretched. "Please, I'm cold and frightened. Please don't turn away from me."

Rowan grunted and groaned from the effort of trying to drag himself closer to her. Her cool tiny fingers caressed his brow and ran through his hair as he rested his head in her lap.

"I thought you were dead, Freydis. The last time they took you...you didn't come back." He cringed at the helpless, childlike tone of his own voice, but he was too exhausted to fully feel the shame of it.

"I am here, Rowan," Freydis cooed, "I'm here now."

When the fever finally broke, Rowan woke to find himself alone once more. *Had he dreamed it all? Was she truly gone, or had she ever even been there to begin with?*

His head was swimming, and his thirst was unquenchable. Mercifully, the pitcher of water had remained where the guard left it, full of cool clear water. If it was poisoned, he no longer cared. What was real and what was fantasy had blurred during his time in Midhir's dungeon. Perhaps he'd gone entirely mad. Perhaps he wasn't even alive, and this was his own personal version of *Tech Duinn* or Hell. With his mixed blood, he couldn't be certain.

Keys rattled in the cell door, and four large guards entered.

"Get up," said the one now kneeling to undo his shackles from the stone wall. "The king wishes to have an audience."

They hauled Rowan from the cell and up from the bowels beneath the Winter Palace to the great hall. Gathered inside was a large contingent of the guards, many of whom he'd watched drag Freydis out each time. As he walked, he made a mental note of the ones he would kill for torturing her if he ever found his freedom.

All eyes were on him, the disgraced commander and favourite of the once-crown prince. He ignored their snickering and focused on the king's empty throne. The guards shoved him to his knees and fastened his shackles to a large iron ring that had been bolted to the floor at the centre of the room. A smaller contingent of guards gathered at one side of the large group, and Rowan recognized them as his former soldiers. Each of their faces creased with varying degrees of rage and pity.

Rowan looked around but didn't see the king until a herald opened the great obsidian doors. The king entered, escorted by Winter's most feared general, Dullahan. It wasn't the general that made him want to retch but the woman on the king's arm...*Freydis.*

She was dressed in a resplendent black gossamer gown that fell to the floor. Its plunging neckline and high slit heated Rowan's blood. She had betrayed them all. She was no longer frail-looking, and she smiled at the sight of him chained to the floor.

As the king and Freydis reached the dais, Midhir kissed the back of her hand, releasing her before ascending the steps to sit on his throne.

"Welcome, Commander," Midhir crooned, "consider this a pre-trial of a sort."

Rowan kept his eyes on the floor, remaining silent as the king taunted him.

"Come now, you haven't lost that bright Summer spirit, have you? After all, I sent you this gift," the king gestured to Freydis, now perched on the steps before the throne. "Did she not please you?"

Rowan's voice cracked as he replied, "You are most gracious, Your Majesty, to offer such a comfort."

Midhir steepled his fingers in front of his chin. "Pity some of the guards had to ruin all our fun."

The words had no sooner left the king's mouth than the small group of ex-soldiers was surrounded by the remaining guards and forced to their knees. The one guard who had faithfully brought Rowan water remained stoic, looking ahead, without a hint of regret on his face. Freydis stood and walked over to them. Her lithe fingers traced that same loyal soldier's jawline, encouraging him to his feet. She turned to glance at Rowan before slicing the lesser fae's throat slowly, with a fingernail much too long and sharp to be Freydis's.

She dipped her fingers in the blood that flowed freely from the dead fae's throat and sauntered over to where Rowan knelt before the king. Freydis knelt to face Rowan and, one by one, licked the blood from each finger, stopping at the last to trace Rowan's lips with the soldier's blood. Before he could turn away, strong hands held him in place, and Freydis kissed his mouth, licking the blood from his lips. Bile rose in his throat. He managed to look away as Freydis stood up, remaining in front of him.

The king's voice echoed through the hall, "That's enough, Leannán, you are riling up the courtiers."

Rowan's eyes shot up to where Freydis had been only moments before to find Leannán Sídhe looking down at him with a feline grin.

"I told you we'd get to know each other better," she pouted and then giggled sadistically before stalking back to her place at the king's feet.

"Yes, and thanks to Leannán Sídhe," the king snarled, "we discovered traitors in our midst."

With a simple, almost imperceptible gesture from the king, the remaining ex-soldiers-turned-guards had their throats sliced by their captors. Leannán clapped and squirmed with a giddiness that made Rowan want to rip her throat out.

"So, now that we've covered the first order of business, we can move on to the details of your trial." The king cleared his throat, "The trial will take place in the next several days. In the meantime, you shall remain chained here, before my throne, to prevent any further opportunities for traitors to intervene with your punishment."

The king stood, descended the dais, and left the great hall. All those who had been in attendance of the king's spectacle filed out behind him, leaving Rowan and the slain bodies of men he'd served with for centuries lying on the floor.

Chapter Thirty

The Winter Queen loved babies. Despite reassurances from Vetus and Ophelia that Maeve would not whisk little Aoife away to some unreachable part of the Otherworld, and even though Maeve was Cass's grandmother, Cass kept a close watch whenever the queen was with Aoife. She knew fae were a cunning people, and human children were worth more than their weight in gold to them.

"You look like you're going to grab Aoife and run," Ophelia chuckled. "Maeve's arms are probably the safest place she could ever be."

Cass nodded, keeping her eyes on her grandmother, "I know. I just...it's a lot to digest. The Winter Queen is cooing and cuddling my daughter. It's very surreal."

Ophelia laughed, "I can appreciate that. How are you settling in otherwise?"

Cass sighed, "Even surrounded by so many people, I still feel so alone."

Ophelia poured more tea into Cass's cup. Everyone had been so welcoming since she'd arrived at Arbor Castle. She and Aoife had their own rooms, and Ophelia ensured all their needs were met. Vetus, her uncle, didn't speak much, but when he did, it was kind.

Cass had missed seeing Freydis by only a few days, and she found it hard to adjust to all the new and unfamiliar pieces of her life. She still woke up every morning looking for Ethan. Still waited to hear his laugh or feel the comfort of his arms around her.

"Grief has no rules, Cassandra," Ophelia said. "You are welcome to stay here as long as you need. You and Aoife will want for nothing, and should you ever feel as though the castle is too crowded, we will arrange for you to have a place of your own. We take care of each other here."

"I wish Freydis was here," Cass stirred her tea absentmindedly. "I wonder what her family is like. I'm happy she has finally found them, as I have found mine."

Ophelia glanced quickly to where Maeve stood, humming to Aoife with a conspiratorial smirk on her face. Cass watched the exchange and added, "Am I missing something?"

"We are happy for you and Freydis both," Maeve replied. "Have you received any more updates from her?"

"The most recent one was more of the same...she's doing fine, learning so much, misses everyone," Cass sipped her tea. "No details really, and I don't want to pry."

Queen Tarynn had sent her general, Diarmuid, to summon Vetus to the Summer Palace for the Autumn Equinox. The entire force of Summer's army was camped throughout the countryside surrounding the palace. Tarynn was preparing for war. The fact that it was Diarmuid, *the* Summer General, who came to retrieve him gave Vetus an inkling about the nature of his summons.

Kerridwen decided to tag along and "pay her respects" to the Summer Queen, and Vetus was grateful for the company. The last time the siblings had visited their aunt, she had been in a prickly mood.

Tarynn sat regally on her ancient oak throne. The beauty of her gold-and-crimson chiffon gown rivalled any sunset. In place of a crown, the Summer Queen wore her hair in a French braid halo. Diarmuid approached the throne, but to Vetus's and Kerridwen's surprise, he barely bowed his head in deference, choosing instead to place a kiss on the queen's outstretched hand. The siblings exchanged a curious look, and Kerridwen raised a conspiratorial eyebrow, which Vetus understood meant they would discuss it further later.

Vetus's usual Winter garb had been slightly altered since his demotion as crown prince. He no longer bore his father's sigil on his doublet; rather, he now carried a golden image of the Tree of Life, Tarynn's sigil, on his chest. The crown-of-thorns brooch was replaced by a simple gold leaf, although the rest of his outfit remained recognizable as Winter Court's in origin. The Otherworld had a sense of humour, it would seem, as Tarynn indicated she had not requested the change.

"I must confess, Nephew, I had hoped to see you more often after appointing you my emissary," the Summer Queen pouted, "but I have heard some other interesting whispers that tell me you've been rather busy."

"Happy Equinox, Your Majesty. You look lovelier than the Autumn Goddess herself," Vetus crooned.

"And why should I be happy?" Tarynn sneered. "Your wretched father seeks to usurp my crown and rule over all of the Otherworld. My whisperers tell me he has been meeting with many foreign dignitaries of late. What do you suppose he is planning?"

"I do not know, My Queen, but I will use all the resources I have at my disposal to uncover his intentions."

"And you, Kerri? What have you heard? I know you like to play on both sides." The queen's mouth quirked when Kerridwen calmly accepted the jape.

"You flatter me, Your Majesty." Kerridwen's smile was feral.

Vetus shook his head. Both his aunt and sister were formidable fae women, and Kerridwen was at her most powerful during the Autumn Equinox. It was a significant gesture of respect for her to visit the Summer Court on this day of all days.

"I have not heard about my father's plans," Kerridwen said to the queen, "nor do I intend for Autumn to be involved in his warmongering, if that is what you fear."

Tarynn bristled and motioned for Diarmuid to approach. Vetus watched as the queen spoke quietly to her general, caressing his cheek before he slowly moved away once more. The general was known for the mark he bore, a magical love spot said to make any woman who looked upon him fall madly in love with him. To Vetus it sounded like a curse, but obviously the queen was not immune. He tucked that small piece of information away for later.

"I shall visit the Winter Palace at once, Your Majesty, and I will send word as soon as I have something worth sharing," Vetus said.

With her eyes still on her general, the queen motioned their dismissal with a flick of her hand. Vetus and Kerridwen had just turned to leave when the queen's voice rang out.

"Say hello to my little sister, won't you, Nephew?"

Vetus froze where he stood.

"You didn't think that Maeve could return to the Otherworld without my knowledge, did you? I'm surprised Midhir isn't tearing the place apart to find her. It can only mean that he doesn't know. Use it to your advantage if you can."

Vetus and Kerridwen decided to take their time going from the lands of Summer to the Winter Palace. Vetus was in no hurry to face the Winter King after he'd stripped him of his titles and essentially put a bounty on his head. Fortunately, the position of emissary was protected by older and more sacred magic than the fae possessed, and even Midhir himself wouldn't dare to cross it.

The Otherworld existed for far longer than any one race could claim, and each had their own little pocket to themselves. Legend held that the land was older than the Gods, too, and whatever magic created the Gods, well, Vetus didn't want to know what a power of such magnitude could do in the wrong hands.

The Winter Palace had come alive with the Autumn Equinox, as the balance of power would now shift toward Midhir. Still, no foreign legions were visible, and so far, Winter did not appear ready for war.

Vetus blew out a breath in relief, "Well, at least Father hasn't given marching orders yet. There may still be time to prevent this war."

Kerridwen scoffed, "Don't get too comfortable with that idea, Big Brother. Midhir thinks he has Nuada's sword; war is inevitable."

"You are probably right, Kerri, but let's grab a bite to eat before we cross that bridge. I could use a pint of Dizzy's ale, and we haven't properly celebrated the Equinox together in years." Vetus gave her a mischievous smile.

"All hell is breaking loose around you, and you want to throw care to the wind and drink yourself sideways? I wouldn't miss it for the world."

The siblings sauntered into The Lusty Leprechaun, and immediately, all the patrons stopped and looked at them. Not only was Vetus the now-disgraced former crown prince, but he wore the sigil of the Summer

Queen. He had walked nonchalantly into the viper pit. Kerridwen's hand went instinctively to her blade. Vetus gave her a wink.

"Master O'Gratin, a round for the house on us. Happy Equinox," Vetus announced.

The room erupted with a cheer. As Vetus and Kerridwen made their way to a table near the back, soldiers and other lesser fae shook Vetus's hand and greeted them pleasantly as though they were old friends.

Once seated, Kerridwen shook her head, "You never cease to surprise me. I sometimes forget that you weren't always a stuffy, uptight high fae lord."

A shadow passed across Vetus's eyes, "That part of me died with Solveig, but I can put on a good show every now and again."

Dizzy brought two frothy mugs of ale and sat them on the table in front of the prince and princess. He stood beside their table, picking at the dry skin around his fingernails, his knees trembling so hard they almost knocked together.

"Is something wrong, Master O'Gratin?" Vetus asked.

"I, uh...beggin' yer pardon, milord, uh...Your Highnesses, I just heard a rumour that I was hoping you could deny."

Vetus glanced at his sister, who had pinned the nervous proprietor with a predatory glare.

"Well, out with it," Kerridwen snapped.

"It's about Commander Rowan," Dizzy swallowed. "Word is they've got him locked up and been torturing him. I haven't seen him in here for weeks, and some of the boys who were regulars here, loyal to the commander, ya see...well, they've gone missin', and I thought I ought to tell someone."

All the colour drained from Kerridwen's face as Dizzy spoke. Vetus snatched the poor man by the collar and hauled him close. No one seemed to notice, or at least they knew better than to interfere.

Vetus whispered, "Who else have you spoken to about these rumours?"

"N...n...no one, my prince. Just you and Her Royal Highness here."

Vetus released Dizzy and immediately felt sorry for him as he appeared to have wet himself when Vetus grabbed him.

"Get yourself cleaned up and tell no one what you've heard. Lie low until you hear from me or the princess again. Your life depends on it, do you understand?"

The poor leprechaun nodded and shuffled back somewhere behind the bar, no doubt to change out of his soiled breeches.

"Vetus, he may already be dead," Kerridwen said quietly. "What do we do?"

Chapter Thirty-One

The ringtone from her cell startled Cass awake. Her eyes were unfocused, and her heart raced as she took a moment to figure out what the sound was, where it was coming from, and why someone was calling at three o'clock in the morning.

She grabbed the phone and hit the button to silence the ring so it wouldn't wake Aoife. Looking at the call display, she saw that it was Freydis calling and decided she could forgive her friend. Cass had no idea what time it was in Belize, so maybe Freydis had forgotten it was the middle of the night in Ireland.

Cass quietly answered, "Hi, hang on a sec," and slipped on her slippers and robe before tiptoeing into the hall.

"Okay, I'm good now," Cass sighed. "I hope you know how much I love you. It's 3:00 a.m. here, and—"

"Cass? Cass Walsh?" said an unfamiliar voice.

"Yes? Who is this? Why are you calling from Freydis's phone?"

"My name is Tina, and I am Dr. Marcus Wolfe's assistant. Freydis never made it to Belize. Marcus and the US government kidnapped her and are holding her in a facility in Texas."

"I'm sorry, what?" Cass laughed nervously. "Whoever this is, you can tell Freydis that this prank was stupid, and she isn't funny."

"Please, you need to listen. This isn't a joke. Marcus found out she isn't human, and he's completely lost it. They've been doing test after test on her, and they plan to move her either tomorrow or the next day to another facility where she will be unreachable. She said you would help. Please." The caller was frantic.

"Marcus wouldn't do something like that. He loves her," Cass said dismissively.

"I don't know what to tell you, but Marcus isn't the same. It's like something snapped when his brother died and—"

"You mean when *Marcus* killed him. You do know I'm his widow, right?" Cass hissed.

"I'm sorry, yes, I know, but I just can't stand to watch him become a monster, and Freydis is in rough shape. Can you help me get her out of here?"

"How the hell am I supposed to do that?" Cass asked. "I will need some time. Can I call you back?"

"Marcus doesn't know I have her phone...I can give you an hour. Tops."

"Fine. Call me back in an hour."

Cass hung up the phone. The disorientation she felt from abruptly waking up had been replaced with pure adrenaline. She peeked back into the room to see Aoife still fast asleep. As quietly as she could, she closed the door and broke into a run down the corridor toward Ophelia's rooms.

Cass's lungs burned as her chest heaved, trying to suck in the air. She knocked on Ophelia's door. Once. Twice. Then listened to see if anyone stirred. She knocked again.

"Ophelia? It's Cass. Are you awake?" Cass continued knocking.

"Hello, Cassandra," Ophelia said from behind her. "Trouble sleeping? I always go to the kitchen for tea when I can't sleep. Shall I make you some?"

Cass blurted, "Freydis has been kidnapped. Marcus has her. The bastard is experimenting on her. He knows she's not human, and they have her somewhere, but they're planning on moving her and—"

"Stop!" Ophelia's command echoed off the stone walls. She held up her hand. "Stop talking. I need to think."

Ophelia pinched the bridge of her nose and squeezed her eyes shut. The silence was excruciating. Cass wanted to grab her and shake her. Anything to get her to have a sense of the urgency and desperation Cass felt.

"We need to do something. She is calling back in an hour."

Ophelia opened her eyes and inhaled deeply, "Go wake Maeve and meet me in the kitchen."

"Me? Wake the Winter Queen?" Cass grimaced.

Ophelia rolled her eyes and turned to walk briskly in the direction of the kitchen. Cass cursed under her breath and made her way toward the queen's bedchamber.

Once gathered, Ophelia poured everyone a cup of tea, and Cass recounted the entire conversation to both women. Ophelia's knee bounced, and she tapped the table with her fingers. Maeve stood silent, watching the flames in the hearth, sipping her tea.

"We are running out of time," Cass pleaded.

The sound of brisk footsteps was the only warning they received before Kerridwen burst into the kitchen. Her usually immaculate appearance was replaced with the dishevelled, panicked one of someone who had been running for their life.

"Oh, lovely," Maeve crooned, "we've been waiting for you and your brother to arrive. We have quite a precarious situation at hand."

"Rowan was taken prisoner and locked in father's dungeon. He's been tortured, and he is to be tried for treason," Kerridwen bent over, placing her hands on her thighs as she tried to catch her breath. "Vetus has gone to rescue him. He wouldn't let me help. Mother, you need to help him."

"She can't," Cass interrupted. "Freydis never made it to Belize; she was kidnapped and is being experimented on. She needs to be rescued."

Silence filled the room as all eyes turned toward Maeve. Ice spread beneath her feet, and despite the roaring fire, Cass shivered as the temperature in the room dropped.

Cass broke the silence, "Freydis needs your help. Please. Grandmother, I am begging you to help her. I will do anyth—"

"No," Kerridwen cupped her hand over Cass's mouth. "Do not finish that sentence. Even though you are family, you must never make deals with the fae, and by the Gods, don't say you'll do *anything* they want."

Maeve scowled at Kerridwen, who stuck her tongue out in return.

"Who will help Freydis?" Cass continued. "We can't just leave her."

"We are not going to leave her," Maeve snorted. "Kerri, you and Cassandra will rescue Freydis."

Cass paled, "I am only human. What can I possibly do?"

"Freydis trusts you," Kerridwen answered. "She barely knows me, and if what you say is true, she may not be in her right mind to let me help if you aren't with me."

"I will keep Aoife," Ophelia offered, "if you are willing, Cassandra."

Cass nodded, "How soon can we be ready?"

Vetus pulled his mail hauberk over his head. He decided to go with the shorter version and not the full-length tunic so his movements would be less restricted. His cuirass, worn to cover his chest, was engraved with his own sigil, not his father's or the Summer Queen's. If he was going to die, he would wear his own mark.

A lighter midnight-blue traveller's cloak covered his back. His hand rested on the hilt of his ancient blade as he steadied himself. He felt a bit foolish bothering with the armour as it would do nothing against Midhir's magic, but if he had to fight his way in, or Gods be good, his way out, it would help against soldiers' blades or arrows.

Rowan was the closest thing to a son he would ever have, and Gods be damned if he would let his father imprison and torture him unopposed. All the extra time he'd been spending in the Otherworld had bolstered his own magic and healed his lingering soreness from the injuries he'd received when Fomor attacked him at the Winter King's behest.

Vetus walked through the main entrance of the Winter Palace unchallenged. Using it to his advantage, he pulled up the hood of the cloak and quietly entered the great hall with a crowd of other high fae for what he assumed was Rowan's trial.

From where he positioned himself at the back of the room, he had a clear view of the king's throne and a dozen heavily armed fae that stood around the perimeter. A jury of nine high fae nobles sat to the left of the king's throne, and Lir, Petra, Leannán, and General Dullahan stood on the king's right.

Vetus moved to where he could see the gaunt figure shackled to the floor. Rowan was nearly unrecognizable. His dark-brown hair was a tangled, matted mess, and a dark, unkempt beard covered his face. His sunken silver eyes had lost all their brightness. Vetus had to force his mouth to remain closed to stifle the roar of rage that demanded to break free.

The crowd chatted casually, as if trials of this nature were an everyday occurrence. Vetus felt a stillness flood over him, a killing calm. It was the same feeling he got before all the great battles he had fought in over the centuries.

"My Lords and Ladies," his brother Lir's nasally voice slithered through the air, "Commander Rowan MacArtur has been charged with high treason against His Majesty, Midhir, King of Winter. He has also been charged with the crime of compelling soldiers under his command to assist with the unlawful escape of a traitor and their subsequent murders, as he is directly responsible for their executions."

The crowd murmured with mixed reactions. Even several of the guards seemed to bristle at the charges. As Lir continued to speak, Vetus's grip on his sword tightened.

"Evidence has been provided to the tribunal in advance, and they are present now to hear the traitor's defence," Lir continued, "and if there is anyone else who wishes to speak on his behalf, an opportunity will be provided by His Gracious Majesty."

Vetus watched Lir signal to one of the guards and scowled as the guard loosened Rowan's shackles and forced him to his feet.

"This is your opportunity to give your defense," Lir sneered. "Use it wisely."

"Your Majesty," Rowan's weary voice cracked, "My Lords and Ladies, Honourable Jury, I have served the Winter Court for centuries. I have been a loyal and faithful servant to the crown since I was rescued by our prince, His Royal Highness, Vetus Mac Midhir. I have fought and bled for this realm. I have trained and mentored its soldiers. I helped secure the legendary Nuada's sword and see its return to His Majesty, the King. I am no traitor. The fae who helped me while I was held in the dungeons of the Winter Palace did not act because they were compelled or ordered to do so but out of love and loyalty."

Vetus seethed as the crowd snickered at Rowan's defence. He would slaughter them all if that was the price the Gods demanded for Rowan's rescue.

"Pretty words are not a defence, Commander," Leannán Sídhe grinned. "Is it not also true that you interfered with the king's agents on two separate occasions, preventing them from dispatching a grievous threat to His Majesty and the realm?"

Vetus began moving through the crowd toward the place where Rowan stood, ready to draw his blade, when General Dullahan's terrifying, gravelly voice boomed, "My King, if the legends are true, Nuada's sword not only deals an unhealable wound but can also compel the truth when held against an enemy. Why not use the sword and end this circus?"

Vetus froze.

"General, as always, your wisdom in these difficult matters is a great boon," the king growled. "Lir, get the sword."

Lir retrieved the sword from an alcove behind the throne and handed it to the king. Vetus held his breath.

"General, if you would be so kind." Midhir thrust the blade toward General Dullahan.

The general grasped the sword and inspected it carefully. He turned his empty eyes toward Lir.

"What game is this, boy?" Dullahan hissed. "Bring me the real sword."

Midhir glared at Lir, who to Vetus's delight, had lost all colour from his cheeks.

"F...fa...father, my King...that is the only sword." Vetus could see Lir trembling from where he stood. "This is the sword Vetus gave you. There is no other."

Midhir whipped his head back toward the general.

"I fear you have been deceived, my King. This is a clever forgery, but a forgery all the same."

The gathered crowd erupted at the general's words.

"There is no magic in this sword."

Midhir roared, and Vetus stepped out of the crowd to where Rowan stood and drew his blade.

"Midhir, King of Winter," Vetus bellowed, "I demand you release this prisoner. After all, your quarrel is with me."

Midhir's icy gaze fixed on Vetus as the temperature in the room plummeted. The windows instantaneously clouded with frost.

"You dare challenge me, Vetus Mac Midhir." The king descended the steps from the throne, and a formidable blade of ice and winter magic formed in his hand. His courtly robes shifted before Vetus's eyes into obsidian plate armour.

The king's steps were slow and deliberate. Vetus focused on his breathing and rooted his feet.

"Yes, Father," Vetus embraced that stillness that filled him, "I challenge you. In front of all these witnesses. I challenge you not only for the commander's life but also for your crown."

Midhir's insidious laugh echoed through the halls, "There you are, my son. I thought I'd lost you to that mouthy little whore and the abomination you created with her. At least you are acting like a Prince of Winter again, not some simpering fool."

As father and son faced off, much of the crowd fled the great hall to avoid becoming collateral damage. The guards had surrounded Vetus, who stood with a hand on Rowan's shoulder, facing the king.

"Vetus," Rowan said frantically, "I am not worth your life. Let me face this, I am ready."

Vetus gave Rowan's shoulder a reassuring squeeze before stepping toward the king. "Look after Freydis if this goes ill."

"Stop, damn you!" Rowan pleaded. "I won't let you do this."

Vetus drew in a deep breath and rallied his magic. His sword glowed a brilliant blue as runes appeared along the blade. "It's true I brought you back a forgery, the brilliant work of the dwarven smiths of Svartalfheim. But it is not the only masterpiece I returned with."

For the first time in his very long life, Vetus saw a hint of fear in his father's cruel dark eyes. His brother Lir must have seen it, too, because he hurried to the king's side.

"Father, let me be your champion," Lir begged the king. "Let me prove my worthiness as crown prince."

In a heartbeat, Midhir's sword vanished from his hands, and the obsidian armour faded back into his regal robes. "You honour me with your courage, my son. I must not deny you."

To Vetus's surprise, General Dullahan scoffed at the king's cowardly acceptance of Lir's offer and skulked out of the great hall. Petra remained tensely standing where she had been, and Leannán giggled with maniacal delight.

Vetus angled himself to face his brother, who drew his sword. Lir was a formidable warrior, but he lacked any real mastery of the magic in his blood. It was as if the Otherworld herself abhorred him.

"I will kill you, Lir," Vetus said flatly. "You do not have to sacrifice yourself for his approval. Walk away, little brother. Go to your wife. Await the birth of your child. Go and live—fight, and I will drench this hall with your blood."

"You are a disgrace, Vetus," Lir spat. "I have his approval and his blessing. I am the *fucking* crown prince now. My child shall wear the crown of thorns for thousands of years after me. Your name, dear brother, will melt away like late-spring snow and be forgotten."

The words were barely out of Lir's mouth before he lunged, his sword sweeping toward Vetus's head. Vetus easily deflected Lir's attack, pivoting to the left and using Lir's own momentum to knock him to the ground.

Lir roared, got to his feet, and turned to face Vetus again, "I will make sure I am the one to kill that little *bitch* of yours once I finish you off. I will let each and every one of my soldiers have a go at her, though, before I do."

Lunge, parry, pivot, advance—blades sang as the brothers continued their vicious skirmish. Lir's movements slowed as he grew weary, and Vetus was soaked with sweat. The brothers paused long enough to suck in a few desperately needed breaths.

Vetus tracked his brother's every move, every breath. He didn't notice Petra was no longer standing next to the throne. As he faced off once more against Lir, Vetus noticed Lir's eyes flick briefly to the left over Vetus's shoulder.

Turning a heartbeat too late, Vetus felt a sharp tear near his left shoulder blade where Petra's blade pierced his mail. Had he not turned when he did, it would have directly pierced his heart. His left arm hung limp at his side, so he used the hand clenching his sword to shove Petra back.

The sharp pain made Vetus forget about his brother, whom he had turned his back on. Petra howled and lunged once more, dagger in hand, toward Vetus. Side-stepping her attack, he moved just as Lir brought his sword down. The attack from high above Lir's head came down with all his force and lodged itself into Petra's clavicle, severing an artery.

The sound was sickening, and Vetus staggered back a few steps. Lir's face blanched as he realized what he'd done. He grabbed the dagger from Petra's limp hand; black ichor pulsed out onto the cold stone floor.

In a rage, he threw himself at Vetus, who once more parried the attack. He slashed the backs of Lir's heels, bringing him to his knees. Vetus stalked around to face his brother and placed the tip of his sword at the centre of Lir's throat.

"Surrender, Brother," Vetus's breathing was laboured, "and I will give you a quick, clean death. You can join your wife and child in the next life."

"Stop!" a loud, clear voice called out. Vetus turned his head in time to witness his mother, in all her Winter Queen glory, enter the great hall.

Midhir, who had been sitting on the edge of his throne, seething, fell to his knees.

"No more bloodshed," Maeve spoke sternly. "What madness is this?"

The room was silent and still as death, like the whole world held its breath. The Winter Queen ascended the steps toward her husband, who remained in a stupor on his knees.

"Is it really you, *mo ghrá*?" Midhir whispered as he looked up at her, "Or a spirit sent to taunt me?"

Vetus stood silently, sword still at his brother's throat, as his mother knelt down and took his father's face into her hands.

"Yes, *my love,* it's me." Maeve kissed him gently and said softly, "End this."

Midhir kissed her again and once more on her forehead as he stood. Maeve returned to her feet and stood beside him.

"Vetus, accept your brother's surrender, but spare his life, and I will return your position and your titles. Your brother has suffered enough."

Vetus leaned a little into his blade, and a trickle of blood ran down his brother's skin. He knew Lir would never forgive him for Petra's death even if she didn't die by his hand. It would be better to end the threat for good.

"Husband," Maeve's pleading tone gave Vetus pause, "as a gift to me, to celebrate my homecoming, release Commander MacArtur. Let him serve the crown prince once more and let us put this dark day behind us."

"Your beauty is surpassed only by your wisdom, *mo ghrá*," Midhir crooned. "Guards, release the commander to the crown prince. Take him from my sight, Vetus Mac Midhir, and once you have tended to your wounds, you are commanded to return here for an audience with the queen and me."

Vetus sheathed his sword and bowed deeply to his parents. Without looking at his brother or Petra's bloody corpse, he bent down and helped Rowan stand. Vetus put his good arm around Rowan for support, and they walked toward the large obsidian doors that stood unmanned and ajar. His father's voice rang out in the silence.

"Bring your sister with you."

Chapter Thirty-Two

In the courtyard of the Winter Palace, Vetus struggled with his one good arm to keep Rowan upright and walking. Weeks spent chained and malnourished had taken their toll on his strength.

"Gods, I thought you'd be lighter," Vetus grumbled. "You look like skin and bones."

Rowan chuckled, "Perhaps your old age is catching up with you."

Vetus lowered Rowan gently to rest against a statue of the Dagda and sat beside him to catch his breath.

"I guess you know the queen has returned," Rowan murmured.

"Mmhmm," Vetus sighed.

"Once more, I find myself owing you a life debt, My Prince. You should not have interfered."

"As if I would let them kill you, boy. You are *my* family." Vetus levelled his gaze with Rowan's. "This life isn't finished with you yet."

Tears streamed from Rowan's face, "I am not the man you used to know, My Prince. I am changed."

"We all are changed by our experiences, Rowan. Every choice we make changes us. You will regain your strength and be twice the man you were before you were imprisoned." Vetus nudged him.

"It was not the dark or the hunger and thirst that stole my spirit. They had that fae woman pretend to be Freydis. Over and over again, they would drag her away from me, screaming, to be tortured where I could hear and do nothing." Rowan wiped his face with the dirty sleeve of his linen shirt. "Her screams are all I can hear, awake and in my dreams."

"I am so sorry that knowing me has caused you such pain," Vetus said, resting a comforting hand on Rowan's shoulder. "I'm unworthy of your loyalty, but I vow to help you find your way out of this darkness."

"Serving you has been the honour of my life, and I regret nothing," Rowan gestured toward Vetus's limp arm. "Except that. At least that Fomorian witch got what she deserved."

"Indeed—and painted yet another target on our backs. Lir will never forgive or forget this loss, but that is a worry for another day. We will never get to Arbor Castle using the old ways in our conditions," Vetus stood and stretched his one good arm. "I'm going to use the last of my strength to create a portal, but I warn you, it will not be pleasant."

Before Rowan could respond, Vetus gripped his shoulder, and the courtyard faded away into darkness.

Cass curled over and vomited. The closest passage from the Otherworld to where Freydis was being held was still too far to walk, so Kerridwen used magic to create a portal to make up the difference. The magic didn't agree with Cass. Kerridwen, however, emerged looking flawless, as usual. Cass wiped her chin with her sleeve.

"Please tell me I won't have to do that again," Cass groaned.

"I'm sorry, doll, I went very basic to conserve my magic in case we need it to get Freydis out. Normally, it would be less jarring on your human body." Kerridwen looked around in the fading twilight. "Are we sure this is the right place?"

Cass followed Kerridwen's gaze to a nondescript four-story building. The stone cube had no windows and only one visible entrance. The parking lot was still full of vehicles. Tina had led them to believe that it would be practically deserted at the time they'd agreed upon.

Cass's heart thundered in her chest. There was no way they'd just walk in and walk out like she had hoped. Kerridwen worried at her lower lip.

"What now?" Cass muttered as they stood awkwardly across the street.

"I am not leaving here without her," Kerridwen scowled. "But I had hoped I wouldn't have to use my magic so soon."

Cass was startled as a fork of lightning ripped apart the sky. Kerridwen's fingers sparked with electricity as the wind picked up. Thick dark clouds rolled in, filling the sky above them, as thunder rumbled in the distance.

"Remind me not to piss you off," Cass let out a nervous chuckle.

A slight figure dashed across the street and approached them. Cass recognized Tina from seeing her tag along after Marcus when they'd been at the hospital with Ethan.

"Tina, right?" Cass raised her voice above the wind, extending her hand. "I'm Cass."

"We have a major problem," Tina's face was pale. "They've decided to move her, tonight...well, now actually. She is heavily sedated, and there are government representatives everywhere. We are too—"

Tina's voice cut off as she noticed Kerridwen, the picture of a badass ancient magical being about to exact her infernal vengeance upon her enemies. Her chestnut hair was flawless in the wind that howled around them, and her onyx eyes were luminous as her power surged through her.

Tina gaped; a mixture of awe and terror painted her expression as she turned to look at Cass once more.

"I know," Cass said flatly.

"Is she a...," Tina shuddered. "Is she like Freydis?"

Cass rolled her eyes, "Look, we aren't leaving without her. Just make sure she is ready when we go in."

Tina nodded, "Marcus made them put a tracking microchip somewhere inside her. I didn't have time to find out. They won't stop looking for her, Cass."

Cass's stomach gurgled as if she was going to vomit again.

"Just tell us where she is and get out of the way; then you can go back to believing that magic isn't real and there are no monsters living in your closet or under your bed."

"Third floor. Last door on the right," Tina murmured, unable to take her eyes off Kerridwen.

"Your Highness," Cass shouted over the wind, "we need to go now."

Kerridwen raised her hands above her head and, with a clap, brought her hands together. A bolt of lightning struck the building, taking out the power.

"Get inside and find her," Kerridwen commanded. "I will busy the guards."

Cass and Tina watched Kerridwen walk across the street straight toward the main entrance. Thunder continued to rumble like ancient drums of war.

"There is an emergency exit we can use and take the stairs," Tina offered.

Cass nodded. The two women hurried across the street, keeping to the shadows as best they could.

Tina swiped her pass, and the emergency door opened. The halls were black as pitch, except for the red emergency lights. Cass followed Tina closely as she moved through the dark.

Tina swiped her pass again to open the doors leading to the stairs. Up three flights, they entered the chaotic third floor. Doctors, attendants, and government officials scurried about in the dim red light. Cass was on Tina's heels, as she expertly navigated the sea of bodies. They were approaching the last door on the right when a familiar voice hollered Tina's name over the din. Cass froze and Tina turned around toward the voice.

Marcus was making his way toward them, hindered by the people filling the hall. As Tina brushed past Cass, she handed her the key card she'd been using to open the doors. Cass casually continued to the last door. Marcus had almost reached them when raised voices erupted at the other end of the hall, drawing his attention.

Cass quickly swiped the card and stepped inside, shutting the door behind her. She leaned her forehead against the cool door and took a deep, steadying breath. When she turned around, her legs nearly went out from underneath her.

The room was empty, except for the monitors that beeped quietly and the bed on which Freydis was tightly secured. Cass hurried to the bedside.

"Freydis," Cass started unfastening the restraints; tears blurred her vision. "It's Cass. I'm here to take you home, okay. I'm gonna get you outta here."

Cass's fingers couldn't move fast enough. Freydis lay naked, covered by a thin sheet. The wrist and ankle restraints were tightened to the last available hole. If the monitors weren't showing her vitals, Cass would have thought Freydis was dead.

Tears flowed freely now as Cass continued to undo the straps. "What did they do to you?"

"Cass?" Freydis's weary voice slurred her name. "You came."

The weak grin that followed Freydis's words broke Cass's heart. Finishing with the last strap, she moved quickly to the head of the bed and tried to help Freydis sit up.

"You need to put your arm around my neck so I can get you up," Cass grunted as she tried to lift Freydis's nearly dead weight. *Skin and bones shouldn't be so heavy*, Cass thought.

"Everything hurts, Cass, I can't," Freydis moaned.

"Yes, you can, you just need to swing your legs...here," Cass gently removed Freydis's arm from around her and moved to grab her bare legs and pull them off the bed before returning to prop her up again. "Can you stand?"

Freydis tried to pull herself into a sitting position and managed to get her feet on the floor with Cass's help.

"Just go easy and put a little weight on them," Cass held her tightly. "Use me for balance."

Freydis made a move as if to stand, and her legs gave out. Cass barely had time to wrap her arms around Freydis to keep her from falling to the floor.

"Cass, what are you doing?" Marcus's low voice made her heart stop. After sitting Freydis gently into one of the chairs, Cass turned toward Marcus and the government agent who tailed him.

"You disgust me, Marcus Wolfe," Cass hissed. "Killing Ethan wasn't enough? You had to try and take Freydis from me too?"

"Ethan was gone before I tried to save him, Cass," Marcus crooned. "Don't you see? If we had known how special Freydis was, we could have used her to save him. But she was selfish and hid it from us."

"Have you lost your fucking mind, Marcus? Listen to yourself." Cass scoffed. "You loved Freydis. The Marcus I knew would never torture someone the way you've tortured Freydis. You've become a monster, Marcus, and I am glad Ethan isn't around to see who you've become."

Marcus turned to the agent and motioned toward Freydis, "Secure the subject."

The man hesitated. Marcus grabbed him by the arm and shoved him forward. "She is sedated. Secure the damn subject."

Cass moved to block him, but he pushed past her.

"I am not going to let you do this, Marcus."

"You can't stop—"

Marcus's words stuck in his throat. His hands flew to his throat, and Cass could see the whites of his eyes. She turned to see Freydis standing with her hand around the agent's wrist. He hung limp in her grasp. Freydis's stormy eyes burned as she glared at Marcus.

"You asked once what I am," Freydis's insidious chuckle made the hair on Cass's nape stand on end. "I am fury. I am wrath."

Cass watched in horror as the agent crumbled to dust in Freydis's hand and she nonchalantly brushed his residue from her palm.

"I have laid in that bed planning this moment every day since you brought me here," Freydis spoke calmly as she approached Marcus, who appeared frozen where he stood. "This is where your story ends, Marcus Wolfe."

Cass stepped in front of Freydis, "You don't need to do this, Freydis. You can walk away. I will take you home."

A gust of wind entered the room as Kerridwen appeared in the doorway. Freydis ignored Cass's plea and brushed by her. She placed her hand over Marcus's heart. Cass looked at Kerridwen, whose face remained indifferent.

"Kerridwen, you need to stop her," Cass was frantic. "Freydis, you are better than this!"

Freydis turned and gave Cass a sad smile.

"No, I'm not."

As soon as the words left her mouth, Marcus crumpled before them. Freydis stumbled, and Cass grabbed her, wrapping her arms around Freydis to keep her on her feet. Kerridwen placed a hand on Cass's shoulder, and everything went black.

Vetus's portal landed them in the courtyard of Arbor Castle, startling two sentries who'd been playing a game of dice. Vetus and Rowan collapsed in a heap. The sentries launched to their feet and scurried to the prince and their captain.

"Hard at work, lads?" Rowan chuckled as he and Vetus were helped to their feet. "The prince is injured. Fetch Lady Ophelia immediately."

"But, sir, you are hardly in better shape yourself," said the taller of the two. "Let us bring you inside."

Vetus grunted his approval and gave Rowan a look that told him to shut his mouth and accept the help.

Inside, the castle buzzed with urgency at the sight of their bloodied and battered prince. Ophelia practically sprinted down the stairs into the large great room where they stood. A young nymph followed close behind, carrying a sleeping infant in her arms. Ophelia gave orders like a seasoned battle commander.

"Get Commander Rowan to the kitchen. The cook will see you fed, boy; you look terribly thin," Ophelia barked.

"I have missed you, *Aintin*," Rowan murmured as the sentries ushered him to the back stairs leading to the kitchen.

"I shall see to the prince myself," Ophelia muttered dismissively to the nosy few who'd been milling about, drawn to the commotion of the abrupt arrival. Her sharp teal eyes assessed his injuries. Vetus wrestled to keep the smile from his face. She was worse than an old mother hen.

"I will live, Ophelia. It's just the arm that needs a little attention. Nothing a good meal and a long nap can't fix." Gesturing to the sleeping baby, Vetus quipped, "I hadn't realized you were expecting?"

She scoffed, "You're insufferable. It's Aoife, Cass's baby. That arm will need magic to help it heal, since you insist on living in the mortal realm. At least, Her Majesty the Queen got to you both in time."

"I had it well in hand," Vetus winced as she tore the fabric near the wound left by Petra's blade that rendered his arm a decoration, "I was winning."

"The loss of blood has muddled your senses, My Lord. Come," Ophelia guided him to a chaise longue that sat in front of the large unlit hearth.

"Are you going to tell me why you are looking after my great niece?"

"First, you have to promise you won't go running off to save the day," Ophelia gave him a look that made his Winter blood turn to ice.

"Hasn't he already saved the day?" Rowan's voice interrupted them as he crested the stairs from the kitchen. He held up Vetus's walking stick, "Cook thought I could use it."

Vetus nodded and said to Ophelia, "You have my word; now tell me."

Ophelia sighed deeply, "Freydis never arrived in Belize. Marcus, her human lover, kidnapped her."

"Where is she? Where did he take her?" Rowan snarled.

"I don't know, but—"

Rowan interrupted her, "I made no promise not to act. I will find her and make him pay for his betrayal."

Rowan tossed the walking stick to Vetus, who barely caught it with his one good arm. Slowly but determinedly, Rowan turned to make his way toward the undercroft when a strong gust of wind and a bright flash filled the great room.

The light faded in time for them to see Cass vomit on Kerridwen's boots. Vetus was sure Kerri was about to vomit herself, but his eyes darted to the limp body in her arms.

Ophelia gasped and moved quickly to take Freydis from Kerridwen's arms. Gently, she lowered her to the floor.

Freydis's limp naked body was barely covered by a thin white sheet. Her hair was drab and dishevelled, and for a moment, Vetus thought she was dead.

Rowan fell to his knees as Kerridwen approached Vetus, where he stood frozen, gaping at his daughter's crumpled form.

"Is she…," Vetus's voice was barely a whisper.

"No, Big Brother, she lives, but I fear that it's the damage we cannot see that will be the worst."

"They experimented on her, drugged her," Cass's voice faltered. "They had her strapped to a bed, naked and alone in a windowless room."

The temperature plummeted as Vetus filled with rage. He had warned her. So many times. If only he had told her who she really was, that the home she had longed and looked for had been here all along. She belonged here. Belonged to him.

"Human kindness, at its finest," Ophelia hissed. A castle attendant had fetched several blankets intuitively, which Ophelia used to cover Freydis's fragile body. She turned to where Rowan still knelt, pale and staring at Freydis. "Make yourself useful, boy, and start a fire. The prince will have us all frozen to death."

Kerridwen stooped to help Rowan stand, "I will help, come on."

"They gave her a microchip," Cass blurted. "Some sort of a tracking thing. I think they expected her to try and escape."

"Where is it?" Ophelia said, giving Vetus a worried look.

"Tina didn't know," Cass murmured.

Dragging his fingers through his dirty hair, Vetus looked around at the people he loved and tried to collect his thoughts.

"Ophelia, do we still have connections at that tech company in Dublin?" he asked.

"It's been a few years, but I will reach out first thing in the morning." Ophelia gave Cass a reassuring smile, "We will figure all of this out, Cassandra."

Chapter Thirty-Three

Freydis woke in a strange room, with her head in a fog. She vaguely remembered Cass helping her out of her restraints, but everything after that was missing. Her body felt heavy as she tried to raise herself into a sitting position. A warm hand on her back made her nearly jump out of her skin.

"You are safe, Fierce One, you're safe," Rowan's low voice cooed.

She hadn't realized he'd been sitting near the head of her bed. She frantically looked around the room to try and get her bearings.

"You're at Arbor Castle. Cass and the princess brought you here after they rescued you," Rowan reached toward her face, and she moved instinctively away from him, putting the strand of hair that fell into her face behind her ear herself.

Pain flashed across his face, "No one is going to hurt you, Freydis."

"Where is Vetus?"

"I will get him for you," Rowan offered, retreating from the room like a beaten dog.

She laid herself back on the bed, trying to pull the missing pieces from the recesses of her memory. As twisted as it was, she longed for the drug-induced oblivion of the past several weeks. At least she would be numb. At least she might forget.

A gentle knock on the door drew her attention. Vetus entered the room and moved quickly to the edge of her bed. He placed a kiss on her forehead, and she burst into tears.

He cupped her cheek and gently wiped her tears with his thumb, "I am so sorry, Freydis."

She wiggled over in bed, giving him room to sit beside her. He sat leaning against the headboard with his legs crossed on the bed. She tucked herself into his side, breathing in his cool, crisp scent that always reminded her of a winter forest and continued to sob.

"You have suffered an unspeakable betrayal, Dea, but you are strong enough to survive this."

Vetus murmured more comforting words as she cried. She wanted to believe him. She wanted to believe this wasn't some drug-induced beautiful dream and that she was safe.

"You need to rest and recover your strength. We can have someone stay with you if you don't want to be alone. We can all take turns. Rowan hasn't left your side since we got you back."

Freydis wasn't sure she wanted anyone other than Vetus anywhere near her. She couldn't stop the overwhelming sense of violation she felt. The only person who had always made her feel safe was Vetus.

"I should have listened to you," she sobbed. "I just wanted to belong somewhere."

"You are where you belong now, Dea, with people who love you and accept you for who you are. Sometimes those people are family, and often, they are not. At least, not your family by fate, but your family by choice."

"I see that now," Freydis looked up at him. "I just wish I didn't have to learn the hard way."

"The most important things in life and the worthiest are never easy. Sometimes the lessons life must teach you require going through the underworld and back." Vetus kissed the top of her head, "You survived, which means all is not lost. You need to rest. I will stay until you fall asleep. And when you're ready, I will make sure you arrive safely to meet your mother's sister if that is still something you want to do."

Freydis had fallen to sleep, so Vetus carefully eased himself off her bed and made his way to the kitchen. Ophelia had just finished pouring tea for the others. Kerridwen stood to give up her chair.

"I will stand, Kerri," Vetus smiled at his younger sister. "I just spent a very long time sitting and need to stand."

"How is she now?" Rowan asked.

"Her physical wounds will heal quickly, but I am afraid of the damage that's been done to her spirit. The light has gone out from her eyes." Vetus ran his hand through his hair, "It will take time for her to find her way back."

"She killed him...them," Cass murmured. "How will she come back from that?"

Vetus looked at Kerridwen, who nodded confirmation. He inhaled deeply.

"We will find a way, Cassandra." He gently squeezed her shoulder.

Kerridwen cleared her throat, "I wish I could stay, Big Brother, but now that Freydis and Rowan are safe, Leila said, if I don't return home, she will leave me for the blacksmith." She stood on her tiptoes and kissed him on the cheek, "I have offered for Rowan to come to the Autumn Court. I am impressed with the security he has arranged for you and would like him to oversee the creation of my own personal guard. With your permission, of course."

Kerridwen winked at Vetus, and he was grateful that she had offered to give Rowan something to take his mind off Freydis. He knew Rowan needed to recover from his own nightmare, and staying at Arbor Castle would only prolong the process, while Rowan worried about Freydis the whole time.

"There is no finer choice for such a task," Vetus squeezed Rowan's shoulder. "I will take care of Freydis for you. When you are both healed, not that you need it, but you have my blessing, if she'll have you—if you think you can tame her."

Vetus fought his own tears as Rowan's eyes welled up, looking at where Ophelia and Cass sat, fussing with Aoife. Ophelia nodded her approval and gave Vetus a comforting smile.

"I would be honoured to help you, Princess," Rowan inclined his head to her, then looked at where Vetus stood, "and I will never tame her. I would have her wild or not at all, but I will prove that I am worthy of her, My Prince."

Vetus embraced Rowan and said, "You already have, son."

Kerridwen and Rowan agreed to head out for the Autumn Court at dawn, and everyone said their goodnights. Vetus sat sipping his tea, and Ophelia waited with him until they were alone.

"It means a lot to him, what you said about giving your blessing," Ophelia murmured.

"I know," Vetus sighed. "I should have told him long ago."

"We all make mistakes, Vetus; you can't bear everyone's burdens."

"Have arrangements been made to remove the microchip?" Vetus asked her.

"Our contact has agreed to come tomorrow morning. Do you think she will allow it?" Ophelia's words dripped with obvious concern.

"I don't know," Vetus bowed his head and covered his face with his hands. "That is not going to be the hardest part."

"She will come around, Vetus. She is strong, like her mother. And her father," Ophelia smiled.

"I know," Vetus dropped his hands but remained staring at the floor. "There will be withdrawal, and possible relapse. They drugged her for weeks. I still have nightmares about the last time she dealt with something like this."

"You are not alone, Vetus," Ophelia took his hands into hers, and he raised his gaze to meet her eyes. "We will face this together."

Vetus stood, kissed Ophelia on the cheek, and left the warmth of the kitchen behind.

Ophelia had woken Freydis early to meet with the technician who came to remove any tracking devices. Fortunately, they were easy to locate, just under her skin. All three of them. Marcus was smart; she'd give him that. But he would never torture another living being. He was dead. She had killed him. The memories of that night had returned to her.

After thanking the technician and Ophelia, Freydis decided to indulge the grumbles in her stomach. Cass and Aoife were in the kitchen when Freydis arrived to eat breakfast. She was shocked at how big Aoife had grown since she saw her last.

"How are you feeling?" Cass's bright, bubbly voice was one of the sweetest sounds Freydis ever heard. "Say hi to Auntie Freydis, Aoife."

Freydis poured herself a hot cup of tea and sat across from Cass, "I owe you my life, Cass. I don't have any words, I—"

Cass clucked, "Don't be silly. Having you here, knowing you're safe.... That's enough for me."

"Where is everyone this morning?" Freydis asked, looking around. She spotted buttered toast on a plate and grabbed a slice. "I expected the kitchen to be bustling."

"Vetus was summoned to the Summer Court. Apparently, the Queen of Summer wants an update on the events that took place before and during Rowan's rescue. Ophelia is like a ghost sometimes, appearing and disappearing as she pleases," Cass paused and swallowed deeply.

"Rowan and Princess Kerridwen left at dawn for the Autumn Court. He gave me this letter to give to you."

Freydis took the letter from Cass's outstretched hands and finished her tea and toast. The two friends chatted easily and followed breakfast with a walk around the island with Aoife.

When Cass announced it was time for Aoife's nap, Freydis made her way to the castle library and sat at the old stone table where the stack of books she'd taken out months ago still sat. Holding the envelope in her hand, she traced the words *Ceann Fíochmhar* that he'd written on it. His name for her. She wished she felt the way he saw her.

She set the unopened letter on the table and stared at it. She had been cold and distant upon seeing him after her rescue. She wished she had acted differently now. She had been overcome with shame and disgust knowing what Marcus and the others had done to her. How could Rowan ever love her now that she had been violated and damaged? What if she panicked every time he touched her?

She held the envelope to her lips; then tucked it, unopened, inside one of the books. It would be easier this way. She'd never been good at goodbyes. Freydis breathed in deeply, the smell of old books steadying her, and she stood and left Rowan's words to her behind.

On her way to her room, she found Ophelia speaking with several of the castle's attendants. Upon seeing her, they said their goodbyes and dispersed, leaving Ophelia and Freydis alone in the corridor.

"I want to leave for Belize as soon as possible once Vetus has returned," Freydis said. "He promised to get me there safely when I was ready. I can't think of a better place to begin healing than with my mother's family."

Ophelia nodded and gave Freydis her best fake smile. It didn't fool Freydis, but she returned the smile and thanked Ophelia before returning to her room. She needed to face her demons on her own, and she needed to learn more about her magic. Perhaps then, she would finally know who she was meant to be.

A calm had settled over the Winter Court with his mother's return. Vetus stood in the courtyard, watching the palace sentries lob playful banter back and forth as the guard changed. The mood was a stark contrast to the tempestuous Summer Court from whence he'd come.

The Summer Queen had always been prickly, but she was mad as a March hare as of late. Between his duty as her ambassador and the drama unfolding with his family, he'd hardly had any time to give Freydis during her recovery. He hoped, when this family meeting was done, he could concentrate on helping Freydis heal and, when she was ready, meet her mother's people at last.

A subtle whiff of cinnamon tickled his nose only a few seconds before Kerridwen wrapped her arms around him from behind. They had been inseparable as children. She always seemed to sense when his thoughts were getting the better of him.

"One day, this will all be yours," she teased.

"Hmmm," he grumbled. "I'd rather not."

"I've been wanting to chat about Freydis," Kerri's teasing smile left her face. "What do you know about her magic?"

"I've only ever seen her use a glamour. But I imagine she would have some affinity for Winter magic, maybe even be able to influence the weather a bit, if she practised," Vetus mirrored Kerri's pensive expression. "Why?"

"Vetus, I don't know what magic Solveig possessed, but when Freydis killed Marcus...," Kerri dropped her gaze and shook her head, "she should have been too weak; you saw how she was when we brought her back."

"Out with it, Kerridwen." Dread crept up Vetus's spine.

"She drained the life out of a man. Literally turned him to dust and then used that strength to kill Marcus. He didn't disintegrate like the first human, but she killed him all the same. I've never seen a power like it."

Vetus swallowed deeply, "Impossible. Solveig was incredibly powerful, but she never killed anyone. Her power healed others, not drained them."

"I don't think we should ignore it, Big Brother. Perhaps Rowan might know something. I can ask him."

"Don't tell anyone else, Kerri. Not until we have more answers," Vetus pinched the bridge of his nose and sighed. "How is Rowan? I feel his absence greatly."

"He is distant and drowns himself in training my new guards. He will come around, but it will take time. In the meantime, Leila loves having someone to take care of."

"I've made a mess of things with Rowan and Freydis. Perhaps Lir should be father's heir. He has the stomach for it."

Kerridwen laughed, "Oh, bite your tongue. You will be a good and honourable king. Now, stop dawdling, and let's go face the music."

Arm in arm, brother and sister entered the palace. Inside, attendants bustled through the halls, updating decor and transforming the grim relic into a proper Winter Court. Vetus watched as Kerri sauntered over to a young lesser fae and began chatting easily. She had a regal grace that put everyone at ease.

As he waited for her, his guts churned as he recalled Kerridwen's words about Freydis. *Death magic. Is that what Midhir fears?* Vetus would have to get to the bottom of this, and quickly. Death magic always exacted a steep toll.

The lesser fae curtsied to his sister and hurried away. Kerri motioned for Vetus to join her.

"The meeting has been arranged in the king's *private* quarters," Kerri said in a conspiratorial tone, to which Vetus shook his head.

They made their way down the main corridor and up the spiral stairs leading to Midhir's tower. The King's Tower boasted two bedchambers, a small galley, a personal library, and a parlour, all crowned with a rooftop cellarium where night-blooming flowers danced in the moonlight. Vetus had loved this place as a child.

In the parlour sat a low stone table around which stood five high-backed velvet chairs. A crystal decanter full of honeyed wine sat on the table, accompanied by bowls of nuts, berries, and several dishes of sweets.

Kerri strolled in unabashedly and poured herself some wine. Vetus stood stoic by the door. They didn't have to wait long before Lir, the youngest of the three, skulked in. Kerri greeted her younger brother by placing her hand against his heart and bowing her head in recognition of his loss.

"Leila sends her condolences," she murmured.

Vetus wanted to recognize his brother's loss and be able to help him grieve as a brother should. He wanted to take him under his wing, having experienced such a loss himself, and tell Lir how time would someday make it easier to bear. But any brotherly love or affection Vetus once had for Lir had died long ago.

"And you, *your highness*?" Lir sneered at Vetus. "Do I have your condolences?"

Before Vetus could speak, the King and Queen of Winter swept into the room, the tension between them palpable. The king was sulking, and Maeve was more aloof than usual.

"Your Majesties," Vetus and his siblings bowed deeply.

The royal family stood around the stone table and surveyed each other in silence. It had been centuries since they'd all been together as a family. Maeve cleared her throat and, reaching for the decanter, poured the king and then herself a glass of honeyed wine.

"It is wonderful to have you home, mother," Lir crooned, "only several hundred years late."

Vetus watched Lir recoil as his father shot him a heart-freezing glare. Maeve could do no wrong in his father's eyes. Midhir worshipped her like a goddess. But Vetus also wanted to know where his mother had been. Especially when they'd needed her most.

"Forgive my brother, *Ard Ri*," the words were sickly sweet rolling off Vetus's tongue, "but I must agree with him. The queen has been absent, and as crown prince, I must insist she give an account of her absence."

"Don't succumb to chauvinism, Vetus, dear; it is beneath you," Maeve corrected. "And I intend to explain everything, which is part of the reason for this audience."

Vetus sat back indignantly and glowered at Kerri, who sniggered openly at Maeve's stinging rebuke. Apparently, the queen was blameless in Kerri's view as well.

"The main reason you are here," Midhir growled, "is to fix the mess you've made of things. The Fomorian princess is dead, and word is spreading throughout the court about the fractured state of our family. Though it has never come to pass, our ancient laws decree that any high fae who wishes to challenge for the crown is free to do so."

"Father, surely you must know it would never come to that," Kerridwen chided. "No one in the Otherworld would even consider challenging the Dagda's heir, let alone risk the Morrigan's wrath."

"I want my family avenged," Lir interrupted. "I demand an equal sacrifice. His only child for mine."

Lir pointed his finger at Vetus as though he were hurling a spear at him. It was not Vetus's fault they were dead. He had given Lir the opportunity to stand down. It was Lir's pride and petulance that sealed Petra's fate. Still, even knowing that, Vetus couldn't assuage the guilt he felt over the innocent child who'd been lost. It had become increasingly rare for new fae to be conceived in the Otherworld.

"Like I believe that was to be your only child," Midhir scoffed. "*Inis Fáil* is likely half full of your bastard children."

"Few use that name anymore, my love," Maeve corrected the king. "And you are lucky to have your head still attached to your body, my son." She narrowed her gaze at Lir, and Vetus tried not to make eye contact with Kerri, who'd been battling the giggles for most of the exchange.

"I will find you a new bride, Lir," Midhir said dismissively, "after I deal with the fallout from the last one's death. Word has already reached Lord Balor; I am certain of it. We must be prepared for imminent retribution. All our resources must be prepared, especially my own flesh and blood."

"You expect my loyalty after all you have done?" Vetus would be damned before he'd pretend like nothing had happened. "You have made attempts on my life, on the life of *my* heir, and tortured one of your most loyal commanders. I owe you much, *Ard Ri*, but loyalty isn't on the list."

"His words are treason, Father," Lir whined. Kerridwen kicked his chair and glared at him.

"Rowan MacArtur is no longer a commander in this court. He is banished from these lands," Midhir's words fell like a hammer. "If he is caught anywhere near this court, I will execute him without fanfare or a trial. And as for that wretch you dare to call your heir—"

Vetus gripped the arms of his fancy chair, the wood groaning as he leaned forward to protest. Maeve silenced him with a glare and turned her attention to Midhir.

"There is a far more pressing matter, my King," Maeve grasped her husband's hand, silencing his tirade, "such as the reason for my sustained absence."

A frozen silence swept through the parlour. Every other person in the room thought they knew the reason behind the queen's departure and separation. Now, they would finally hear the truth.

"The Gods are dying."

Meet the Cast

Freydis (*Fray-dis*) – Main protagonist
Astrid (*As-trid*) – Freydis's human companion, deceased
Solveig (*Sol-vey*) – Freydis's mother, deceased
Vetus (*Vet-us*) – Crown Prince of Winter, Freydis's best friend
Ophelia (*O-feel-ya*) – Head of Vetus's household
Cass Walsh – Human best friend to Freydis
Ethan Wolfe – Cass's boyfriend
Aoife (*eh-fa*) – Cass and Ethan's daughter
Doctor Marcus Wolfe – Ethan's brother
Tina – Marcus's assistant
Midhir (*Mid-here*) – Winter King, Vetus's father
Maeve (*May-v*) – Winter Queen, Vetus's mother
Lir (*Leer*) – Prince of Winter
General Dullahan (*Doo-la-han*) – Right hand of the King
Commander Rowan McArtur (*Row-an*) – Protégé of the Crown Prince of Winter
Dizzy O'Gratin – Owner of The Lusty Leprechaun
Leannán Sídhe(*Leah-nan Shee*) – Member of the Winter Court
Petra (*Pet-rah*) – Vetus's ex-fiancée
Kerridwen (*Care-id-when)* – Daughter of Midhir and Maeve, Ruler of the Autumn Court
Leila (*Lay-la)* – Wife of Kerridwen
Tarynn (*Tear-in*) – Summer Queen
General Diarmuid (*Deer-mut*) – Summer Court general

Acknowledgements

Words seem insufficient to adequately express the gratitude I feel toward all those without whom I would never have written this book. I hope the act of finishing it and my commitment to continue writing, even when it's hard, honour them and the support they've given me.

My belief in myself to write stories worth reading exists in large part due to the encouragement and feedback I received from my ninth-grade English teacher, Mr. Doucette. Though you no longer walk among us, thank you for instilling a deep love of the written word in me.

To my wonderful parents, Linda and Edward. Thank you for raising me to be a stubborn dreamer who believes anything is possible if I put my mind to it.

To my sister, Sam. Thank you for your unconditional support from the very beginning. From inspiring a large part of Kerridwen's character to being the first eyes to read the manuscript and give honest feedback, you helped make this story come alive. I would be lost without you.

To my oldest friend, Caleigh. Thank you for taking time, over and over again, to read each draft and every re-written scene. Your encouragement has been a blessing to my fragile writer's heart.

To my advanced readers. Thank you for taking a chance on me and this story. Your feedback helped this story move from good to great.

To Tannis and Val, my work besties, thank you for covering shifts for me to attend bookish events and cheering me on. It means the world to me.

To The Write Practice and the critique partners I found there. This group was a game-changer for me as a new writer.

To the Irish Pagan School and Morgan Daimler. I am grateful for your tireless dedication to creating and making available accurate information about Ireland and her folklore from authentic sources. Whether it was the podcasts, the IPS YouTube channel or your published works, my research was made easier because of your work. Go Raibh Maith Agat.

To my brilliant editor, Raya P. Morrison. From the moment you accepted me as a client until this very moment, your professionalism, expertise, and shared vision for this story were more than I could have hoped for. You are a gift to the writing community, and I want everyone to know it.

To my children, Kade, Clay, Seth, and Finn. Thank you for occupying each other while I wrote and for not taking the headphones personally. I hope you never stop being yourselves and making your presence known in the world.

To my everything, my husband, Mitchell. You are my muse. Your unconditional love inspires me, and every honourable man I write will be modelled after you.

To my readers, without you, this story is just ink on a page. Thank you for taking a chance on me. I will endeavour always to be worthy of you.

Jeremiah 29:11

Coming Soon

Shadows in Her Heart: Book Two of The Enaid Chronicles, by ATL Doyle

Chapter One

Two pills left.
Freydis squeezed her eyes shut, grasping the pills in her hand like a lifeline. The small Cessna CE-510 plane shuddered as it braved another pocket of turbulent air.

"How much longer?" Freydis called up to the pilot. Her empty hand flew up to cover her mouth as the very-light jet lurched. Her stomach gurgled, threatening to spill its contents for the fourth time.

"We're forty minutes from Big Creek Airport," the co-pilot answered. "We should be out of this rough patch shortly."

Freydis rolled her eyes and twisted the cap off her water bottle. If she was going to die on this tin can, she would not be going down with a clear head. The two little pills dropped onto her tongue, followed by a gulp of cool water. She needed to find more meds, or something a little stronger, when she landed.

Cass had given her a dozen or so pills before Freydis left for Belize. Sweet Cass. She'd been through too much. Her whole life had been turned upside down with a new baby, losing Ethan, and then Marcus's death. She'd been seeing a therapist ever since Freydis's rescue.

Cass's doctor was a pill pusher. He'd given her several prescriptions for sedatives and anti-anxiety meds. They didn't help Cass, but Freydis popped them like candy. Cass was too lost in her own troubles to notice.

If Freydis was a better friend, she wouldn't be leaving Cass to heal alone. But here she was again, focused on herself and running away from her problems. She could picture Rowan gloating that he was right about her.

Her chest tightened at the thought of Rowan. They didn't get a chance to repair things after that embarrassing night she'd spent with Marcus. Freydis cringed at the thought of Marcus Wolfe. He was dead, but the memories and the dreams were ever present, lurking underneath the surface, waiting for her to let her guard down.

Perhaps that's why Rowan wrote the letter—to tell her that he couldn't forgive her and was moving on. Why hadn't she read that Gods-forsaken letter? She'd stupidly left it behind.

The effects of the medication were finally settling in when the pilot turned on the seatbelt light, and the nose of the plane tipped forward. *Great.* This wasn't exactly the first impression she'd hoped to give her long-lost family. Still, at least she wouldn't be a bundle of nerves.

After landing, Freydis looked around amusedly. The airfield, misleadingly called Big Creek Airport, was little more than a farmer's field. It was nothing special, but the palm trees made up for the disappointment. Freydis had spent a long time in cold and wet climates, so she was excited to be somewhere that autumn still felt like summer.

Freydis managed keep all but a little bit of vomit off her sweater. She was overdressed for the temperature—at least, that was the message she was getting from the moisture on her top lip. She pulled the hoodie off over her head and shoved it into her bag.

Stepping into the arrivals area, Freydis pulled her suitcase behind her through the stanchions, trying not to look like a lost puppy. She had no idea what her aunt looked like. Perhaps the butterflies in Freydis's stomach would recognize her.

She walked toward a small cluster of people. Sophia, her mother's sister, was unmistakable. The same sharp yet delicate features and chestnut hair. Sophia's dark eyes reminded Freydis of the mouth of a cave at sunset, deep and inviting. They were not the stormy eyes of her mother—Freydis's eyes.

The woman walked up to her with a brilliant smile. "You are the picture of your mother," she said, cupping Freydis's cheeks. "I am overjoyed to meet you."

Sophia pulled her into a tight embrace. A cascade of emotions rushed over Freydis at her touch. The happiness she felt conflicted with the way her body stiffened. She breathed through the discomfort. Freydis had never been much of a hugger, and since the Marcus situation, physical touch wasn't always easy.

"The joy is mine," Freydis said. "I've waited my whole life for this moment."

"Come," Sophia placed a hand on her shoulder. "Mattias and Isabella are outside. We've all waited a long time for this moment, and we have so much to talk about."

The short trip from the airport to Sophia and Mattias's bungalow was uncomfortable, to say the least. Freydis struggled to keep her eyes open and, every time she spoke, she felt like she was slurring her words a bit.

Mattias seemed kind and fatherly, asking about her flight and making small talk. He reminded her of Vetus a little. Isabella did not speak to her at all.

When they arrived, Sophia gave Freydis a brief tour before showing her to the guest room. Freydis walked in to find her things unpacked and put away or laid out around the room. Freydis fought to swallow her anger at the violation of her privacy when Sophia's calming voice cooed behind her.

"I am sorry about your things. The *parum amicis* like to help occasionally, even when they are not asked."

"*Parum amicis*?" Freydis asked.

"House spirits," Sophia smiled. "I call them my *little friends*. Mostly, they keep to themselves, but they are curious about you. Are you hungry? Dinner isn't for a few hours yet, but I will make you something."

"No, thank you," Freydis said. "My stomach hasn't settled since the plane."

"Alright. Why don't you get some rest?" Sophia suggested.

Freydis nodded and lay down on the bed. Her eyes fluttered shut before Sophia closed the door.

The clash of metal on metal pierced the crisp autumn air, echoing across the lake. Rowan grunted as the soldier he was training slammed into him. Wetting his dry lips with his tongue, he braced himself to hold his ground.

Training new recruits was Rowan's primary task. Princess Kerridwen, who was absently watching the melee, had given him full authority over her soldiers. He would make elite warriors of them all.

Rowan preferred to be in the ring with them. He refused to do it any other way. *A leader serves.* That was his motto. His opponent feinted, catching Rowan off balance, landing a staggering blow.

"Well struck!" Rowan gave the recruit a reassuring grin and dismissed him. The poor lad looked as though he was either awestruck or scared senseless. Rowan wiped the sweat from his brow and turned toward Kerridwen, who perched on a rough wooden bench against the outside wall of the barracks.

The beauty of the Autumn Court's warm browns, fiery oranges, golds, and crimsons faded in her presence. Despite the radiant glow of her power surrounding her, Rowan noticed how she picked at her long fingernails and fidgeted in her seat. He could smell a storm in the air. Ominous clouds congregated above the looming mountains, and Rowan wondered if the two were connected.

"Your Highness, I didn't expect to find you checking in. Do you like what you see?" Rowan schooled his features, trying to hide his smirk after lobbing the shameful flirtation at her. This was their game, and she looked as though she could use the distraction.

"You are working hard, Rowan," Kerri said absently. "You should be proud."

Rowan balked at her lack of flirtatious retort. Something was eating at her. She always teased him about his infatuation with her. From the first time he saw her, he thought he'd seen an angel—the dark and kick-your-ass type, but an angel all the same. The day he'd met Leila, Kerri's wife, was the worst day of his adolescent life. True to her nature, Kerri goaded him about it ever since.

"My lady, I have never seen you so troubled," Rowan murmured.

"My daughters arrived this morning," Kerri mumbled.

"Now, Your Highness, I'm sure they aren't that bad," he teased. "They are *your* children, after all."

"Don't you stick up for those two," the princess scoffed. "They're not children anymore."

"Are they not?" Rowan feigned shock. "Where has the time gone?"

"Indeed." Kerri seemed to consider that very thing before she blurted, "Did you and Freydis ever talk about her magic?"

It was an abrupt shift in the conversation, but Rowan had been expecting it. Cass had recounted the conversations and events of Freydis's rescue to him in vivid detail. Rowan had felt a chill skitter through him at the mention of her pestilent magic. He wanted to believe she could handle it, but a tiny whisper of doubt crept into the recesses of his mind.

He couldn't forget their argument the night he'd found out she'd slept with Marcus. He'd accused Freydis of running from her problems, leaving others to clean up her messes. What if he'd pushed her too hard?

"I have never seen Freydis use dangerous magic. At least, not with my knowledge," Rowan levelled his gaze at the princess, "but I believe what Cass has told me about her power. I believe she could be in terrible danger by having such magic...But if anyone can handle it, it's Freydis."

"You must miss her terribly," Kerri mused. "I can sense your grief."

"I wake up each day, and a piece of me is missing," Rowan said. "Sometimes, I feel like my heart briefly stops beating, or my breath becomes shallow. There are times I can't speak and times I can't stop screaming at the Gods for their cruelty."

"Difficult times don't last forever, Rowan." Kerri squeezed his shoulder. " I've arranged for the remainder of your possessions at the Winter Court to be brought here. You are welcome to stay as long as you need."

Kerri met his gaze and placed her hand on his chest for a heartbeat before walking away toward her stately gothic manor house.

Rowan inhaled deeply and let his mind wander, trying to recall the look of Freydis's stormy eyes so he could drown himself in them.

It was dark when Freydis awoke from her sedative-induced sleep. How long had she slept? Her stomach growled in reply. Freydis flicked on the lamp by her bed. A small stack of books sat on the nightstand. She instantly recognized the top book as her worn copy of Marcus Aurelius's *Meditations.*

She thought she'd forgotten it and even had a little meltdown about it at one point on her trip. She opened the book, and tucked neatly inside was the folded note containing her mother's last words to her, written so many years ago. She closed her eyes and silently thanked the Gods that it somehow made the journey.

The next book she didn't recognize, but a hastily written note was taped to its cover:

> Dearest Freydis,
> I thought you might need this.
> Love, Ophelia

Freydis carefully removed the note. The book's leather binding looked like it had been done by hand. The cover had no title printed on it, but there was a faint impression of a symbol Freydis thought she recognized but couldn't remember the name of.

She opened the book and ran her finger over the jagged edge of what remained where the first page had been torn out. The remaining thick pages were covered in rich black calligraphy, clearly written by hand. It was beautiful. As she flipped through the pages, an envelope fell out onto the floor. The familiar handwriting made her heart race.

Rowan's letter was inside the envelope now starring up at her. She shook her head in disbelief as she bent down to retrieve it. Vetus always spoke fondly of Ophelia. *She always takes care of everything.*

Freydis didn't dare read the letter now, before dinner. She wasn't sure what state it would leave her in, and she'd already made a lacklustre first impression. Rowan would have to wait.

Freydis checked herself in the mirrored bureau before leaving the bedroom. Her eyes were dark-rimmed and sunken in appearance. She hadn't been sleeping properly.

She rubbed her eyes and sauntered to the kitchen, where she found Mattias pouring two glasses of wine. He smiled at her.

"Freya."

"It's Freydis, actually." She smiled tightly.

Mattias took a sip of his wine and swished it around in his mouth a little before swallowing. Freydis watched and waited awkwardly for him to respond. He smiled at her again.

"I know." His voice was smooth and deep. " I said 'Freya' because that is who your mother named you for." He leveled his gaze at her. "Did you know that?"

Freydis shook her head.

"Do you mean the goddess Freya?" she asked.

He nodded.

"Freya was a dear friend of Sophia's and your mother's." Mattias topped up his glass, retrieved the second, and gestured for her to follow with his chin. "Come. Sophia is in the garden."

Behind the bungalow was a beautiful vegetable and herb garden bordered by a small orchard. The nearly full moon lit up the night. Sophia's silhouette was visible at the farthest end of the garden. Freydis paused to take in the scene.

Mattias murmured, "Whenever it is clear, she communes with the night sky. A part of her created those stars, and somewhere out there is home."

He continued to stroll toward Sophia, and Freydis followed slowly behind. She watched Mattias hand the second glass of wine to his wife. They clinked their glasses, and he kissed her on her cheek. Mattias followed as Sophia approached Freydis. Sophia looked like a goddess herself in the moonlight.

"I have been searching for you since my mother died," Freydis said, cringing a little at the half-truth. She wasn't sure if she would have accomplished anything if it hadn't been for Vetus.

"There is so much I want to tell you," Sophia sighed, "but we will go at your pace and start with what you want to know."

"I barely remember the things my mother told me about herself. I think the years have muddied my memories. I don't know fact from fantasy anymore."

Sophia pointed toward the stars. "We came from out there, somewhere...a very, very long time ago."

Freydis remained silent. She had dreamt of this moment.

"Ninety-nine Oraculian sentinels and our autarch...sent here by our creators for rebelling against them."

Freydis's confusion must have shown on her face because Sophia clarified, "An autarch is the equivalent of a monarch on this planet."

"So, you were sent here as punishment?"

"Ours was not the first rebellion," Sophia sighed. "The first rebellion led to the death of our mother and Archon, Saranya. Her death revealed a previously unknown truth. We discovered that when an Archon dies, their portion of Údarion's essence is passed to their offspring."

"What is an Archon?" Freydis asked.

"The Archons of Enaid are the incarnations of the creator, Údarion. Our histories tell us of events that lead to Údarion rending itself apart to interact more intimately with creation. Each Archon is a living, breathing portion of that essence, including your grandmother and grandfather."

"But how could she die? We are immortal."

"Like us, the Archons are eternal. We do not age past maturity, so we will never grow old and die. We will simply last unless we are killed." Sophia paused. "The next Archon to die was our father, Custor."

"I'm so sorry," Freydis murmured.

Sophia shook her head and continued, "Our brother, Hakon, learned that our father and several other Archons had become corrupt and killed him for it. With two Archons dead and their essences passed on to their children, Enaid was in a state of confusion and turmoil."

"Custor wasn't the only corrupt Archon, and when Solveig learned the truth of everything, she led the rebellion that we lost and were exiled for," Mattias added as he approached them.

Freydis met Sophia's concerned gaze. She was at a loss for words as she tried to process what she was hearing. Her head was spinning.

Hugging her face with both hands, Freydis huffed out a breath, "I don't even know where to begin my questions."

Sophia laughed, "Our family, just like our history, is complicated—everyone's is. But don't worry. I will tell you everything I know, and what I can't remember, I'm sure, Mattias has it written down somewhere."

From where they stood, they saw Mattias raise his glass in confirmation, and they both laughed.

"How long did I sleep?" Freydis asked. "I don't even know what day it is."

"It is just after dinner. Come, you must be starving," Sophia said and hurried into the house dragging Freydis with her.

About the author

ATL Doyle is a voracious reader and lover of large cups of tea. With inspiration from authors like Tolkien, C.S. Lewis, Jim Butcher, and more, she discovered her love of writing as a teenager. Early work included a poetry collection and several short stories. *Magic in Her Blood* is her debut novel. Writing has become her best form of therapy for living with mental illness. When she isn't writing, she enjoys reviewing books on her blog and trying to balance the busy life of a wife and mother of four boys on Canada's beautiful East Coast.

Contact the author through her website:
WordHaven.ca

Help independent authors and small presses by leaving a review of this book at your favourite online retailer or review site, or sharing on social media.